Touched by passion . . .

Sarah's heart hammered as she stared at the gold buttons climbing up Sergeant McCauley's chest. They were right in front of her. When she took a hasty step back, he put out a hand to steady her. His fingers on her arm kept her on her feet, but unsettled her more than any chance touch should. Or was it chance?

His thumb caressed the inside of her elbow, a slow, sensuous motion that urged her to sway toward him in a dance with silent music. When she bit her lower lip to keep her gasp from escaping, the sparks in his eyes glittered like burnished gold.

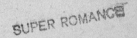

Jove titles by Joanna Hampton

THE COMING HOME QUILT
WOVEN DREAMS

Woven Dreams

JOANNA HAMPTON

JOVE BOOKS, NEW YORK

This is a work of fiction. Names, characters, places, and incidents are
either the product of the author's imagination or are used fictitiously,
and any resemblance to actual persons, living or dead, business
establishments, events or locales is entirely coincidental.

A QUILTING ROMANCE is a trademark of Penguin Putnam Inc.

WOVEN DREAMS

A Jove Book / published by arrangement with
the author

PRINTING HISTORY
Jove edition / January 2000

The Penguin Putnam Inc. World Wide Web site address is
http://www.penguinputnam.com

ISBN: 0-515-12727-2

A JOVE BOOK®
Jove Books are published by The Berkley Publishing Group,
a division of Penguin Putnam Inc.,
375 Hudson Street, New York, New York 10014.
JOVE and the "J" design
are trademarks belonging to Penguin Putnam Inc.

PRINTED IN THE UNITED STATES OF AMERICA

10 9 8 7 6 5 4 3 2 1

For Kathy,
to fulfill a long overdue promise

Thank you for believing.
I will never forget you.

Woven Dreams

∞

1

AT THE SCREAM, HE leaped off his horse without thinking.

Benjamin McCauley pulled his nightstick, ran around the corner, and crossed the street in two steps to where a woman was crumpled on the cobbles. Knowing it was useless, he put his fingers against her neck. No pulse. He cursed as he stared at the knife in the middle of her chest. At least her death had been quick. Just like most of the murders here in Five Points.

Coming to his feet, he looked along the street where the tenements threatened to topple at any moment. Laundry wafted high above his head, but the people, who usually sat on the stoops, had vanished. Not a dog barked. Not a kid shouted. The whole street, in the middle of the busy Irish slums, appeared abandoned.

That was no surprise either. Folks had a way of being busy whenever he tried to talk to them. He understood the Irish mistrust of authority, but they were not in Ireland any longer, suffering under the heavy-handed British rule. They were in New York City, and the Metropolitan Police were here to protect them and keep the peace.

Too bad the Irish in this slum had no interest in keeping things peaceful.

Benjamin tensed. Who was huddling in the shadows? He doubted if it was the murderer, contrite about what had happened, but he had seen stranger things in his five years with the Metropolitan Police. He had joined the force a year after it was started in 1857 and had since learned that he had had no idea to what lengths some people would go to get money or prestige. Shading his eyes, he saw nothing in the alley. The murderer might be there, but first he had to see what he could discover here, before the site of the murder was disturbed.

And it would be disturbed if he went to check every shadow. Other corpses had been stripped before the police found them.

He glanced back at the dead woman. His eyes slitted as he noted the quality of her clothes. This woman could not be from Five Points, unless she had stolen that light-blue gown and matching slippers. He doubted that, because they fit her perfectly. When he saw a purse by her side, he picked it up. He bit back a curse when he saw money in it. This had not been a robbery, so why had she been killed?

He squatted again, trying to see something that would give him an idea of who had killed this woman and why. There always was a reason for murder. All he had to do was figure out what it might be, and that answer might lead him to the murderer.

"Is she dead?"

His head jerked up. Where had this other woman come from? He had thought the street was empty. He stared. He could not help himself. The vivid sapphire of her eyes could not be muted by the gold-rimmed glasses balanced on her slender nose. Hair as black as her gown edged her cheeks and drew his gaze to the curve of her lips. It was as appealing as her other curves, which he could view above the full bell of her skirt.

"Sir, is she dead?"

"Yes! Who in the blazes are you?" He cursed silently when those incredible eyes widened. He should have hidden his irritation, but he also should have heard her before this.

She took a step back, then another. "I can get someone— someone to help."

He was on his feet and seizing her arm before he could stop himself. If this woman had seen something, he was not going to let her disappear back into the labyrinth of Five Points. She stiffened, and he saw those blue eyes rivet on the badge on his chest, the copper badge that identified him as one of the Metropolitan Police.

Faith, when were the people here going to understand that the police wanted to help stop the criminals who preyed on them?

"Oh, thank goodness," she whispered.

"Thank goodness?" He took a deep breath and discovered it was flavored with a light flowery scent that was doubly appealing among the stench of the open sewers along the street.

"You *are* a policeman, aren't you?"

Not releasing her arm, he tipped his low cap to her. "Benjamin McCauley, miss."

"Sergeant McCauley?"

"Yes." He eyed her up and down again. Surely he would have remembered encountering this woman with eyes that could sear right through him, but he had to ask, "Have we met?"

"No, Sergeant, but your reputation is well known in Five Points." She glanced back at the body in the street. "Shouldn't we be sending for someone to help you?"

He flinched at her polite reminder that he had a job to do that did not include admiring her. "I shall as soon as I discover any clues to what might have happened here. You didn't see anything, did you, miss?"

"I heard a scream." The cool fire in her eyes dimmed, and all color sifted from her face. "I thought someone might be being robbed. I came here and saw . . ." She put her hand over her mouth as if she feared she would be ill.

Benjamin turned her, so he stood between her and the dead woman. All his instincts were wrong today. This woman had not been tranquil, simply so shocked that every emotion had drained from her. Now it was flooding back, sweeping over her in waves of pain and disbelief.

"I must investigate," he began, resisting the temptation to draw her against his wool coat, which was too hot for late May.

"I understand." She slipped her arm out of his grip and squared her shoulders. "Let me find someone to give her last rites."

"You know—?"

"Sergeant McCauley, almost everyone in Five Points attends Father O'Leary's church. I'll get him."

"Thank you, miss."

"Granger. Sarah Granger."

"Of the Second Avenue Mission?" He smiled. "*Your* reputation is well known here in Five Points, as well."

"That is no surprise."

Benjamin watched as she gathered up her black skirt to keep it out of the sewers that ran across the street and hurried in the direction of the church on the next corner. So that was Sarah Granger. Not at all as he had expected; he had assumed Miss Granger was much older, maybe a gray-haired widow. For, reputedly, she planned to devote the rest of her days to taking care of the children ignored by the fancy so-called aid societies over on Broadway and Fifth Avenue. Enjoying the sway of her skirts as she stepped up onto the uneven walkway, he decided he needed to pay the Second Avenue Mission for Needy Children a visit soon.

Sarah Granger struggled to breathe as she walked away. In the two years that she had been overseeing the Second Avenue Mission beyond the edge of Five Points, she had heard about other murders, but this was the first time she had seen a corpse lying in the street. Pausing by a stoop, she put her gloved hand on the rail. The last few flakes of paint cracked and rained to the ground, but she ignored them.

Dear God, she didn't want to be ill here where Sergeant McCauley could see. Or anyone else, for that matter. She had worked hard to build her reputation as tough, but fair.

To be sick now could wipe away what respect she had won here.

Something moved in the alley in front of her. She almost screamed. *Don't be a fool!* Sergeant McCauley would not have let her come this way if the murderer were lingering about, would he? She had tried to avoid any interaction with the Metropolitan Police, because anyone who was connected to the police force was considered suspect in Five Points.

She tightened her grip on the railing and looked back at where Sergeant McCauley was squatting beside the dead woman and making notes in a small book. Her stomach threatened to revolt again at the sight of blood on the cobbles. No, she would not be sick. No, she would not.

Think of something else. How many times had she told Rachel that, when her assistant was sickened by the stench of Five Points? But she could not think of anything else. She had to get Father O'Leary and—

The cry was so soft she might have missed it if she had been walking by at a normal pace. Peering into the alley, she saw a child hunched next to a basket about the length of a man's arm. She forgot her own despair when she heard the child's sobs.

She paid no attention to the filth as she knelt by the child and put her hand lightly on his small arm. He was, she guessed, no more than three years old. When he looked up at her, she almost choked on her gasp. The shape of his face and the golden color of the curls were identical to the dead woman's. Was this her child?

"I am Sarah," she said in the soft voice that seemed to work best with frightened children. "What's your name?"

"Conlan." His little fist was clenched onto a partially finished quilt that was draped over the edge of the basket, and he stuck his thumb in his mouth as he whimpered. His wide eyes tried to see past Sarah. She edged between him and the view of the street, exactly as Sergeant McCauley had done with her.

She almost looked back to where Sergeant McCauley was. She had not been completely honest with him. Al-

though they had never spoken, she had seen him several
times during her visits to Five Points. It had been impossible not to notice his easy control of his chestnut horse or
how his hair of the same color caught the sunshine that
slipped past the tenements. When they had stood so close,
she had found it even more impossible to ignore the firm
line of his rigid jaw. She prayed he had not been aware of
her reaction when he touched her, sending some unknown
sensation through her. Powerful and dangerous, but taunt-
ingly like when her dear, late Giles had offered his arm.

"Where's Mama?" asked Conlan.

Sarah forced a smile. "I think we should wait here for
her."

"But where is she?"

Instead of answering, she asked, "Where is your papa?"

"Gone."

Her smile faded. She had heard that too often. Some
of the lads here had joined up to fight in the War of the
Rebellion, but most of them just took off when the responsibilities of a wife and family became too heavy. The
women were left to try to make a life for their children in
this slum . . . and to die. Then the children came to the Mission until she could find them a place to live.

The little boy stared past her. "Who are you?"

Sarah turned awkwardly and looked up at Sergeant
McCauley. He seemed impossibly tall from this angle as
she raised her eyes past his knee-length coat and the single
row of polished buttons closing it. When he knelt beside
her, she saw that the bulky shoulders of his uniform coat
were not an illusion. Yet, as he held out his hand to brush
curls back from Conlan's face, she sensed a gentleness in
him that was in contrast to everything she had heard about
the policemen who were supposed to be only a shade more
reputable than the criminals they sought.

"I'm Sergeant McCauley." He glanced at Sarah, arching
a ruddy eyebrow.

She understood what he did not say. The child must be
newly arrived in Five Points, because the kids here, even
ones this young, knew all the policemen who patrolled the

streets and how to avoid them when they wanted to get into mischief.

"This is Conlan," she said quietly.

The little boy stuck his thumb in his mouth again, then asked around it, "Where's Mama?"

Sarah ignored the nausea that returned doubly strong when Sergeant McCauley's face became as stony and unemotional as one of the statues in Father O'Leary's church. "He wants his mother," she whispered, watching how the little boy never released his hold on the patchwork quilt in the basket.

Quilt . . . Why did it have to be a quilt? She pushed another wave of sickness and grief aside. She must not let her own pain keep her from helping this child. How often had she repeated the warning to herself since she had come to work in New York City?

"I have to find out what he saw," Sergeant McCauley said, bringing her gaze back to him.

"Can't that wait?"

"Maybe. Maybe not." His smile returned, looking as forced as her own. "Conlan, did you come here for a walk?"

Conlan nodded.

"A long walk?"

He nodded again.

Sarah put her hand on Sergeant McCauley's arm. When he glanced at her, surprise stealing the hard edge from his face, she knew he had every reason to be shocked. However, this was no time for propriety. This was the time to make sure this child was helped.

"Sergeant," she said quietly, "even a single block would be a long walk for a child this size. You may be making bad assumptions if you base them on his information."

A smile curled along his lips as he put his hand over hers. Caught anew by the ebony power of his gaze, she could not look away. That uncontrollable sensation surged through her again.

It vanished into icy embarrassment as he chuckled and said, "Thanks, Miss Granger, but trust me to know what I'm doing." Before she could say anything, he turned back to the little boy. "Conlan, can I see what's in your basket?"

Thumb tight in his mouth, he shook his head. "Where's Mama?"

"Let me try," Sarah murmured.

"If you think—"

"Trust me to know *my* job."

Again that brow rose, but he motioned for her to take over.

She did not smile at Conlan. She was not going to act as if nothing were amiss. Children had a wondrous knack for knowing when adults were lying to them. It was too bad she had lost that skill herself.

"This is very pretty," she said, pointing to the quilt. The pattern was complete, but the quilting was not. Another surge of pain threatened to send shudders through her. It seemed a lifetime ago that she had looked at a quilt with delight. It *had* been a lifetime . . . the one she had lived since Giles's death two years ago. "May I look at it?"

"Yes, very pretty."

"So many colors."

"So many colors, yes."

She was astonished to see the rough shimmer of silk among the patches in the quilt. Where had someone gotten silk in Five Points? She looked at Sergeant McCauley, understanding now why he had asked about a long walk. He did not believe the child and his mother lived in Five Points. That made no sense. No one came here unless absolutely necessary. Trying to keep her astonishment out of her voice, she added, "Can I touch the yellow spot here?"

"Touch it. Yes."

She smiled. He was like a mockingbird, repeating back what he heard. Running her fingers along a patch near the edge where an unusual pattern seemed to have been sewn into it, she realized this quilt was as well made as the child's clothes and as clean.

"Can I look at the blue spot here?"

"Look. Blue spot." He peered at the quilt. "Here?"

She smiled when he pointed to a green paisley piece. "No, here."

"Blue here," he insisted.

"May I touch *this* blue spot?"

"Touch *that* blue spot."

"You have more patience than I," Sergeant McCauley whispered near her ear. The pulse of his breath swirled past her bonnet and against her skin, sending another pulse exploding through her.

"Something I need with children, especially chatterboxes like this one," she replied as if she had taken note only of his words. She swept her hand over the quilt to the blue patch. The basket was not empty, she realized as she leaned forward and saw that the unfinished quilt was tucked around something inside it.

"May I look at the rest of it?" she asked.

He slid his hand across the quilt, but did not release it. "Look at it. Yes. Be careful. Mama says Conlan be careful." Tears dripped again from his wide eyes, and she fought her temptation to throw her arms around him and offer comfort. She had seen too many children scurry away in dismay when an adult approached too quickly.

Sergeant McCauley pulled a handkerchief out from under his coat. When he leaned toward the child, the little boy recoiled.

"Here," he said, putting the handkerchief in Sarah's hand. "Maybe he'll let you."

She took Conlan's hand and drew him to his feet and toward her. "See what's in the basket while I wipe his face." Her smile was not as uncomfortable as she dabbed at the little boy's cheeks and asked, "Do you need to blow your nose? Can I help you with—?"

Sergeant McCauley choked back a gasp. She looked at where he was drawing back the patchwork quilt. There was a baby in the basket!

The baby could not have been more than a few days old. Soft curls as golden as Conlan's peeked from under the quilt where embroidered blackbirds flew along the sides. *Four-and-twenty blackbirds baked in a pie,* came the nursery rhyme in her head. She shook the words away.

"No!" shrieked Conlan as Sergeant McCauley reached for the baby. "My baby!"

Sarah offered the flustered man a sympathetic smile. If circumstances had been different, she doubted if she could have kept from laughing at the sight of a strong, confident man like Sergeant McCauley being baffled by this little boy. But today she had no interest in laughing.

Wiping Conlan's tears again, she asked, "May I take your baby out of the basket so I might see her? She is so pretty."

"Pretty. My baby is pretty."

"Very pretty." She gave him the handkerchief. "May I?"

"Yes. See my pretty baby."

As Sarah reached into the basket, Sergeant McCauley asked, "How do you know it's a girl?"

"Just a guess."

He tilted his hat back on his head as she cradled the baby in her arms. "I thought you might have some way of figuring that out before you even touch the baby."

"Usually I know because the children that are left at the Mission have a name pinned to their clothes or blanket." She glanced into the basket. "Is there any note in there?"

"Nothing but this quilt."

"Peculiar, isn't it?"

"That there's no note?"

"That is an odd design for a quilt, don't you think?" With her elbow, she gestured toward the blackbirds.

"I know less about quilts than I do about babies." Coming to his feet, he picked up the basket. He quickly handed it to her when Conlan opened his mouth to protest. "That little fellow sure doesn't hide his opinions, does he?"

Sarah slipped the basket over her arm and reached for Conlan's hand. When he placed it trustfully in hers, she breathed a prayer of gratitude that she had happened to stumble upon these children before someone else had. Conlan might have trusted the wrong person. Although the only crime of most of the people in Five Points was being poor, too many lurked ready to take advantage of anyone who was not careful.

"I will check with Father O'Leary if he knows the children," she said.

"I doubt he will."

She nodded. Again she understood what he did not say. These children were too well dressed to be from these rough streets.

"Will you take them in at the Mission until we can find their father?" Sergeant McCauley asked.

Sarah wanted to say no, that the Mission was already overcrowded, that there was no crib for the baby, that she was not sure if she would have enough money to buy food for next week for the children living at the Mission. She said, "Of course. We never close our doors to needy children."

"Just don't let the little fellow here see . . ." He gestured with his head toward where the body still lay on the cobbles.

"I won't." Looking down at Conlan, she said, "I'd like to take you to meet a friend of mine. Father O'Leary is—"

"Mama!"

Sarah gasped as he pulled his hand out of hers and raced out into the street. "Sergeant McCauley!"

He pushed past her even before she finished his name. Holding the baby tightly, she followed. Horror clamped around her throat, strangling her as Conlan ran toward a woman on the other side of the street. If he turned and saw—

Her worst fears became reality as the child froze in the middle of the street. His cry was primal and heart-wrenching and went on and on.

Sergeant McCauley scooped him up and brought him back to the side of the street. Handing him the baby, Sarah knelt again to put her hands on either side of the little boy's face. She tilted his eyes toward hers and almost recoiled. She had never seen such terror. Fighting not to look away, she spoke softly.

"Conlan?"

He made a mewling sound, then reached out to the quilt.

Pressing the quilted corner to his face, he stuck his thumb in his mouth.

"Conlan?"

It was as if she had said nothing. His eyes did not blink at her voice. He simply clung to the quilt and stared through her.

"Is he going to be all right?" Sergeant McCauley asked as he put his hand lightly on her shoulder.

Grateful for his touch when she was sure she had lost touch with the little boy, she whispered, "I don't think so."

2

AS SARAH TURNED THE corner onto Second Avenue and the block where the Mission was, she noticed dozens of eyes peering out from behind curtains, watching the strange parade she led. Here, beyond Five Points, those eyes could see Sergeant McCauley's frustration as he walked behind her, keeping an eye on the little boy who seemed unaware of anything but the quilt he clung to. Eyes like these must have been peeking out of the windows of the tenements in Five Points, but no one would admit that to him or the other policemen who had arrived to help with the investigation. Nobody, it seemed, had seen or heard anything when the woman was killed.

She was glad when Sergeant McCauley had quickly turned the corpse over to the priest and the investigation to one of his fellow policemen. With Conlan lost in his pain, she was not sure she could have managed to get him and the baby back to the Mission alone.

She listened to the hoofbeats of Sergeant McCauley's horse, whom he called Rogue. Their hope that the chance to ride on the policeman's mount might pull Conlan out of his prison of terror had been for naught. The child sat on the back of the horse, Sergeant McCauley making sure he did not fall off, but looked neither left nor right. He clutched the quilt to him like a shield.

She should have held more tightly to the little boy's hand. Then he would not have seen his mother lying dead in the middle of the street. Tears bubbled at the edges of her eyes. If only she could turn back time and keep the little boy from rushing out of the alley . . .

She continued to walk in silence. The afternoon was edging toward evening, taking the day's worst heat with it. She wished it would take the horrid stench that came from the open gutters and the charnel houses, but the rotten stew of the streets would remain until cold suffocated the odors.

Gritty sunlight fought its way through the maze of tangled streets and tumbledown buildings. Slowly, as they had come toward Second Avenue, the tenements became better maintained. It was a subtle change, for even the best buildings were in dire need of paint and masonry work. What altered most was the traffic on the streets. In Five Points, most people traveled on foot. Once they left the slum, carriages clogged the roads. Teamsters shouted to their horses. The iceman was here; the fruit peddler, and the ragman, too.

The baby gave a soft cry. Sarah adjusted the basket, and the baby girl wailed with righteous fury. Thank goodness the Mission was just ahead.

She paused by the four steps leading up to the front door. Through the open windows, she could hear laughter and singing. She smiled. The Second Avenue Mission for Needy Children was an island of compassion, offering a sanctuary to those who needed it most. Now there would be two more mouths needing food, two more rapidly growing children needing clothes. She needed a way to raise money quickly.

She glanced at the quilt Conlan held. Every time her father's church had been trying to raise funds, the ladies of the church had gathered to make quilts. She could . . . No, she could not! She just could not!

"Thank you, Sergeant McCauley, for helping me bring the children home," Sarah said as he lashed his horse's reins to the railing.

He lifted Conlan down from the saddle, but cradled him as if he were as young as the baby. "You're not all the way home yet."

"If you're busy—"

"I am." He flashed her a smile that warned he would not be budged on this. "I'm busy helping you."

"I don't need—"

"*I* don't need more trouble today, Miss Granger, from you or anyone else." He glanced past her, and she turned to see her assistant on the stairs.

Sarah smiled. Thank goodness, Rachel had been watching for her return from Five Points.

Rachel Nevins was a vibrant elf whose hair was too bright to call auburn. Sunshine emphasized the generous serving of freckles splashed across her full cheeks, but, Sarah noticed with a pinch of dismay, her customary smile was missing.

What else was going wrong? Sarah wanted to run up the stairs and into the house to find out what had stolen Rachel's smile.

No need, she realized when Rachel said, with unusual coolness, "I did not expect we were having callers, Sarah."

"Sergeant McCauley isn't calling," she answered quickly, too aware of the many ears that eavesdropped on every conversation on the street. Rachel should know better than to discuss something like this outside. As if she had not heard the tension in her assistant's voice, she added, "Rachel, come and meet Sergeant McCauley. Sergeant, this is my assistant, Miss Nevins."

He smiled even though Rachel did not move from the top step. "It's a pleasure to make your acquaintance, Miss Nevins."

"Rachel, can you take this baby and check her?" Sarah asked when Rachel remained silent. This was no time for Rachel to start acting strangely. "I suspect she is in need of both food and a diaper change."

When her assistant's face softened as she reached for the baby, Sarah relaxed. Rachel wrinkled her nose when she settled the baby in the curve of her arm, but began to mur-

mur hushed sounds as she carried the baby into the house. No matter what disturbed Rachel, all thoughts of it vanished when she held a baby.

"Not very friendly, is she?" Sergeant McCauley asked as Rachel went into the house.

Sarah's smile wavered when she faced him. "I can take Conlan now, if you wish."

He shook his head. "I've got him. If you'll show me where to take him . . ."

"Of course." She wished she could think of some excuse not to invite him into the Mission. Any that she spoke, even the truth that it would do the Mission no good to have a policeman loitering about in front of it, would sound petty and cruel when he had been so kind.

Starting up the stairs, she paused when she heard a whimper from the little boy. She turned and held out her hands. When Sergeant McCauley placed the child and the quilt in her arms, she cuddled the frightened child close. He grew rigid for a moment, then melted against her. Hot tears sifted through her bodice as Conlan pressed his face to her breast. She whispered softly to him, guessing that what she said made no difference when he was this upset. Yet, if her voice reached him, it might draw him out of his terror.

"Will he be all right?"

She raised her gaze from Conlan's ashen face to meet Sergeant McCauley's eyes. The grief in them was as riveting as the little boy's and threatened to undam her own. When Sergeant McCauley put his hand on the railing close to her elbow, she suddenly yearned to edge down a step and let him cradle her as she cradled the child. She ached for arms around her, strong arms that would hold back the rush of pain of losing someone dear, someone she had thought she would spend the rest of her life with. Then, while his broad shoulders protected her from the past that haunted her, she could release the tears that had waited two years to fall.

"Shall we go in, Miss Granger?"

His words tore apart the sweet fantasy. Blinking, she

nodded. Thank goodness he had no idea what she had been thinking. Gathering her skirt up, she climbed the last few steps to the door.

He reached past her to open it. When his sleeve brushed hers, she recoiled.

"I thought you might want help," he said, his voice as rigid as his face.

"Yes, I do. Thank you." Her words were a jumble as she entered the Mission before he could guess that she had not been offended by the chance touch. She had been astonished by the quiver rushing through her. If the mere touch of his coat against her sleeve elicited such a sensation, she did not want to think what . . .

She was too upset by what she had seen. It was nothing more than that. And the quilt brought back all the memories she had spent two years trying to forget. Now they flooded over her, happy ones she longed to savor, but they had been shadowed by grief. She tried to dam them once more.

Here in the Mission she would regain her serenity as she always had, here among those she loved and who needed her as much as she needed them.

As she set Conlan on the bottommost step of the steep stairs leading to the upper floors, she heard the familiar clatter of footsteps. She scooped him up just as five children came racing down the stairs.

"You should not be running in the house," she said automatically as she moved back toward the door to her office.

"Miss Sarah, I saw a policeman outside," the tallest girl cried. "Did you see—? Oh, my!" She gulped loudly.

"Children, this is Sergeant McCauley. He helped me bring our two newest children here." She motioned toward the kitchen at the back of the house. "Rachel has a baby out there."

Benjamin stepped hastily aside as the children careened around the newel post and down the narrow hallway that ran between the stairs and the two rooms at the front of the house. Their footsteps clattered on the tiled floor before they disappeared behind a swinging door.

"This way, Sergeant McCauley." The prim tone had returned to Miss Granger's voice as she pointed to the door on the left. At least she was not showing him to the front door.

He took another glance at the room on the other side of the hall. A rod and rings waited for portieres, but the doorway was bare. A trio of chairs and a settee whose cushions sagged almost to the floor were arranged in front of the simple hearth. Everything was threadbare, but clean, including the rack of children's clothing drying in front of the windows in what he guessed had been the house's parlor.

As he followed Miss Granger into the room on the opposite side of the hall, he looked upward. More children were up there; he could hear giggles and cheerful voices. He grinned wryly to himself. Those were sounds he did not encounter often when he was working.

This room was half the size of the parlor. Two doors were set across from the single window. Between them, atop a patternless gray rug, were a desk and several chairs. Another old sofa, this one having given up all pretense of supporting its cushions, was pushed against the side wall. There was, he noted with amazement, no hearth. This room must be freezing during New York City's damp winters.

Miss Granger placed Conlan on the sofa and knelt in front of him. Taking off his cap and locking his fingers behind his back, Benjamin watched in silence. There was a sense of love and welcome in this house for children who had lost everything. Maybe that warmth would reach Conlan, too.

"This is my house, Conlan," Miss Granger said with a smile. "I have some small cakes in the kitchen. Would you like one?"

The little boy continued to suck his thumb as he rubbed the quilt between his fingers.

Benjamin frowned when he saw how Miss Granger glanced at the quilt, flinched, then looked hastily away. Why? The answer came as quickly as the question. This quilt might be the best clue they had to finding the murderer. She must have realized that. He should have, too, but he had been too caught up in admiring her delicate lips and strong chin. It was time for him to think about his job.

"Why don't we make you more comfortable? It's hot, don't you think?" She reached for the quilt.

Conlan screeched, and she drew back, her face as colorless as the little boy's.

Benjamin swallowed roughly. Saints on high, the kid had the lungs of a banshee, and his cry was as unsettling. He had never heard such a sound from a child, this wild keening. Putting his hand on Miss Granger's shoulder, he was not sure if she was trembling or if he was. Or maybe both of them.

She looked up at him, despair dimming her eyes. When he held out his hand, she placed hers on it and let him bring her to her feet with a rustle of black satin. He did not release her fingers as he led her to the far side of the room. Just now, he wanted a human touch to erase the taint of that heart-breaking shriek.

"Are you all right?" she asked.

"Me?"

"Yes, you. Right now, you look as gray as a Johnny Reb's uniform."

He tried to smile, but had no more success than she did. When her gaze shifted back to the little boy, he asked again, hoping she would give him the answer he wanted to hear, "Will he be all right?"

"I wish I knew." She undid the ribbons of her funereal bonnet and lifted it off. Setting it on the desk, she said, "I have never seen—"

"What was that?" came a gasp from the door.

Miss Granger rushed to the door, where her assistant was surrounded by what Benjamin guessed might be an even dozen children. It was not easy to tell, because they all were pushing and jostling to see into the office.

Miss Nevins frowned as she looked past Miss Granger to him. "Did *he* do something to the child?"

Before he could defend himself, Miss Granger retorted, "Of course not! Rachel, Conlan is frightened enough already. I don't think we should distress him more with the excitement of the other children."

"Of course." Her scowl lengthened her face. "I'll take them up to help me find a drawer to use for the baby's bed."

"Rachel?" Miss Granger's fingers clenched on the door. "Did you see anything on the baby to give us some clue who they might be?"

"The baby comes from a middle-class or better home, because there is lace on her little dress and her diaper is made of finer material than half of the clothes we have in the Mission."

"But nothing to identify them?" Benjamin asked.

For a moment, he thought Miss Nevins would not answer him. Then she said, "Sarah, that's all I can tell you right now. Maybe the little boy will know—"

"I'll speak to him as soon as he calms down," Miss Granger answered. "Thank you, Rachel." She smiled. "Children, will you help Rachel find a place for our new baby to sleep?"

Benjamin folded his arms over his chest as he watched the children rush up the stairs, the youngest ones helped by the bigger children. Their excited voices suggested that they had no reason to be afraid now that they were here in Miss Granger's protection. They had been right . . . until now.

Walking to the sofa, he bent over to examine the quilt. He did not need the instincts that had served him well since he joined the Metropolitan Police. Even Miss Granger had seen that this quilt had answers for all the puzzles surrounding this murder. He saw no bloodstains on it, so he guessed the children had been safely hidden in the alley before the woman was attacked. That could mean but one thing. She had realized she and the children were in danger. But how? Again the answer was simple—because she had recognized the murderer and knew that person was a threat to her and her children.

What other clues could the quilt offer him? As he lifted one corner, slender fingers halted him. He looked up to see

Miss Granger. By all the saints! She was as quiet as a sneak stalking his prey.

"Not now," she said softly.

"Miss Granger—"

"Not now." She put her hand on his arm and steered him away from the little boy, who was nodding with fatigue.

He halted by her desk and faced her, again folding his arms over his chest. "Now see here, Miss Granger. I know you mean well, but obstructing a policeman in his duties is against the law."

"I'm sure it is," she said with quiet dignity, "but my duties include protecting that child from any additional pain today. Let him be comforted by his quilt and sleep. Maybe when he wakes, he'll be more himself."

"That could take hours."

"Or days."

He scowled. "I don't have days to wait. There is a murderer out there who has so far been successful. If we delay too long, that murderer may strike again."

"I realize that." Sarah sighed as she wrapped her arms around herself and watched Conlan drifting off to sleep. "I've lived here long enough to know that, but I know what that child needs."

"Do you?"

She was startled by the question. Facing Sergeant McCauley, she said, "I hope so. Each child who comes here brings a unique past that is filled with problems and grief and loss. Although I pray that none of the others have had to suffer what this dear child has today, none of them have been exempt from pain. It is my job and Rachel's to give them a chance to learn to love and trust again, so they might be part of a family again."

"That's a huge task."

"I know, but it's one that matters deeply to me. Just as I know that your work matters deeply to you."

"How do you know that?"

"I know because of this." She tapped the badge on his chest and almost smiled when he gaped at her in amazement. She knew she was being brazen, but she needed to make her point. "You wear it proudly, although a Metropolitan Police badge can bring more abuse and accusations than those wearing it could ever be guilty of."

"Then you know why I need to examine that quilt more closely."

"Yes."

"Then—"

"But not now!"

His hands curled into fists at his sides, and she wanted to say she understood his frustration. Dear God, she wished she could hand him that quilt and send him on his way and have him capture the murderer and take the taint of this horrendous crime away from the Mission.

She could not.

Grief clogged in her throat when she went to lean the little boy back onto the cushions, so he might sleep and lose himself in what she prayed were dreams as pretty as the fabrics sewn together in his quilt. Her fingers lingered on the blackbirds along the edge. How odd that someone had added such an elegant design to an otherwise simple quilt! Maybe "Sing a Song of Sixpence" was Conlan's favorite nursery rhyme, and the border had been added to please him.

She could not help smiling. She had made her first nursery rhyme quilt when she was only a few years older than Conlan. The stitches had been uneven, slanting the quilt to one side, but she had kept that quilt for years. Her smile faded. She had planned to use that quilt for her first child, even though, in the years since, she had become an expert quilter, winning prizes at the local fair and making quilts to give to friends who were getting married. Then she had started on a special quilt of her own just as her life had fallen apart. She had pushed quilting out of her life along with everything else when she came here.

For the first time, she missed it. *Really* missed it. Her fingers itched for the smooth sensation of a worn needle in them as she made the small stitches that created magic out of simple fabric. When was the last time she had thought of magic?

Conlan whimpered in his sleep, and she brushed his hair back from his salt-stained face. Bending, she kissed his cheek lightly. Tonight, Rachel would have to oversee putting the children to bed by herself, because this child needed someone to sit by him as he slept and to hold him when he woke.

"Sarah?"

She straightened and stared at Benjamin, wide-eyed that he had used her given name without asking her permission. No doubt, after her bold actions, he thought he need not beg her leave for such an intimacy.

When he took her hands, folding them between his, she knew he must be able to feel how her fingers shook. Maybe he would think it was caused only by the remnants of her fear. She wondered why she expected him to believe that, when she did not. Something about this man, this *policeman* who could cause all kinds of trouble for her and the Mission just by being here, something about him created sensations she had thought had died with Giles.

Don't be silly! She had known Giles for years and had come to love him. When he had given his life for his ideals on a Southern battlefield, she had been certain she would never savor those feelings again.

"Sarah," he whispered, "you cannot ignore the truth. That woman's murderer must even now be plotting what he will do next. A man who has killed has nothing left to lose."

She pulled her hands out of his. "I don't want to hear this."

"I'm sorry if it disturbs you."

"I know you didn't intend to frighten me." She struggled to smile, but failed.

"You're wrong." He tilted her chin up with the crook of his finger. "I want you to be scared, very scared, because I believe someone knows who killed Conlan's mother."

"Conlan?" she whispered, held by the raven fervor of his gaze.

He nodded. "And, Sarah, I suspect someone else may be realizing that, too."

With a choked gasp, she drew away. "He's just a little

boy. A terribly scared little boy." She faced him, clasping her hands. "He won't even speak now! Why would anyone worry about him?"

"Because Conlan might be able to identify his mother's murderer." He grasped her shoulders and tugged her a half step toward him.

"Even if he could identify the murderer, who would believe a little boy of his age?"

"I would."

"Would a judge and a jury?"

He shrugged as his hands drifted down along her arms to cup her elbows. "I cannot say, but I would be willing to risk it if there were any chance that the murderer would hang for his crimes. That's why you must help me."

"I will help as much as I can, but you cannot have the quilt tonight."

His hands fell away, and the familiar sense of being utterly alone struck her like a blow. "I hope you don't come to regret that decision, Sarah."

She stared after him as he walked out of her office. Dropping to sit in a chair by the window, she watched him swing into his horse's saddle and ride down the street. She fingered the edge of the quilt, then pulled her hand back. Why was it a quilt that Conlan held to his heart? She had pushed quilts from her shattered heart.

Conlan stirred, and she looked back at him. *Let the past go.* She had to think of *this* child in *this* place at *this* time. She had done the right thing to help him.

Hadn't she? She was no longer sure.

3

"NOT A WORD." RACHEL shook her head. "Not even when I asked him what he wanted to eat."

Sarah gathered up Conlan in her arms and sat in the rocker in the middle of the parlor. He was stiff in her arms. Not a sound came from him but the sucking of his thumb as he rubbed the unfinished quilt against his cheek. Looking over his head, she asked, "How's the new baby doing?"

"She ate as if she hadn't in days."

"She's not much more than days old."

"What are you planning on calling her?"

Sarah smiled. "Why not Birdie? Who knows? That may have been her name, which would explain the blackbirds on the quilt."

"Birdie?" Rachel's freckled nose wrinkled with her smile. "I like that. She's as little as a bird."

"And eats like a hungry young bird!" She smoothed Conlan's hair back from his forehead, but he did not look up. Thank goodness, he would eat when she put food in front of him. He simply did not talk or react to anyone.

"Sarah, these two children in addition to the others are going to take so much time that you are going to need to hire a girl to help in the kitchen."

"You know we can't afford that." She sighed. The benefactors of the home were giving less each month. With
the uncertainty of the war, only fools did not horde their
money. Some of those who had donated regularly had sent
letters to let her know that they could not give again until
the war was over. Others simply never responded to her
letters. Only Mr. Winslow was giving as much as two years
ago.

She had to find a way to raise money. She could hire the
older children out, but she did not want to send them to
where they would be treated no better than the slaves had
been treated in the South. There must be something they
could do here in the Mission, but she was not sure what.

"I can't cook *and* watch the children." With a laugh,
Rachel held up her hands. "And don't you offer to help.
You don't have the time either. If you hire a girl to work
in the kitchen, I can handle the children and laundry. Then
you can concentrate on just the children and the mending
and raising funds for the Mission."

"Just?" She chuckled.

"Maybe the girl could help with the mending, too."

"Maybe before the end of the year."

Rachel groaned. "By the end of the year, we'll have
worked our fingers clear to the bone and beyond."

"I know, but I can't spare the dollar a girl would expect
each week."

"If we could find someone who would accept less—"

"You know that's impossible. I don't know anyone who
would work for less."

"If I asked around—"

Her voice grew stern. "No, Rachel, don't get someone's
hopes up when I can't pay anyone but you now." She
leaned her cheek against Conlan's hair. "I really wish I
could tell you to go ahead and find a girl, because I know
that this little fellow and Birdie are going to need a lot of
help to grow strong."

Rachel shuddered as she glanced toward the door.

"What is it?" Sarah asked.

"Is *he* coming back?"

She sighed. The emphasis warned her that Rachel was speaking about Sergeant McCauley. "I'm sure he'll be back. He wants to find out what happened to the children's mother."

"It would be better if he stayed away."

That she could agree with, for every reason that came into her head except one. How could she explain that a thrill erupted through her at Sergeant McCauley's chaste touch? How could she suggest that she was willing to risk the fury of her neighbors for another sampling of that excitement?

She was saved from answering when the rest of the children rushed into the parlor. The tallest girl, whose name was Fiona, held a book. If only Fiona were another year or two older, then she could have been just the helper they needed, but she was only nine years old.

While Sarah read fairy tales to the children, as she did each evening before they went to bed, she wished she could have told Rachel to hire a girl. They must soon, because, although Rachel had not spoken of it today, Sarah knew that her assistant would not be returning after she married at the end of the year. There had to be some solution, but she was not sure what it might be. Going without sleep most of last night was not making it easy to think of anything but Goldilocks and her three bears.

". . . And they lived happily ever after." Sarah closed the book and smiled at the eager faces. She loved the time when she had the luxury to sit with the children like this. Putting the book on the table beside her, she leaned back against the worn upholstery of the chair and listened to the children chatter about the fairy tale.

They seemed so untouched by the life they had known before they came here. She shivered at the thought of any of these dear children behaving like Five Points urchins who believed robbery and fighting were customary childhood activities. But what future could there be for Irish orphans in a city that despised immigrants? She hoped that they would be able to find positions in a shop or in one of the elegant homes along Lafayette Street or Lexington Avenue.

She fingered the quilt Conlan held. The patches of silk drew her eyes again and again. Were he and Birdie from one of those wondrous houses such a short distance and another world away?

"Read us one more story," urged Missy, who was only a month or so younger than Fiona and ruled over the younger children like a matriarch.

"One more?" she asked with false amazement. "I've already read you four. Aren't you getting tired of hearing about princes and princesses and evil witches?"

A loud chorus of "No!" widened her smile. It faded when Conlan did not respond to the other children's excitement. How could she reach this child? She ran her fingers along the section of the quilt that was not finished. Maybe she could persuade him to talk to her again by using this quilt.

But how? She shivered at the very thought. She must get past this lingering pain, this final remnant of her grief for Giles. How she wished Conlan had been clutching a stuffed toy instead!

As she opened the book, the gaslight flickered. The front door must be opening. She put her finger in the book to mark her place and rose. Setting Conlan on the chair, she quieted the children with a promise that she or Rachel would read them one more story before they went upstairs to bed.

"Good evening, Miss Nevins. Is Miss Granger in?" Sergeant McCauley's deep voice resonated through the hall that was more accustomed to the soprano trill of the children's laughter.

"She is busy with the children," Rachel replied primly.

"Is she now?"

Sarah fought not to smile when he looked past her assistant. Putting her hand on Rachel's arm, she wished she could ease her assistant's scowl.

"Sergeant McCauley wants to speak with you, Sarah," said Rachel in the same strained tone, "but I told him you were busy."

"This is very important," he said, taking off his cap. "I need to speak with you, Miss Granger."

Handing the book to Rachel, she replied, "Of course. If you will come into my office." She took one step toward her office on the other side of the hall, then said, "Rachel, one more story before they go to bed." She turned and said, "Only . . ."

Her heart hammered as she stared at the gold buttons climbing up Sergeant McCauley's chest. They were right in front of her. When she took a hasty step back, he put out a hand to steady her. His fingers on her arm kept her on her feet, but unsettled her more than any chance touch should. Or was it chance?

As she met his steady gaze, she could not mistake the smile sparkling in his eyes. His face remained stern, so Sarah would not guess at this hint of amusement without becoming lost within his eyes as well. As if this were a very intimate jest between them, he held her gaze as gently as he held her arm.

His thumb caressed the inside of her elbow, a slow, sensuous motion that urged her to sway toward him in a dance with silent music. When she bit her lower lip to keep her gasp from escaping, the sparks in his eyes glittered like burnished gold.

"Just one story before bed," Rachel said as she walked away.

Sergeant McCauley chuckled. "Sounds like an excellent idea. Shall we take advantage of this time to ourselves?"

"I think not!" Sarah lifted her chin. "I don't know what gave you the idea that—"

"We should talk while Miss Nevins is reading to the children?" His brow threaded with bafflement. "I thought you would not want the youngsters about when we speak of what brought the two children here."

"Of course." How could he fluster her so much that she forgot everything but his touch? Even when Giles had kissed her, she had been aware of the breeze crossing the front porch of her father's parsonage. "If you'll come into my office, we can talk."

Benjamin swallowed his laugh as she went into the room and closed the door after he had entered. Flustering Miss Sarah Granger was easy when she reacted so strongly to everything. Not just to him. He would not flatter himself with that assumption. Since he had left the children with her yesterday, he had spent his time learning more about this woman and her work.

She had been at the Mission for almost two years. In that time, she had made an impression on every person she met. Those who had not spoken with her still had an opinion of this determined woman. She was offered the same respect as the priests in the church down the street, not quite part of the day-to-day life of the others here, but an inseparable facet of life along Second Avenue.

He admired the soft curve of her lips as she motioned for him to sit on the sagging sofa. Those lips could grow straight when she was sure she was right. He watched them as he said, "My captain asked me to bring the quilt to the station."

He was surprised they did not grow taut when she replied, "No."

"Miss Granger, you are interfering with the investigation of a murder."

"You needn't remind me of that." She drew her chair out from behind her desk and sat facing him.

Again he was amazed. He would have guessed she would keep the desk between them as a shield. Then he realized that she was so accustomed to being honest with people, she expected the same from them. How could she be so foolish? Half the people who lived in Five Points would not recognize honesty if it were introduced to them personally by President Lincoln.

"Captain Potter wants that quilt delivered to him immediately."

She shook her head. "Captain Potter will have to be as patient as you. And as patient as I, because until Conlan is himself again, I will not deprive him of the sole bit of comfort he has."

"Do you know what you are risking?"

"Yes." She ran her fingers along the curved arm of the chair. It was a motion she must do often, because the varnish was wearing off the wood.

"You could be sent to jail."

"I know, but I consider that highly unlikely." She smiled as she gestured toward the door. "Who would take care of these children if I were sent to jail?"

"That would not be a consideration."

Folding her hands in her lap, she smiled. "Sergeant McCauley, there is no need to argue about this because I shan't change my mind. As long as Conlan needs that quilt, he shall have it. The moment he returns to his prattling self, I shall have the quilt delivered to you and Captain Potter."

He stood and released his breath in a slow, deep sigh. He should go into the other room where the children were laughing about the story Miss Nevins was reading to them. He should simply take the quilt. He should, but he could not. Maybe if he had not seen the little boy's bright-eyed delight in it and his baby sister, that look that had become dull and withdrawn, maybe then he could have taken the quilt.

Maybe . . . His gaze was caught by hers, and he was drawn to it like a thief to treasure. Resting his hands on the arms of her chair, he leaned toward her. Her eyes widened, and her mouth opened. Whatever she had intended to say went unspoken when his leg brushed hers through her wide skirt. She looked hastily away. He cupped her chin, bringing her face back toward him.

"Sarah, you must listen to me," he whispered, his fingers slipping along her cheek.

"What gave you that idea?" Sarah swept his hand aside as she came to her feet. For a moment, she thought he would not move away. She was not certain what she would do if he did not.

Then he edged back, but only a single step. She was caught between him and the chair. When she started to push the chair out of the way, he reached past her and clasped its arm. His sleeve stroked her arm, each fiber of the wool sending a pulse of something delightful through her; urging her to forgive him for being so outrageous.

"Sergeant McCauley—"

"Benjamin," he murmured as his finger edged up her cheek again.

"I shouldn't."

"Shouldn't what? Call me Benjamin or let me touch you like this?" He ran his finger along her lips, which quivered at his light touch. "Or do this?"

His arm around her pulled her up against the line of buttons down his chest and swept her mouth to his. As gently as he had cradled the baby, he sampled her lips. She raised her hands to push him away, but, as she touched his shoulders, her fingers curved along their breadth, eager to explore them. He deepened the kiss until her breath grew frayed. Her fingers sifted up through his hair to savor the pleasure she had not enjoyed since—

With a cry, Sarah pulled away. Had she lost her wits? She barely knew this policeman. He endangered everything she had created here at the Second Avenue Mission for Needy Children, a haven for the children and for her heart, which must not be jeopardized again.

"Good evening, Sergeant McCauley," she said, keeping her back to him. Her cheeks were on fire, and she did not want any blush betraying her.

His hands on her shoulders brought her to face him. When she stared at the buttons on his coat, he tipped her chin up gently. She did not have to look at him, but she knew how childish it would be to fight him. He deserved this courtesy while she told him how he should expect no other.

"Sergeant—"

"It won't compromise you in any way to call me Benjamin, Sarah." His lips tilted as he spoke her name. "And I'm just following orders."

"Orders? Whose orders?"

"Captain Potter told me to offer you whatever I must to get that quilt."

She stared at his grin. She began to speak, then halted.

How much more outrageous could he be? Walking around her desk, she picked up the basket Birdie had been in. She shoved it into his arms.

"Tell Captain Potter that he will have to be satisfied with this for now," she said coolly.

"The baby's basket?"

"It might offer some clue to where the children are from." She ran her finger along the handle. "It is well made, and this pretty design is fancier than anything I've seen around here."

His smile disappeared as he tipped the basket one way and then the other. The intensity in his eyes matched what she had seen when she met him by the murdered woman. "I believe Captain Potter will find this interesting," he said. Raising his eyes, he added, "Thanks, Sarah."

"As soon as I can, I shall let you have the quilt." She arched her brows. "You don't have to try and seduce it from me."

"Why not? Because it won't work?" He closed the distance between them again as he reached past her to set the basket on the chair. "Or because it will?"

She never had been so glad to be interrupted by the door opening. Hurrying to it, she bent to give Skelly a kiss on the cheek. The little boy refused to go to bed without one. She took his hand as she turned to where Benjamin still stood.

He picked up the basket. Offering Skelly a smile, he said only, "Thanks for the basket, Sarah."

"I hope it will satisfy Captain Potter for a while."

"That's about as likely as me being satisfied with only one kiss from you." He brushed her cheek with a quick kiss as she had the child's.

"Are you going to bed, too, Sarah?" asked Skelly, looking up at her, wide-eyed.

"Not any time very soon." She fought to smile for the youngster. How dare Benjamin act so in front of the children!

Benjamin laughed. "I get the message. Loud and clear."

He winked at the little boy. "See you sometime not very soon."

She bit back her irritation as he walked out into the hall, collected his flat-topped hat, and closed the front door behind him. He would be back. He would not leave her alone until he got his hands on the quilt . . . and her.

∞

SARAH TIPTOED OUT OF her office and closed the door quietly. At last, Conlan was asleep. The little boy had been inconsolable tonight. His cries had disturbed the other children so much that she had finally brought him down to her room and tucked him and his blackbird quilt beneath the covers on one side of her bed, something she had vowed she would never do. All the children had tried to devise excuses to sneak into her bed, so she had insisted that no one would be allowed in. That pledge had held . . . until tonight. She could no longer tolerate the soft weeping and the intermittent howls of grief. Giving the child two drops of laudanum in a glass of cider, she had held him until he slept.

Rubbing her brow, she tried to remember when this headache had started. Two days ago—or was it three? Probably it had begun right around the time when she had received the letter from the Granville family letting her know that they could no longer make any donations to the Mission.

We regret this, but the extreme expenses incurred by our business because of the ongoing war . . .

She had seen those words or something similar too many times in the past year. At the beginning of the war with the Confederacy, she had heard so many people say that they did not expect it to last very long. She had wanted to believe they were right, but she could not. General Lee had been well known as a brilliant man around the military academy at West Point. When he went to fight for the Confederacy, many of the cadets went with him. They knew they faced hanging as traitors, so they would not surrender easily.

Now the war had been going on for over two years. All the excitement, all the certainty that the Yankee forces would triumph, all the patriotism were gone, along with jobs in the shipyards where once ships had sailed to Southern ports to get cotton for Northern mills.

Sarah could no longer put off finding another way to raise money to pay for the children's needs. She would not have them on their hands and knees scrubbing floors in one of the fine homes on Fifth Avenue. Nor would she consign them to a long day's work in one of the factories. There, they would sew in dim light until their eyes were strained nearly to blindness.

Sewing . . . She already had taught the older girls rudimentary sewing skills. If she taught them to quilt and to make the fine quilts that her father's church had used to raise money, Mr. Pettigew might sell them in his store on the corner.

Her first pulse of excitement vanished. Even if she could force herself to return to quilting, she had no money to buy fabric. She must save what little money they had to pay for some help with the kitchen work. Not a full-time girl, but someone who would come occasionally to handle some of the heaviest cleaning.

So what other ways could she raise money for the children?

"Come in," Rachel said from by the front door.

Turning, Sarah saw it was open. The day's last heat surged in, but she ignored it as she stared at a blond woman. Hope pulsed through her. Maybe this woman had come looking for Conlan and Birdie.

"You'll want to speak to our director," Rachel added.

Stepping into the dim light from the single lamp in the foyer, Sarah smiled even as her hopes faded. The woman was bulging with pregnancy. "How can I help you, Mrs. . . . ?"

"Mrs. O'Brien. Doreen O'Brien. Are you the director?"

The woman's Irish brogue told Sarah that she must be

from Five Points. "How can I help you, Mrs. O'Brien?"

"I hear you're looking for a girl to work in the kitchen here."

"Where did you hear that?" She glanced at Rachel, who avoided meeting her eyes. Apparently Rachel had decided not to listen to good sense.

Mrs. O'Brien shrugged her thin shoulders. Sarah guessed she was seventeen at the most. "Heard it here and there. I thought I'd see if you'd gotten a girl yet."

"Not yet. Rachel, will you check on the children to be sure they are in bed?" Keeping her voice even, she added, "We'll speak about this in the morning."

"Sarah—"

She put her hand on Rachel's arm. Her assistant only wanted to help, she knew, but that did not give them the money to pay for more help. Looking at Mrs. O'Brien, she said, "If you'll come into the parlor, Mrs. O'Brien."

The woman glanced around with candid curiosity as they went into the room that was oddly quiet now that the children were in bed. When they sat, Sarah noticed how the young woman stroked the blue settee. She suspected that the frayed material was finer than anything Mrs. O'Brien had ever seen.

"My man's gone with the army," Mrs. O'Brien said in answer to Sarah's question.

"Does your family mind you working out while you're pregnant?"

Again she shrugged. "I need to live, Miss Granger. They can't help me, and I can't afford to live on what my husband sends me."

"I'll be honest," Sarah said as she leaned forward to meet the woman's brown eyes. "I can't pay much, Mrs. O'Brien."

"You can call me Doreen. Everyone else does." She fumbled with the strings on her bag. "I thought you might offer me room and board and two bits a week in exchange for helping you in the kitchen." She hesitated, then said, "I can cook and clean, but I don't want to tend your children. I've spent the last ten years raising my younger sisters and brothers." Her fingers settled on her stomach. "And I've got this one to take care of soon."

Sarah wanted to cheer. For what she could squeeze from the budget, she was going to get someone to oversee the kitchen and relieve her and Rachel to look after the children. There would even be some money left over. It might be enough to put a down payment on the fabric she would need for the children to make quilts. She ignored the twinge at the thought of facing what she had put out of her mind for two years. She must think of the children first.

Rising, she smiled. "Doreen, I think you'll find working at the Mission is hard, but very rewarding."

"I know I shall find it very rewarding," agreed the young woman with an answering smile.

As Sarah led her to the kitchen at the back of the house, she hoped things were about to take a turn for the better at the Mission. It was about time.

∞

SARAH WOKE WITH A start. Something was wrong. She had heard something or smelled something or . . . She was not sure, but there was a change in her room. No, Conlan was still asleep, nearly lost in the pillows with the comforter pulled half over his cheek. Poor dear. He wanted to hide like a little creature seeking its burrow. She wished she knew some way to help him. If—

The sound came again, rustling near her bedroom door. Sitting, she held the sheets close to her breast as she reached for her wrapper. She pulled it around her and listened for any sound.

Slowly she slid across the bed to reach the table where a kerosene lamp sat. The lamp was gone! Straining to see, she was sure something stood near the door. Slow breathing told her it was some*one*. Her fingers closed over a letter opener.

"Who is it?" she whispered as she lifted it.

No reply came. There was someone else in the room.

Every inch of her could sense that. The person must be tall, for the shadow loomed over her.

"I know you're there. Who is it?"

The shadow remained between her and the door. She had no other way to escape.

No noise came except the steady pulse of breathing.

Taking a step away from the bed, she whispered, "What do you want?"

A soft scratch was her only warning. Light burst outward from the door.

"No!" She stared at the profile she had treasured in her memory. It could not be him. There were no ghosts in the Mission!

As the man turned toward her, light from the gas lamp sparkled off his hair, which was the same ebony as his clothes. The only bit of color came from his blue eyes twinkling on either side of his patrician nose. Then she saw the white tightness of a scar on his left cheek.

"Lorne!" Sarah choked. This man could be more dangerous to the Mission now than a ghost.

"How are you doing, honey?" His tenor drawl was as warm as she remembered it. "Surprised, Sarah?"

She rushed past him into her office. For a moment, she was not sure if he would follow. She lit the lamp as he sat in the chair behind her desk. Without asking permission, he pulled out his pipe and began filling it.

She sank to the settee. When her wrapper flared around her, she tightened the sash and adjusted the neckline so the lace on her chemise was hidden. His lips quirked with amusement.

"I guess I startled you," he said, leaning back in his chair. "I doubt if you get many callers here."

"I've never made it a practice to invite midnight callers into my bedroom."

He lit the tobacco and took several puffs until the bowl glowed red. The acrid smoke curled from his mouth. "I didn't mean in your bedroom, Sarah. I meant in this purgatory you've made for yourself. I never expected to see you in a place like this."

"And why not?"

"Oh, I know you're the good Reverend Granger's daughter, but there's a huge difference between church teas in West Point and ministering to Irish orphans in a New York slum." He chortled as she waved aside the smoke. Noticing stitching on his sleeve, she recalled how he once would never have worn a coat that had been torn and resewn. But once he had been her friend. "If Giles saw you now—"

"Leave Giles out of this."

He ignored her sorrowful voice. "If he could see you now, he'd drag you out of here. When I saw you on the street dressed like a crow, I could not believe my eyes. You used to look so pretty in that candy-striped dress you wore when—"

"Enough!" When he cocked a black eyebrow, she asked in a calmer voice, "What are *you* doing here?"

"It's been more than two years since I visited New York. I thought I'd see how the folks up North were doing." He smiled through the smoke ringing his head. "The Irish are at the throats of the coloreds. New York is a lovely place to spend the summer."

In a whisper, she gasped, "You're staying all summer? Are you mad?"

"Hardly, my dear Sarah." He rose, leading her gaze upward with him. Bending, he kissed her cheek. "Don't worry. I'll see you soon."

"But what are you doing? Where are you staying? Lorne, what—?"

"Hush," he answered as he put his finger to her lips. "Why don't you go to bed? You look tired."

She pulled back, shocked, for his teasing brought to mind Giles's. How they used to enjoy fooling everyone—one pretending to be the other, although they had never done that to her. Or, at least, she had never caught them in such a jest. That had ended when Lorne was hurt during a ride along the Hudson River, and he was left with that scar on his cheek. "But, Lorne, don't you think—?"

"If anyone notices the broken window in the pantry, I suggest you call the Metropolitan Police." He put his pipe between his teeth and smiled. "It's a shame they don't protect you better."

She froze when he mentioned the police. Why hadn't she thought of this as soon as she saw Lorne? She had been shocked. And not only by Lorne's call, but because she could not shake off the dream he had interrupted. In it, Benjamin had held her again in his arms. His kisses had been but a preamble to the bedtime story he was offering to share with her.

If Benjamin and Lorne chanced to meet, it would be disastrous. Benjamin would not hesitate to arrest a Southerner who had skulked into the city.

"Why are you here, Lorne?" she asked.

"Don't be so curious." His smile grew taut. "Giles always said that was what he liked least about you. How you always poked your nose into other folks' business on the pretext of trying to help them." He turned off the gaslight.

"Lorne?" She whirled toward the door to the hall as she heard his footsteps in that direction. He was silhouetted for a moment in it, then gone.

She raced after him. When she reached the foyer, even his shadow had vanished. She hurried to the kitchen. If he had slipped out that way, the only sign was the broken window.

Trying to peer through the shadows, she pushed at her eyeglasses and realized she had left them by her bed. As she turned to return to her room, she heard footsteps on the back stairs. She spun. With a sigh of relief, she smiled at Doreen. Thank goodness she had not come down a few seconds earlier.

"I thought I heard a prowler." Doreen pointed to the broken window. "Do you want help cleaning up the mess?"

"Go back to bed. I can manage." She tried to smile. No one must guess Lorne had been here. He could be arrested.

Doreen nodded and hurried back up the stairs.

Sarah took a ragged breath as she reached for the broom by the long table where the children ate their meals. "Why now?" she whispered as she swept the shattered glass into a pile.

There was no answer, but she had not expected one. All she expected was more trouble.

4

"THERE SHOULD BE PLENTY of good material left on these bolts." Sarah fingered the cotton. It was not smooth, but it was thick. When several layers were quilted together, it would offer enough warmth for a New York City winter.

"I won't charge you for the faded fabric." Mr. Pettigew pushed his thick, dark hair out of his eyes. Not that it mattered. She suspected he needed spectacles even more than she did, but he refused to wear one of the sets he had for sale. Instead, he squinted at each of his customers until he resembled, with his bushy whiskers, a well-fed mouse.

"Thank you." She touched the section that had given up its color to the sunshine that poured through the glass in the store's door. This would work for the inner layers of the quilts.

He set two more bolts and a small box of thread next to it. When he added up the figures on the paper on the nicked counter, she hoped he did not hear her gasp. She had known how expensive everything was getting with the war, but she had not guessed the cost of cotton had doubled in the past six months since she last had bought material for the children's clothes. Since then, she had been lengthening hems and patching elbows and knees with scraps.

She pushed a few coins across the counter. She had enough left to pay for the fare to Mr. Winslow's house later in the week. Once she collected his donation, she would be able to pay Mr. Pettigew. The storekeeper allowed her to buy on credit because she always paid him within a few days. That had been easier when she had more benefactors for the Mission. Now she had to live week-to-week on what Mr. Winslow donated until she could persuade someone else to help.

"What are you doing with all this fabric?" he asked as he wrapped it in brown paper and tied it so she could carry it more easily.

"The children are going to be making quilts."

"You can make a lot of quilts with all this." He peered over the top of one bolt. "How many children do you have sleeping there that you need so many quilts?"

She laughed, hoping she sounded more confident than she felt. "I am going to teach the children to quilt so they can make quilts to help raise money for the Mission."

"Do they sew well?"

"Some of them do."

"I might be interested in a few to sell here." When she smiled, he wagged a finger at her. "No promises, of course. Folks around here don't have a lot of money, but they might be interested in some well-made quilts. So many of the women are hiring out that they don't have time to do the sewing they used to do for their families. I've heard them complaining about that right here."

"So have I."

He chuckled and lifted the large packages to hand to her. "I should have guessed that. You're a quick-minded lass." He hesitated, then added, "Full payment at the end of the week as always?"

"As always." Her knees almost buckled under the burden of her purchases, but she kept smiling as she went out of the store and down the street toward the Mission. This project should be the Mission's salvation . . . even if it broke her heart.

∽

SARAH PAUSED IN MIDSTEP. A mistake, she knew, when Birdie began to cry again. Maybe it had been nothing more than the baby's colicky stomach that she had heard.

Thunder rumbled faintly. She laughed at her own skittishness. Since Lorne's visit two nights ago, she had flinched at every sound.

"Maybe he listened to me," she murmured as she watched the baby's eyes close again. "Not that he ever did before. I wish he'd be more like Giles. Giles would have known how stupid it is to be here now."

She sighed. She had thought she knew Giles well. After all, she had accepted his offer of marriage. Everything had been planned for the end of April. Then shots were fired in South Carolina, and he was gone to defend his home state. And then he was dead, along with every dream she had had.

"But if I'd married him, I wouldn't be holding you, would I?" she cooed, not sure if she was trying to comfort the baby or herself. She would not be walking another woman's child to sleep. She would be cradling her own child—hers and Giles's—conceived beneath the wedding quilt lying forgotten in her parents' attic.

She turned to look at the stacks of fabric on the settee. Holding Birdie in the crook of one arm, she lifted one end of the material. Her fingers tingled with the memory of creating something beautiful out of nothing more than this. She had taken scraps of material and sewn an exquisitely simple design before quilting several layers together with the stitches she had perfected for years.

Her fingers clutched on the fabric as she heard a sharp, staccato sound. "Dear God!" she whispered. She knew that sound, for she had heard it often when she lived near West Point. A gun!

She started to put the baby in the drawer just inside her bedroom door, but faltered when Birdie began to whimper. Glancing at the bed, she saw Conlan shifting. She did not want him to wake now. He had seen too much already.

Holding the baby close, she settled her glasses in place as she hurried into the front hall. She swung the heavy door open. Even after dark, heat from the cobblestones struck her face. Above the dim light of the street lamps, streaks of lightning severed the night.

A shiver ran down her back as she balanced on the narrow top step. It was too quiet. Never had she been outside, even on the coldest winter nights, when the streets were not woven with sound.

She held her breath, seeking any sound to let her know she was not alone. It was as if the world were doing the same, waiting, not moving, anticipating . . . what?

A furtive shadow moved past St. John's Church. It avoided the candlelight coming through the church's windows, so she could see nothing but its speed. A flash of light exploded. The crash of a gunshot detonated the night.

Watching someone leaping through the puddles of light, she reached for the doorknob. She must not be seen!

Another shot echoed along the street. Closer. She cringed against the door. A scream climbed into the thunderheads. It went on and on until she wanted to shriek for the pain-filled voice to stop.

Birdie began to cry. Sarah groped for the doorknob, then halted when she saw more forms along the street. Here, she was hidden in the shadows. If she opened the door, she might be seen.

Shouts from beyond the massive church were lost in the thud of thunder, but the malevolent sound of triumphant laughter resounded. Something she could not understand was called out with an undeniably Irish accent. Horror threatened to strangle her. If the violence of Five Points spilled out here, her children would not be safe.

Again a gun fired. And again and again. The screeches vanished as acrid gun smoke drifted past her. Footsteps faded into the distance. Running, exultant, free from the fear that paralyzed her.

Lightning flared, releasing her from her terror. She took a half step forward, and her foot slipped. The baby chirped, and she held Birdie close again. Every bone was jarred, but she did not dare to moan. Any sound might call back the madman who had danced with the devil's own delight along the street.

Slowly she edged down the stairs. Her fingers tightened on the iron railing until bits of rust cut into them. She should go back into the Mission, but she could see someone lying in the street. Hadn't she learned anything from last week? Then she had let the sight of Birdie's mother draw her into Benjamin's investigation. But she could not let someone die because she was afraid to do anything.

"Miss Granger, go back inside."

She whirled to meet an unsmiling face that was nearly lost in a dark beard. "Father Tynan!" She had met the priest, who was new at St. John's, only once.

"Go back inside."

"Father, I have a few medical supplies—"

"You don't want the Mission involved in what's happening here in the streets."

"The Mission is here to help people."

When she stepped off the bottom riser, she realized he was not much taller than she was. His eyes burned in their sunken sockets, but he was not old. Just tired of the battle here. As she was.

"Don't get involved with what you don't understand," he said.

"Someone has been shot!"

"I'll tend to it. Guard your children, Miss Granger."

"If you need something—"

His smile was there for a moment, then gone. "Thank you, but no. Go back to bed and pretend to be surprised when you hear the news in the morning."

Watching him race away in his long robes, she scowled. A priest who suggested she tell falsehoods was the least peculiar thing about tonight.

She scanned the street. Every window was dark. It was as if her neighbors had fled, so she would not be the only one feigning astonishment when the sun rose. She had thought this section of Second Avenue different from the Irish slums, but she had been wrong.

She climbed the steps as gingerly as she had come down them. At the top, she paused to watch Father Tynan drop to his knees. If no one helped to find the criminals who had done this, it might be only the beginning of trouble. The city was a powder keg waiting to be ignited by the summer heat, too few jobs, and too much whiskey.

Sarah closed the door behind her. She gasped when she saw Rachel standing in the hallway, holding a candle that threw grotesque shadows across her face.

Rachel whispered, "I heard something outside."

"It's nothing," Sarah lied.

"I heard—"

"Thunder!" she interrupted more sharply than she intended. "The storm's getting closer."

"If it's nothing but thunder, then I'll go back to bed. Unless you want to me to check that all the windows are closed."

"No, I'll do that. Go to sleep." She forced a smile. "I was just checking that the door was secure."

"Good night."

Sarah leaned her head against the carved wood on the front door as Rachel climbed the stairs. Thank heavens it had not been Doreen. *She* would not have believed the ridiculous story. No one raised in Five Points would mistake gunfire for thunder.

As if in answer to her thoughts, thunder exploded overhead. She took Birdie into the bedroom and put her into the narrow drawer that served for her bed. Going to the bed, she checked on Conlan.

She gripped the headboard. Her legs would not stop shaking. Closing her eyes, she took a deep breath. Maybe this was all a dream. A nightmare! She could not believe she had witnessed a murder.

Her eyes widened when she heard a knock on the front door. Hurrying out into the foyer, she glanced at the clock on the parlor mantel. Just past two A.M. Only criminals would be out at this hour. When the knock grew more frantic, she reached for the door. How many times had she bragged that no one was turned away from the Second Avenue Mission for Needy Children?

A flare of lightning illuminated the street. Wind-driven rain pelted her. On the steps, a man and a woman huddled against each other.

Benjamin! Something pinched at her when she saw his arm around the woman, whose head was leaning on his shoulder. Not jealousy! It could not be jealousy.

"Can we come in?" he asked.

Thunder crashed around them. "Of course." She stepped back to let them enter. Who was this woman with him?

Only when Benjamin turned to close the door did Sarah realize he was supporting the woman. The woman's feet dragged across the floor, and she sagged. Sarah reached to help him balance her.

"Get back!" he ordered. He lifted the woman into his arms, cradling her as Sarah had the baby.

Sarah stared at her hands in disbelief. Thinned by the rain, crimson ran along her hands and colored her cuffs. The woman in Benjamin's arms was covered with blood.

"What happened?" Sarah gasped. "Has she been shot?"

He gave her an odd look, but said, "I'm not sure. Do you have a place—?"

"Yes." Picking up her skirt, she grimaced. The fabric would be stained with blood. She opened a door past the parlor. "Use the table here." She lit the lamp above the sideboard. "We never use the dining room."

"Sarah—"

"Let me get our medical bag." She put her hand on her belly so she would not give in to her roiling stomach. Rushing up the stairs, she knocked on Rachel's door. She hoped she did not wake the children.

A bleary-eyed Rachel opened the door. "Sarah, what is it? I was almost back to sleep."

"Go and get bandaging and anything we have to stop bleeding."

"Who?" she gasped, pulling on her robe as she came out into the hall.

Sarah shook her head. "Not one of ours. Sergeant McCauley—"

"He's hurt?"

"Go! You can ask questions later."

Running back down the stairs, she went into the dining room. The light from the gas lamp shone on the blood soaking into the tablecloth. When Benjamin turned, he continued to hold an edge of the tablecloth against the woman in a futile attempt to stanch the blood. Sarah's gaze was caught by his. She paused in midstep, unable to move, unable to think, barely able to breathe.

It had been several days since she had last seen him, when he had held her so close. Her memory had not been able to contain all the strength he possessed. He needed that to help keep order on the streets. Yet, when he had drawn her against him, his gentleness had been almost as sweet as his kiss.

"I think she's lost consciousness, Sarah."

His whisper rumbled like the thunder and broke the spell he had cast over her. She hurried to the table, glad that she did not have to warn him to be quiet. They had too much trouble without the children crowding around the doorway, demanding to know what had woken them in the middle of the night.

"What happened to her?" Sarah asked as softly.

"You guessed already. Shot."

"But the person shot in front of the church wasn't a woman."

Again he aimed a frown at her. She readied herself for his questions, but he looked back at the woman. "I found her half a block from here. Do you know her?"

Bending so her shadow did not conceal the woman's face, Sarah recoiled when she saw the woman's mouth was contorted with agony. "No," she whispered, "I don't know her."

"Sarah?" called Rachel from the door. Gingerly she edged closer.

"Rachel, don't dawdle!" As she took the bag of medicines and bandages, she said, "We may need the doctor."

"I'll go!"

"It's dangerous out there."

"I'll go! I can't stay. All that blood . . ." She ran out the door.

A flash of sympathy weighed on Sarah's shoulders. She would comfort Rachel later. All of her attention now must be on this poor woman. Opening the bag, she withdrew some rolled bandages. She ripped a piece.

"Benjamin, we need—"

"Is there a water bucket in the kitchen?" he asked.

She nodded, glad he had guessed what she needed. "By the back door. Please . . ." She realized he had disappeared.

As Lorne had done.

She stiffened at the thought of him. Surely Lorne would know better than to come here tonight, with all the trouble along the avenue and the lamps lit in the Mission.

Dabbing at the blood on the woman's face, she frowned. A woman? She was little more than a child, probably not much older than Doreen.

"How is she?" Benjamin asked as he came back into the dining room.

"Not good."

While Sarah continued to wash blood from the bruises on the woman's face, Benjamin watched her hands. They were competent and not squeamish. He smiled tautly when he heard her whisper an apology for what would have been excruciating if the woman had been conscious. Tender-hearted Sarah Granger somehow managed not to be crushed by the poverty and crime along the streets.

"It looks as if she were struck by a teamster, too," she murmured.

He flinched. She could not have just guessed that. Glancing at the medical bag, he wondered how often she patched up those who had no one else to turn to. Helping the wrong person could bring catastrophe here. But how could he tell her to turn someone from her door? She would not heed him, and, if she did, she was not the woman he guessed her to be. A woman who surrounded herself with children to keep everyone else far from her. A few questions along

Second Avenue had gained him that information. No gentlemen callers, no family visiting, no one but the children.

"She may have been beaten," Sarah continued.

"It's possible. We see it too often in the tenements. When men are stripped of their pride by bosses who pay them too little and work them too hard, they often take out their anger on their women." He wrapped bandaging around the woman's scratched arm. "I'm sure you know all about that."

"Yes." She glanced toward the ceiling, and he guessed she was thinking of what awaited her children when they left the safe cocoon of this house.

"I found her by the road," he said. "She was barely conscious then."

"I'll finish cleaning her so the doctor can examine her, if you'd be kind enough to step outside."

"You need help."

"You're not a doctor or a woman. I don't think—"

"You need help. This isn't a child with a skinned knee."

Sarah did not answer. As she reached for the buttons closing the senseless woman's collar, he loosened the ones at her cuff. With the storm crashing around them, it might be hours before the doctor arrived. If he came at all. Charity customers always had to wait.

She checked for the feeble heartbeat in the center of the woman's chest. When she did not find it, she put her fingers on the woman's wrist. Nothing. She touched the woman's neck. Again nothing.

"Do you need another cloth?" Benjamin asked.

"No." She drew one side of the tablecloth over the woman's face. Unless they could learn her identity, which seemed as unlikely as snow falling from this storm, the tablecloth would be the woman's shroud in the pauper's cemetery.

A broad hand covered hers, and she watched her fingers being lifted away. Slowly she was turned to face his navy coat. The buttons wavered before her eyes. She followed the small chain from the third one to the copper badge in the middle of the dark wool. Her gaze would rise no farther, for she had no strength left.

"I think you could use a drink of something, Sarah. I think we both could."

"It's very, very late."

"And it's getting later." He put his arm around her shoulders and steered her toward the door.

"Should we leave her—?"

"She will be fine."

"But if the children come down, they might see her."

He reached into the bag she carried. Pulling out a length of string, he wound it around the doorknob and the knob of the kitchen door. The only way to open the dining room door now would be to cut the string. "That should keep them out."

She said nothing else, not because words were so difficult to speak, but because the silence offered an odd comfort.

When he led her into the parlor, he said, "Sit while I get you something to put some color back into your face."

"If you want—"

He put his finger over her lips. She pulled back in shock when she realized how it echoed Lorne's motion. Another shiver cut across her stiff shoulders. Thank goodness Lorne had not come here tonight. If he had . . . She did not want to think about that.

"If you'll tell me where to look for something stronger than lemonade or milk," he said as he lit the lamp, "I'll bring it in here after I get the priest to have her moved out of here."

"Over the icebox. There's a bottle of wine there. The glasses are in plain sight."

"Are you all right?"

At his compassion, she looked at him squarely. She must not let him guess that her fear of Lorne returning was as strong as her dismay at the woman's death. "I won't swoon. If it makes you feel better, you'll find smelling salts in the third drawer past the dry sink."

Benjamin chuckled. "I don't think I need to clutter my

hands with them." He became somber. "If you want to cry, don't let me stop you."

"If I wanted to, you wouldn't halt me." She smoothed her bloodstained skirt across her lap. "Weeping is one feminine frailty I don't indulge in."

"Never?" he asked as he paused in the doorway.

"Seldom."

His eyebrow arched, but she added nothing else. To do so might reveal the truth she kept locked in her heart. She had learned tears did not ease sorrow. It had taken many endless nights after Giles's death to teach her the lesson she did not intend to forget again.

Sarah stared at nothing as Benjamin's footfalls were swallowed by the thick walls. Vagrant thoughts fought to come to the forefront of her mind, thoughts of Giles. How proud he had been to wear the cadet's uniform and then to receive his commission. That evening, he had asked her to marry him the next spring. Her father had insisted that they wait, so she could decide if she really wanted to be an army officer's wife. She had decided she wanted to, but, by then, the war was sweeping over the country.

She did not have to close her eyes to see the perfect symmetry of the wedding ring pattern she had designed for this most special of wedding quilts. Sweet, flowered patterns intersecting with gentle pastels in an endless circle within a circle.

A moan slipped past her lips. She wanted to return to that simple joy of creating beauty with a needle and thread. The need was an ache within her soul, almost as strong as her grief.

She pushed the thoughts aside, wondering how she could even imagine being happy when that woman was dead. She wanted to think of nothing. The emptiness within her was comfortingly familiar.

When the front door opened, she rose.

Rachel came into the parlor, brushing rain off her cloak. "Sarah, the doctor won't come out tonight."

"It doesn't matter."

"She's dead?"

"Yes."

"Can I help with anything?"

Sarah shook her head. "You did all you could. If—" The faint sound of a baby crying intruded. "That's Birdie."

"I can take care of her, if you want."

"No, you go to bed. You sat up with Innis last night." Patting her assistant's arm, she said, "Get some sleep."

"Is *he* still here?"

She did not want to argue about Benjamin now, so she said only "Yes," then hurried to her office, and through it to her bedroom.

"Hush, my dear," she whispered as she knelt by the drawer holding the baby.

Birdie wiggled with her distress over whatever had kept her from sleeping. Sarah gathered the baby up in her arms and sat in the rocking chair. She glanced toward the bed. Conlan was still asleep; she could hear his soft, slow breaths.

"Hush, hush," she whispered.

"Sarah?"

At Benjamin's soft call, she glanced around the doorway and answered lowly, "In here."

Benjamin eased into the dark office. He wished that, after all these years of patrolling the streets in the dark, he could have gained a cat's ability to see through the night. Too much hid in the shadows, including a low table. He cursed under his breath when his leg struck it.

His fingers tightened on the wine bottle as he set it and the glasses on the low table. Another murder! While he was in the kitchen, Father Tynan had come to take the woman's body, wrapped in the bloody tablecloth, to the church, but was as doubtful as Benjamin that anyone would come to claim it. The captain was not going to be pleased to hear about this. Neither would the mayor, who had quietly let it be known that no crime must leak out of Five Points, because his constituents in the fancy houses on Lexington and Fifth Avenues would be inconvenienced. In addition, the trouble might creep toward City Hall.

Benjamin glanced at the light flowing across the floor

from the other door in Sarah's office. Why hadn't she stayed in the parlor? What could be so important that she was here in her office now?

He had his answers as he paused in the inner doorway and saw that this room was not a continuation of her office but a bedchamber. It was as simply furnished as the rest of the house, but a sampler was hung on the wall. From where he stood, he could not read what it said. He had had no idea that Sarah slept here behind her office, although it made sense. Long hours of work were as much a part of her life as his, and here, on the first floor, she could hear anyone who came to the door.

"Hush, hush," he heard her whisper.

Seeing Sarah in the rocking chair just inside the bedroom, he leaned his shoulder against the doorjamb. He wanted to enjoy this sight for a moment. Surrounded by trouble whenever he and Rogue were out on the streets, it was delightful to see this warmth as she harbored Birdie against her, trying to soothe the baby.

As the baby's distress eased to a whimper, she whispered, "You just want to be held and loved, don't you?"

"I assume you're talking to the baby," he replied, "but I'd be glad to answer that for you."

She stopped rocking and looked up at him. Her brilliant blue eyes urged him to throw caution aside and answer her whether she wanted to hear it or not. Answer her by tugging her to her feet and bringing her into his arms as he tasted her luscious lips again. The very thought sent a pulse to every muscle, but he struggled to ignore the craving. He was not a man to throw caution aside. Doing that could be fatal on the street.

Here . . . He brushed back a strand of her black hair from her soft cheek. Tingles teased his fingers to curve around her nape and tip her mouth under his.

Maybe she read his thoughts, because she edged away as she stood. Putting the baby back into the drawer that was lined with a blanket, she gestured toward her office.

He was about to speak when she glanced back at the bed. For the first time, he noticed a small lump in it. The boy! A flash of color as the child shifted revealed that the blasted quilt was right here.

"Sarah—"

"In my office, please."

He recognized the obstinacy in her voice. Stepping back, he was not surprised when she came out, carrying the lamp, and closed the door behind her.

"I'm not going to snatch the quilt and run out of here with it," he said.

"What are you talking about?" Her eyes grew wide. "I'm shutting the door because I don't want the children woken up again." Walking past him, she drew the door to the hallway closed, too. "Until everything is cleaned up . . ."

"Father Tynan and his helpers came for the body. When they left, I wiped down the table and tossed the rags in a bucket out back."

"Thank you." Sarah grasped the settee as she tried to force her legs to take another step.

Benjamin's fingers on her arm guided her around it, so she could sit. When she thanked him again, he poured a glass of wine and held it out to her. For the first time, she noticed that he had taken off his heavy coat. Because it was bloody or because of the heat? His shirt was plastered to his body with the night's humidity. Each muscle was outlined by the shadows that the dim light could not fight back. Giles had been strong, as befit an army cadet, but . . . She hastily looked at the white wine in her glass. She should not be staring like a common strumpet.

"I'm glad Father Tynan was able to come," she said as he sat next to her.

"I am, too, because, like you, he mentioned this was not the only shooting tonight."

She glanced away again as guilt washed over her. She had witnessed a murder. Benjamin would be furious that she had not reported it.

Knowing she must say something, she said, "Father Tynan is willing to listen to new ideas."

"Not like Father Monroe?"

"Certainly not like Father Monroe."

He twirled his glass, but his gaze held hers, refusing to let her escape. "Even Father Monroe would know enough to realize it's stupid to rush in to halt the fighting among the Irish."

"Was that who was shot tonight? How—?" She closed her mouth as she saw his swift smile.

"So it *was* you. Father Tynan slipped and admitted he had warned away a witness to that murder." His mouth turned down in a scowl. "How stupid can you be, Sarah? Running out into the street when there's a battle going on! If those fools think you can identify them, you're dead. With any luck, they'll believe you left your glasses inside and couldn't see them."

"Leave off!" She started to rise, but his hand on her arm halted her. Through clenched teeth, she ordered, "Sergeant McCauley, I said leave off!"

"How can you be so stupid? You've heard about the violence on the docks! Just imagine what a lovely woman like you would suffer if she fell into their drunken, bloodied hands."

"I don't want to think of that."

"You should! You've seen that firsthand for yourself. Twice." His voice tightened with rage, but did not rise. "Are you aiming for sainthood or simply martyrdom?"

"All I'm trying to do is protect my children."

He stood and refilled his glass. "Captain Potter thanks you for sending the basket to police headquarters, but he is very anxious to see that quilt. Very, very anxious."

"When I can, I will give it to you."

"By then, it may be too late."

Sarah took a deep drink of her wine. It could not loosen the cold bands of horror clamped around her chest. When he picked up the bottle, she held out her glass. She bit her lower lip as he put his hand over hers to steady it. Were her fingers trembling with the dregs of her fear or the anticipation of his touch? Thanking him for the wine, she drew her hand back, expecting to see it quiver with the sparks still shooting along it.

Sipping again in hopes of regaining her composure, she

said, "It just seems so wasteful. All those lives. Coming to the United States in search of a dream and finding it isn't here."

"But it is. I've made my dreams come true."

"You did, but how can you expect a child from Five Points to think of the future when he's desperate for his next meal? How—?" She stared at him. "You lived in Five Points?"

"Not far from the corner of Worth and Baxter in the very heart of Five Points." He grimaced. "Or perhaps I should say, in the very gut."

"I didn't know."

He chuckled coldly. "How could you? You're so timid around me, you wouldn't ask me the time."

She wanted to retort, but the words died unspoken. He was right. Something about his untamed strength scared her. He governed it closely, and she dared not think what would happen if he unleashed it. The swift sample of pleasure she had savored in his brazen kiss warned her that those powerful emotions would engulf her.

When she did not answer, he continued, "My family came over with the rest when the potato fields failed. My father got a job in a tannery. Not the work he had been accustomed to, but he told us that he found nothing disgraceful about working as a laborer to provide for his family. After a few years, he had saved enough to buy a livery store."

"McCauley's belongs to your family?"

"You know it?"

She smiled. "I've walked past it many times. The black-haired man there—"

"Is my brother Julian." His grin returned.

"I never would have guessed!"

"That I came from Five Points, or that a policeman would have relatives in such a respectable trade?"

"I don't think I want to answer that." She laughed softly. "Whatever I say will probably come out wrong." She set her glass on her desk and closed her eyes. How could she be jesting with him when a woman had died here tonight?

Everything was jumbled, and she could not think straight.

His hands glided along her arms to her elbows. Tilting her back so her head rested on his chest, he wrapped her arms and his in front of her. His cheek leaned against her hair, each breath sifting through it.

"You did all you could," he whispered.

"I wanted to save her."

"You want to save everyone. You give and give and give. Sometimes you give too much. Sometimes you can't give enough. By the time I found her, nothing could have saved her."

"I thought . . ."

"That I expected you to work a miracle?" He turned her to face him, his arm curving around her waist. "Maybe I did, but I brought her to you because I knew you'd open this Mission to anyone who needs it." He bent toward her. "Including me."

His lips brushed hers. The gentle touch was thrilling, but disquieting. Seeing the feverish longing in his eyes, she had been sure . . . All thoughts were eclipsed as his tender touch vanished into a demand to delight in this stolen pleasure. His mouth moved along her face, sampling, sending spiraling sweetness cascading over her. As her arms curled up his back, he recaptured her parted lips to explore her mouth. His tongue probed each succulent secret.

A small moan of longing escaped past her lips as he tangled his fingers in her hair. When she opened her eyes to stare up at his smile, she wished this moment would last forever. She could imagine nothing more wonderful than being in his arms, knowing she was daring a danger she could barely imagine.

"Don't be so foolish again, Sarah," he murmured.

Baffled, she realized he was not speaking of this kiss, but of going out onto the street when trouble started. She stepped out of his arms. "It's not foolish to try to save someone's life."

"Your job is to watch over your children. Mine is to watch over the street." His lips curled into a beguiling smile. "And you."

"Until I give you the quilt?"

His smile evaporated as his eyes burned cold again. "I've already told you how much you risk by not letting me show that quilt to Captain Potter. I don't like to think of the danger you've put yourself in if someone else learns you have that quilt here."

"Conlan won't even let me look at it at this point. He clutches it to him." She put her fingers on his sleeve. "I'm trying to help him *and* you."

"I know." Putting his arm around her shoulders, he opened the door to the hall. He lifted his coat off a peg by the door and folded it over his arm. "I'll drop by tomorrow after I get off duty to see how you're doing."

"Tomorrow?"

He chuckled softly. "Today, if you prefer, seeing as how the night's nearly over." He pulled on his coat. "I'll bring Rogue over so the children can see him."

"They'd like that."

"And will you?"

Leaning on the door, she asked, "Will you stay for supper tomorrow—tonight?"

"How can I resist the chance to sup with you and a bevy of children? I'm sure Mrs. Galway will excuse me from her table."

"Is that where you live? At Mrs. Galway's boarding-house?" A warmth rose along her cheeks as she realized how inappropriate her question was.

He touched the heated spots. "This is very, very lovely, Sarah. Tonight then?"

"At six."

His kiss was swift, but the fire it left on her lips would burn through her dreams. He grinned and pushed her glasses up her nose. "These sure do get in a man's way."

"Go, or it'll be suppertime before you're gone," she replied with a laugh.

She did not close the door as he went down the steps. Watching as he strode along the sidewalk as if he were its master, she was not surprised when he turned toward the parish house next to St. John's.

His dire warnings rang through her head. She hoped he was wrong, but feared he was right. The trouble was only beginning.

5

"LOOK AT THIS, SARAH! Isn't it beautiful?"

Sarah smiled at Fiona, who was thrilled with the lengths of cloth, even the sections that were faded or water-stained. The little girl pointed out that one stain looked like a cat. Another was made by her imagination into a mountain. She motioned for the little girl to come closer to the settee.

As Fiona clambered past the other older children sitting on the parlor floor, cutting the squares to match the paper patterns Sarah had cut out last night, Sarah glanced at Birdie and Conlan, who were huddled in the far corner of the settee. Nothing had changed. The baby was sucking on the bottle as if she had never eaten before. Her brother clutched the rolled quilt and held his thumb in his mouth.

She sighed, but forced a smile when Fiona sat in front of her. Holding up a threaded needle, she said, "Fiona, you have the neatest stitches of any of the children, so I want to teach you how to quilt so that you may help me teach the others."

"That sounds like fun."

"It is." She wished she could be so sure of that. Quilting *had* been fun before it became a focus for her grief. *Forget that!* She needed to help her children, and this was the best skill she had other than loving them.

She handed Fiona another piece of paper. It was smaller than the slip of fabric, but in the same octagonal shape. "Hold it against the back of the fabric and baste the edges of the fabric over until they are the same size as the paper." She demonstrated, folding the fabric over on one section. "See? You can judge if you've gotten the right size all around pinning by the paper in the very center."

"Look!" Fiona grinned. "The flap of material is just as wide as my finger."

"Then you have the perfect measurement. We'll make our basting one Fiona-finger wide."

The little girl giggled, but bent to watch Sarah stitch all around the fabric with quick, easy strokes. "You do that so well, Sarah."

"I've been quilting for a long time."

"But you've never quilted here."

"You children keep me too busy." She ruffled the hair that had loosened from Fiona's braids, then handed her the needle and thread. "You do one now."

Sarah watched as the little girl tried to copy her motions. Seeing that Fiona was struggling, she helped guide the little girl's fingers.

"The thread is like a river following a storm cloud," Sarah murmured. "The needle is the storm. It can cut through anything, but the river can only follow it, connecting the pieces together. You want to let it flow through the fabric without changing anything except making it stronger."

"I like doing this," Fiona announced as she finished one corner of the octagon.

"So do I." The words burst from her with more emotion than she would have wished. When Fiona glanced at her, startled, she motioned for the little girl to try the next section by herself.

Sarah leaned back against the cushions and blinked away the tears that filled her eyes. She *did* love quilting, the play of colors, the richness of the textures, the shapes of the individual pieces that became a wondrous pattern when put together. Her fingers quivered so hard that she clenched them in her lap. To open herself to that joy would mean opening herself to the pain again as well.

She looked at the children huddled on the other end of the settee. "Your baby is growing. Don't you think so, Conlan?" She had been saying things like this to him—babbling, really—since the little boy woke up this morning, just as she had every day since he and the baby had arrived at the Mission. Not once had he responded. Her expectations that he would begin talking again were flagging.

"Birdie is so pretty. Don't you think so, Conlan? She's getting more hair every day. Soon it might be as thick as yours. She loves her bottle. I bet you did, too, when you were a baby."

He looked up.

Sarah's voice faltered. What had she just said? Whatever it was, it had reached past his horror. Baby! He had looked up when she mentioned how he had been a baby, too. Looking down at Birdie, she went on quietly, "I love babies, Conlan. I wish there were more babies in this house."

She glanced at him from the corner of her eye. His head was still up.

"We only have two babies now, Conlan. I wish I had three." She kept her voice light. "Would you like to be one of the babies, too?"

He loosened his grip on the quilt and leaned toward her.

The poor dear! He needed to be cuddled. She had held him so often, but as a toddler, not as a baby. Knowing she must do nothing to frighten him back behind the wall that could not hide his terror, she continued to talk as Birdie finished her bottle. She set the baby on the floor on a blanket and held out her arms to Conlan.

For a long moment, he did not move. Then he edged into her arms. With a smile, she drew one edge of the quilt around him like a baby's blanket and held him as she had his baby sister. She did not slow her prattle, talking about what a beautiful baby he was and how she loved having him as her baby here.

At the same time, she ran her fingers along the quilt. Benjamin was so sure the clue to the murderer was here in this square of cloth that was no more than two feet on any side. What possible information could he garner from a patchwork quilt that was this child's sole comfort?

Her fingers paused as she noted a pattern to the quilting that had not been finished. It was not as abstract as the pieces of fabric. Tracing it with one finger, she realized the pattern was elongated. She could not check it more closely without the risk of spooking Conlan again. Maybe once he began to trust her more again, he would let her see it. For now, she would hold him and delight in the quiet within her office.

Shouts came from the street. Sarah glanced toward the window, but could only see the windows of the house across the street. She hoped it was not another accident. That was what the two deaths last night were being called along the street, although she doubted if anyone believed that.

"Sarah?"

Smiling at Rachel, who stood in the parlor door, Sarah whispered, "Look at this." She pointed at Conlan's hand on her arm.

Rachel did not smile back. Instead, she wrung her apron and said in a strained whisper, "Sarah, come here. Right now!"

"Conlan—"

"Now!"

She frowned. Fear tugged at Rachel's face, contorting it. Had someone else been shot? Impossible! No gunshots had echoed along the street.

Gathering up Conlan, she held him close as she went to the doorway, where Rachel still stood. The woman was staring toward the front door with an expression that suggested the devil himself was paying a call. She almost smiled at that thought, but it was too early for Benjamin to arrive.

She gasped as she stepped out into the foyer. Two children stood by the door with a carpetbag on the floor between them. Fearful brown eyes stared at her from faces the color of the dark oak molding. The older child, a girl who must be close to Fiona's age, wore a tattered gray dress and clutched the hand of a little boy of about six with the fervor of Conlan's grip on his quilt.

At that thought, Sarah handed the little boy to Rachel. He whimpered, but he was not her only problem now.

She walked toward the silent children. "I'm Sarah Granger. What are your names?"

"I'm Ruthie Brown," said the girl with a dignity beyond her years. "This is my brother, Mason."

"Nice to meet you, Mason," Sarah replied, hoping the little boy would smile. When he did, she started to put out her hand to him. She drew it back when Ruthie tightened her hold on him.

"Tell me before I waste your time, Miss Granger. Do you take colored orphans?"

Sarah fought not to smile. The child's pride was touching. Although she needed help, Ruthie refused to beg for it. "Every color but purple."

Ruthie stared at her, then laughed; the sound was like water cascading along a brook. "If you'll take us in, I'll be glad to help with the other little children. I'm not afraid of work, Miss Granger."

"All our children help out. Come in and let me get to know you. Then I'll introduce you to the other children." To Rachel, she added, "Heat some water so these young people can bathe before lunch. There should be two more pallets in the attic. If not, let me know."

"Sarah—"

Cutting her assistant off before she could voice her apprehensions, she smiled. "It's still an hour before lunch, but I'm sure there must be some raisin bread left over from breakfast."

Mason grinned, but Rachel's mouth grew hard. "Sarah, if I could have a word with you."

"Later. This way, Ruthie. It's cooler in my office."

"It was hotter when we were in Mississippi, Miss Granger."

"Hotter than this?" She gave a shudder and was rewarded with another smile from Mason.

As Sarah retreived Birdie from the parlor and carried her into her bedroom where she could sleep undisturbed, she wished she could ease Rachel's distress. They would talk later. Now, she needed to find out why these two children had come to the Second Avenue Mission for Needy Children instead of going to the Colored Orphan Asylum on Fifth Avenue.

Closing the outer door of her office, she waited for the children to sit on the settee, their feet in worn shoes not touching the floor. She pulled her chair close to them. "Where are your mother and father?"

"Pa was killed in the Rebellion." Luminous tears shone in Ruthie's large eyes. "Mama died last week from pains in her chest. We've got no family up North, and we can't go back South where the rest of our folks are. Although President Lincoln freed the slaves, Mama told us she feared some master would try to enslave us again."

"I'm sorry," she said. Dear God, these children were runaways! She soothed herself. Slavery had been outlawed, so Ruthie and Mason were no longer fugitives. "You are welcome here, but I must ask why you didn't go to the Colored Orphan Asylum."

Mason spoke for the first time. "We want to stay together."

"They couldn't promise that," Ruthie added. "Mama told me to look after Mason, and I won't break that promise. Can we stay together here?"

"Boys sleep in one room and girls in another here, but I will not place one of you in a home that will not take both of you."

Ruthie's stiff shoulders sagged. "Thank you, Miss Granger. That's kind of you."

"All the children call me Sarah." She rose and rang the bell on her desk. When Rachel stuck her head past the door, Sarah knew she had been eavesdropping. "Rachel, I think we'd like that raisin bread now. Will you have Fiona bring it in?"

"Fiona? Are you sure?"

Sarah's smile grew rigid. This was no time for Rachel to be rebellious. "Yes."

Rachel did not slam the door, but Sarah guessed that she wanted to.

Regret stole her smile. She and Rachel had been such good friends, and Rachel had helped her through the dark days while she mourned for Giles. But then Benjamin had accompanied her home to the Mission. Rachel might forgive her for that, but her expression warned that she could not forgive her for letting the Browns stay.

Her hope that the children had not noticed was dashed when Ruthie said, "I guess you don't get too many coloreds."

"No."

"If we're going to be a problem, we—"

"You aren't the problem." She hid her astonishment at the amount of education Ruthie must have had. Her ears had become so accustomed to the slang of the street, which was laced with Gaelic and German and other languages, that Ruthie's voice was a pleasure.

At a knock, Sarah opened the door and smiled at Fiona. The girl was carrying a heavy tray topped with a pitcher of milk, a plate of buttered bread, and four glasses.

Taking the tray, she said, "Fiona, thank you. Will you join me and Ruthie and Mason Brown? Ruthie and Mason, this is Fiona Barber."

Carefully Sarah gauged Fiona's reaction. The girl had a huge heart, taking each of the children in the Mission into it as if she were everyone's mother. If she did not accept the Browns . . .

"How do you do?" Fiona asked softly, her eyes wide.

"Fine." Ruthie's wariness returned.

Sarah held out the plate to Mason, who scanned it with the intensity of a general appraising a battlefield. "Take two slices, if you want," she said, then held out the tray to the girls. "Fiona, I thought we might put Ruthie's pallet next to yours."

Fiona sat and met Ruthie's leery gaze. "That's fine, as long as she doesn't snore."

Ruthie's laugh erased the last of the tension between the children. As Sarah poured cups of milk, she smiled. This might work out. Fiona needed to be needed, and Ruthie and Mason must have help to become part of the household.

By the time they had finished everything on the tray, the children were giggling together. She was not surprised that Fiona drew out her quilting and showed it to Ruthie. More and more, Fiona was reminding her of herself as a youngster, delighting in quilting and never going anywhere without a needle and thread and some material.

"I can sew," Ruthie said proudly. She pointed to a bit of embroidery on Mason's pocket. "I did that."

"Can I look at it?" Sarah asked. When the little boy came over to her, she said, "Ruthie, this is very fine work. Have you ever quilted?"

"No, Mama was going to teach me, but she didn't." Tears filled her eyes.

"Would you like me to teach you?" She fought to keep her smile from wavering. "You sew well, and you might enjoy it a lot."

"I do!" Fiona said with every bit of her nine-year-old confidence.

"I'd like to learn." Ruthie smiled shyly.

Sarah watched a few minutes later as Fiona led the others upstairs to show them the bedrooms. Although she was tempted to go along to make sure there was no trouble, she must let the children work this out for as long as she could.

Leaning back in her chair, Sarah smiled. If all problems could be solved so readily, her job would be a joy. She glanced at the papers cluttering her desk. This work would not be a joy. She had several letters to write to plead with benefactors to continue supporting the Mission. Then she had to attack the pile of bills that grew faster than the children. She would write to each of her creditors and ask for a few more weeks, until the first quilts could be finished. She hoped they would sell quickly. Then she would be able to pay her bills.

With a sigh, she knew she could not depend only on the children's enthusiastic efforts. To earn enough money, she must make a few quilts herself. Could she? She was torn between joyous anticipation and trepidation. Neither mattered, for she must do what she must to keep the children from starving.

First, she needed to convince her creditors to give her a few more weeks. If she started now, she might have the worst of it done before Benjamin arrived for supper.

She looked at the stack again. Maybe . . .

∞

BENJAMIN YAWNED AS HE swung down off his horse. Tying Rogue's reins to the newel post on the Mission's steps, he pushed his cap back on his head and scanned the street. People were clumped together, talking furiously and glancing along the street. Not a good sign. Something must be going on.

"Sergeant McCauley!" called a strident voice. "Sergeant McCauley, I must speak with you immediately."

He turned as a bulbous shape in dark robes rushed toward him. Father Monroe seldom left the parish house, preferring to allow Father Tynan to handle the day-to-day work. Something must be going on.

"Good evening, Father," he said, not bothering to smile.

The priest's wide jowls shook with outrage. "I'm glad you are here. Now maybe you can do something about this intolerable situation."

"And what situation is that?" Something bad must be going on.

"It's being talked about up and down the street, and if word reaches into Five Points, there will be more trouble than we need here."

It must be something really bad. He kept his voice even and low, although Father Monroe's words rang along the street, drawing too much attention. "Trouble is something we want to avoid."

"Then maybe you can persuade *her* to listen to common sense."

When the priest glanced at the Mission, Benjamin knew Father Monroe was talking about Sarah. "About what?"

"It's being said she's got colored children living in there."

"Is it now?" He did not speak the curse burning on his tongue. Sarah could not have done something so stupid now. Or could she?

"Maybe she'll listen to you and get them out of here."

He did not reply as he walked up the steps. Until he had the facts, anything he said would be a waste of breath. That had been one of his earliest lessons when he joined the police force.

A lad opened the door and grinned at him. "Sergeant McCauley! Did you bring Rogue with you?"

"He's out front." He ruffled the boy's hair. "Would you take him through the alley and around to the back, Skelly?"

"Glad to."

Benjamin glanced around the foyer. Nothing looked amiss. He could hear the children giggling upstairs, and the rattle of pots in the kitchen. Something was cooking. He hoped it was supper because it smelled heavenly.

Nothing looked out of place.

He walked to Sarah's office door and knocked. When he heard her reply, muted by the thick wood, he opened the door.

She looked up with a smile. A tired one, he noted. He gazed into her blue eyes, which were as clear as a cloudless, autumn sky. His respect for her grew, because she faced alone all the challenges that the policemen did as a team. No one wanted to admit her work helped those who needed her most.

He guessed his own smile revealed his exhaustion when she said, "Come in and sit down. I had no idea it was suppertime already."

"I'm a bit early." He did not look toward the window. "Busy day?"

"They all are." She rubbed her nose and resettled her

glasses on her nose. Joy swept the fatigue from her face. "Conlan let me hold him today, Benjamin. Really hold him."

He stopped himself before he could ask about the quilt. First things first, for now she had invited a different danger upon her. "That's good."

"Good? He hadn't reacted to anything or anyone since the day we found him and Birdie." She closed the book in front of her, and he saw the word *Accounts* stamped on it. When she yawned, she said, "Forgive me. I'm trying to find a way to squeeze a few more pennies out of the budget. I'm not sure how much longer we can open our doors to any child who needs a place to live. I don't want to turn any away, but we are growing crowded."

"So I've heard."

Sarah stiffened at the abrupt tension in Benjamin's voice. Taking a deep breath and releasing it slowly, she said, "I should have guessed you'd heard already."

"So it's true? You have colored children living here?" He sat on one corner of her desk as he unbuttoned the front of his coat. "Father Monroe is nearly beside himself."

"Is he?" She tried to pull her gaze from his fingers as he loosened each button and drew aside his coat to reveal his strong chest. If he undid the buttons along her gown, she could savor his heated kisses all over her skin. And his fingers . . . Those brawny fingers emphasized every word he spoke and tantalized her with the yearning for them upon her.

"How could you be so foolish?"

His sharp voice tore apart her daydream. His touch might be delirious, but he could be overbearing when he acted as if she were one of the Irish ruffians he chased in Five Points.

"I don't want to listen to this again," she replied.

"Again? Who else is trying to put some good sense into your head? Father Monroe?"

She laughed tersely. "He tried, but I reminded him of the first lesson my father taught me: 'Love thy neighbor as thyself.' "

"No wonder he was so livid."

"He accused me of twisting the Bible to my own purposes and being in cahoots with Satan." She sighed as she sat on the sofa. "All this because of two children who had no place else to go."

"The Colored Orphan Asylum—"

"Would not guarantee that they could stay together." She shook her head. "Their father died fighting for the Union, and they are cast out as vermin by those he died to protect. You'd think that would count for something."

"No one wants to talk about the war when every man in the city is waiting to see if his name will be drawn in the draft lottery."

She stiffened again. "Has it been decided when that will be?"

"No." His lips curved in a wry grin. "The longer they put it off, the better."

"I'm not so sure about that. It gives those who like to stir up trouble more time to do that."

His eyes narrowed. "Captain Potter was saying the same thing just the other day."

"Then I guess I'm in good company." Rising, she reached for the doorknob. "And as you are company, would you like something cool to drink before dinner?"

"No!"

The door slammed shut as she tried to open it. Seeing his hand on it, she turned to face him. She did not retort as she stared up at his scowl.

"Sarah, you and the captain may be in agreement about the draft lottery, but I agree with Father Monroe about you having those children here." A shadow of his grin returned. "I don't like the idea that he and I are in agreement."

"Then don't be in agreement with him. Having Ruthie and Mason here isn't that radical an idea."

"Are you insane?"

"Benjamin, what else could I do? It says on the door *Second Avenue Mission for Needy Children*. Not just white children. All children."

He grasped her shoulders, his broad hands covering

them. When she started to spin away, he tightened his grip. "I should have known you'd be a fool! After all, you can't see that giving me Conlan's quilt could help solve his mother's murder."

"I *can* see that, *and* I can see the trouble that could come from opening my door to the Browns, but I shan't do anything to hurt any of these children."

"Just *all* of them?"

"Why does anyone care about the children here?"

"Because so many people have nothing else to concern themselves about. They are so low, so mired in poverty, that they're looking for someone else to look down on." His fingers curved along her face, tilting it toward his. "All that hate. What a waste!"

His lips slanted across hers as he drew her up against him. Her hands slid up beneath his coat to stroke his shoulders. When his tongue delved into her mouth, she swayed against him, caught up in the craving she could not control. She did not want to control it, for she wanted to give herself to this pleasure. Her breath became uneven when he laved her ear and sent his warm breath whirling through her. His fingers glided up her back, pressing her even closer as his mouth sought the pulse line along her neck.

She caught his face between her hands and brought it up so she could see his expression. She was transfixed by the naked longing on it, the same longing that ached within her. With a moan, she drew his mouth down over hers again.

He raised his mouth and whispered, "I knew you were sensible."

"*This* is sensible?" She laughed.

"More sensible than risking yourself for two children."

Sarah gripped his arms, and she saw his eyes widen. Did he think she would walk away from this conversation, when she must have someone—just one other person—agree with what she had done and why? "What if Ruthie or Mason were your child?"

"Sarah, don't cloud the issue."

"I'm not. These two children are the issue. They've lost their family. They need help. So do I."

"What do you need help with?"

"The children are doing some sewing for me, which I hope will bring in some of the money we need so desperately." She tightened her hold on his arms. "Benjamin, I have room for these children. Could I turn them away?"

He walked back toward her desk. Her hands clenched at her sides. Could he not face her—or his own prejudices? Or—and her stomach cramped at the thought—did he know something he was not telling her? Something that dimmed the glow of desire in his eyes and replaced it with anger?

He faced her, his mouth straight with fury. "Sweetheart, don't you know what danger you're putting yourself and the Mission in, simply to help these two children?"

She crossed the space between them. She wanted nothing between them, not angry words, not fear of what might happen if she did not give him the quilt, not the hatred blooming out from Five Points, nothing but their skin pulsing with the same yearning. *Don't be silly!* She must not think of that now when so much else was wrong, but it was not easy to shut out the thought of the one thing that was right. Her hands rose to his cheeks, which were scratchy with whiskers. Exhaustion lined his face, and she wondered when he last had had the luxury of time to shave.

"Benjamin," she whispered, "if those children had come to you for help, would you have turned them away?"

"Of course not, but—"

"No buts."

"You're right." Taking her hands from his face, he held them between his. "I can't convince you to change your mind when I know you're right."

"Thank you, Benjamin. I needed to hear you say that. More than you know." *More than I knew.*

"I still think you're a fool. Just because you're doing what's right doesn't protect you from bigots and blockheads." When he bent to kiss her cheek, she sighed with a longing she could no longer hide. "You're a wondrous woman, Sarah Granger."

"I am?"

"Yes," he answered with a huskiness that seeped into her and teased her to touch him.

His tongue flicked against her lips. Her arms went around his shoulders as one hand tilted his head toward her mouth.

Fiercely she kissed him. For so long, she had been alone, not even trusting her own heart. She wanted to trust it again, to listen to it urge her to seek the echoing beat of another heart. When her breath was swept away by the tempest of his lips, she clutched onto his arms. They enfolded her to his hard chest.

When he reached for the buttons on her collar, her fingers covered his. "No, Benjamin," she murmured.

"Trust me, sweetheart."

Had he been privy to her most private thoughts? That thought was oddly exhilarating, because Giles had chided her often for hiding her true thoughts. Giles! She pushed her loosened hair over her shoulders. He would be outraged to see her acting like a hoyden.

"I trust you," she said, stepping back again. "It's me I don't trust."

"Really?" He smoothed another strand back her from her face. His fingers drifted along it where it swirled along her throat.

When his hand brushed against her breast, she gasped. Her whole body dissolved into rapture. She put up her hand to halt him again, but it settled over his as his fingers moved along her. As if the layers of cotton and silk had vanished, she reveled the magic he was evoking.

Against her ear, he whispered, "Trust yourself, sweet one, and trust me."

Sadly, she drew his hand away. Fighting to control her shaky voice, she said, "Nothing has changed. I can't be anyone but Miss Granger of the—"

"I know," he retorted. His voice grew gentler as he twisted the single strand around his finger. "Forgive me, sweetheart. I'm tired. There's only one thing I'd rather do than go to sleep with you in my arms, and I'd love to do that and sleep with you after, but I know you won't agree."

"Benjamin, would it help if I told you that there's no other man from whom I'd consider accepting such an offer?"

He chuckled. "You sure know how to drive a man insane, don't you?"

"I didn't mean—" The door opened, and Sarah whirled. She yelped when she pulled the hair Benjamin had wrapped around his finger. Tugging it away, she gasped, "Rachel!"

"I knocked . . . I mean . . ." The redhead gulped. "Sarah, I need to talk with you right away."

"What's wrong?"

"Doreen O'Brien's quit. Said she wouldn't work in any place with those children."

Sarah looked from Rachel's tight face to Benjamin's, and she saw his eyes narrow into shadowed slits. Neither of them had to say "I told you so." They had, and she had not listened. She knew that welcoming Ruthie and Mason to the Mission was an invitation to more trouble, but she would not change her decision.

She hoped she would not come to regret it.

6

SARAH WOVE THROUGH THE trash on Second Avenue and around children playing ball. Many men loitered on the steps. Benjamin had told her about the loss of jobs at the docks. If all these men were here, it must mean they could not find work. Rumors called for a boycott until only Irish were hired. It was useless to be so naïve. Employers cared nothing about the bigotry of the slums along the East River.

She paused on the corner. The horse-drawn trolley should be coming soon, but she did not want to ride in one of the "hog-pens on wheels." The vehicles, which had been designed to carry two dozen people, often held more than twoscore. On humid days, the stench was unbearable. She would take a cab. It was her sole luxury.

Stepping over a sewer, she was grateful the Mission was not near the slaughterhouses. There, blood from butchering filled the open gutters along the streets. It was even worse in Five Points, but she was glad she had to go there only occasionally. The children in the Mission had been abandoned on her front steps.

Except for Conlan and Birdie.

She sighed. Her attempts this morning to persuade the little boy to let her touch the quilt had brought such screams from him that Father Tynan knocked on the door to be sure everything was all right. She had to find a way to reach the child again. She was not sure how, but she knew she could not do it if he thought she intended to take his quilt.

Sarah waved to a passing carriage, and it slowed. As she climbed in, she told the driver where she wished to go. She had become accustomed to the astonishment when she spoke the address, so she ignored his stare. Settling back on the dirty cushions, she watched the buildings flow past.

She hoped she was not being foolish with her last pennies. She needed to make this call on Mr. Winslow and return to the Mission quickly. The children could not work on the quilts without her there to oversee them. Rachel's quilting skills were as poor as the younger children's.

A smile swept across her face, bringing a pulse of joy so poignant she wanted to wrap her arms around herself and dance. She so enjoyed the sessions each day with the older children when they sat and cut or pieced together. The time brought her close to the happiness she had known before the war had ripped apart her life. For so long, she had been surrounded by dark colors, and now she wanted to exult in the glorious, albeit faded fabrics that she had purchased from Mr. Pettigew.

She listened to the beat of the horse's hooves on the cobbles. Tonight, Benjamin would be bringing his horse for the children to see. With a smile as she thought of the kisses they had shared before dawn, she gazed out the window.

"Giles," she said so lowly the words would not reach the coachman's ears, "he is a man of honor like you were. I think you would have liked him."

Uncertainty furrowed her brow. Giles had not been happy to discover that her father's church was open to rich and poor alike. Raised in Mississippi, he had believed the classes were meant to be separate. He would have disdained Benjamin for his poor beginnings.

She sighed, then took a deep breath of the flowering trees and the few flowers that grew along the city streets. That aroma told her she was near her destination. The carriage stopped before a brownstone mansion on Lexington Avenue. Marble lintels arched over the windows, and huge columns edged the door. She always was awed by its flashy display of Donald Winslow's wealth.

Paying the driver, Sarah adjusted her sedate bonnet before climbing the steps. Her eyes were caught by those of a fashionable woman stepping into her private carriage. Even from across the street, she could see the derision in the woman's eyes.

Sarah knew her black gown was in keeping with her position, but, not so long ago, she could recall wearing pale colors decorated with lace and bows. Giles had liked her best in light blue or pink, which contrasted with the simple uniform of a cadet. For the first time, she wondered what Benjamin thought of her drab clothes.

"It doesn't matter," she muttered to herself. Those candy-colored dresses belonged to the girl she had been, not to the director of the Second Avenue Mission for Needy Children.

When the door opened, she said quietly, as she did each week, "Good afternoon, Chester. I am expected."

"Of course, Miss Granger," the butler replied. The man, whose hair was iron-gray, never smiled as he took her shawl.

Sarah sighed. This was the most horrid part of her job, but she was dependent on Mr. Winslow's benevolence, especially now when so few others were able to help.

As she trailed after Chester along the luxurious rug, she made sure her smile was firmly in place. She admired the fine paintings that were showcased against the Chinese silk wall covering. Elegant furniture filled the rooms. Portieres framed each doorway. The mixed scents of cleaning fluid and polish were ambrosial after the odors of the slums. This grandeur had been purchased with the profits from Mr. Winslow's textile factories.

Chester paused before a closed door. Opening it, he announced, "Miss Granger."

Sarah's steps slowed as she entered Mr. Winslow's office to find a stranger standing in front of his maple desk. Like the house, the man reeked of riches. His ostentatious gray morning suit was of the finest cut, and jewels glistened on his long fingers. No gray edged his dark hair. His ebony gaze roamed over her in a candid appraisal.

"Come in." Pointing to a chair, he said, "I understand you have an appointment at this time."

She smiled and perched on the chair. She watched as he sat at the desk. His long fingers rocked a pen between them.

"Mr. Winslow asked me to come here this afternoon," she said, not sure why she was being met by a stranger. Until she discovered who this man was and why he was sitting with such ease at Mr. Winslow's desk, she would guard her words. She doubted if even Mr. Winslow's closest business associates knew of his generosity to the Second Avenue Mission for Needy Children.

"You are . . . ?" asked the man in his sharp voice.

"Sarah Granger."

A smile settled on his too full lips, which were almost hidden beneath his thick mustache. Their splash of color made the rest of his hueless face cadaverous. She heard amusement as he said, "So *you* are Miss Granger."

"Sir, you have me at a disadvantage." She realized she was twisting the strings of her bag and stopped before the motion betrayed her discomfort. "You seem to know of me, but I'm unfamiliar with your position in Mr. Winslow's company."

He laughed shortly. "That's because I'm newly arrived to Winslow Enterprises. I'm Averill Winslow."

"Winslow?"

"I assume by your reaction that my father didn't mention me to you."

"No, Mr. Winslow."

"That's hardly a surprise." Dropping the pen to the desk, he leaned back and affixed her with his cold stare. "But you are quite a surprise."

"Excuse me?"

"What's the Second Avenue Mission for Needy Children?"

"Exactly what its name suggests." Her voice steadied, and she sat straighter. "The Mission provides a home for children who otherwise would be without one."

"Any child?"

"We welcome any orphan."

" 'We'?"

"I'm the director. Rachel Nevins is my assistant." Anxious to end this, she asked, "Sir, may I inquire when I shall be seeing your father? I don't have time to tarry."

"My father is ill, Miss Granger."

She stood. "Sir, forgive me. I wouldn't have disturbed you if I had known."

"Stay a moment. My father has spoken of you several times, Miss Granger, but didn't answer a very important question." He rounded the desk. "Why does the director of the Second Avenue Mission for Needy Children come here?"

"Your father is an important benefactor of the Mission."

"Is that so?" He fingered his mustache. "It strikes me as odd that I haven't heard him mention the matter of money in conjunction with your name. Could it be that you knew of my father's condition and have come to prey on his unsuspecting son?"

"Sir, I assure you that I have called here to speak with your father often. Chester can confirm that."

"I see."

She wished he would not stare at her. When he continued, she flinched, for his tone changed abruptly.

"Forgive me, Miss Granger. You clearly aren't one of the vultures."

"Vultures? Is Mr. Winslow that ill?"

He smiled, but his eyes had not yet thawed. "Only a turn of speech. The doctor expects a complete recovery. In the meantime, I'm assuming his responsibilities. And, Miss Granger, one of those responsibilities seems to be you."

"If it'd be more convenient for me to return later . . ." Her voice trailed off as she thought of the bills sitting on her desk. Several were already past due.

"For what?"

Her eyes narrowed as she searched his face. When her gaze met the dark sparkle of his eyes, her breath clogged in her throat. For a single second, his eyes could not hide his thoughts. He was aware of what she wanted and delighted in making her beg for it.

Her chin rose. She could not halt it any more than she could warm her icy tone. "If you'll look in the top right-hand drawer, Mr. Winslow, you should find an envelope with my name on it."

Going to the desk, he pulled out the drawer. He opened the envelope and counted the money inside. "It seems very little for anyone to survive on for a month."

"A week, sir."

"A week?" His dark brows squeezed together above his eyes. "Do you mean to tell me that my father submits to your demand for payment weekly?"

"It was at Mr. Winslow's request that I come each week. Something about the necessity of keeping money for his factories and such."

"I'm shocked my father discussed his business concerns with you."

Deciding the interview had gone on long enough, Sarah held out her hand. He smiled and put the envelope under his dark coat. When he sat again, she hesitated. She did not want to plead for what his father had promised, but she must have the money to pay Mr. Pettigew for the material.

"Mr. Winslow, I—"

"Good day, Miss Granger." He reached for a bell on the corner of the desk. Ringing it sharply, he motioned toward the door, which the butler was opening.

She looked from Chester's placid face to Mr. Winslow's smile. She could not let the children go hungry, even if it meant setting aside her pride. "Mr. Winslow, if you'd give me the donation, I'd be very happy to leave."

"You'll receive no more donations from Winslow Enterprises."

"No more?" she choked. "Mr. Winslow, your father said nothing of this."

He tapped the desk. "I told you that I am now making the decisions for Winslow Enterprises."

"I understand that, sir, but—"

"Miss Granger, as I'm sure you realize, there's a war going on."

"Of course!"

Leaning back in his chair, he clasped his hands over his vest. "Winslow Enterprises is involved in the war effort, as all loyal sons of the Union must be. While there's a profit in this," he continued with a gleam of avarice in his eyes, "it leaves the company somewhat limited for cash. I'm afraid, Miss Granger, you and your Mission are no longer a priority."

"I understand," she answered. "Please thank your father for his past generosity, Mr. Winslow."

As she turned toward the door, she heard the chair scrape. "Miss Granger, perhaps *I* can help you."

"Yes?" Hope careened through her.

"I understand that the Mission owns that house."

"Yes."

He came toward her. "Then sell the house. Property prices are escalating."

"Don't be foolish! Then we'd have no place to live."

Folding his arms over his chest, he demanded, "How many children do you have at the Mission, Miss Granger?"

"As of this morning, sixteen children plus Miss Nevins and myself."

"Eighteen people?" He shook his head slowly. "That building could be rented to many times that number."

"I realize that." She did, for she had visited the tenements in Five Points, where the army of rats did not outnumber the people crowded into dank, moldy apartments. It was not uncommon to find eight or more people living in one room. "I don't want your charity. Nor do I want your useless suggestions."

"I wasn't offering charity. I'm offering to buy the house from you, Miss Granger." He went back to his desk and picked up a slip of paper. "With this, you can go to my bank and sign the necessary papers to turn that house over to Winslow Enterprises."

"Why would I do something like that?"

"Because you need money. You and your orphans can

have the uppermost floor of the house for a nominal rent. Winslow Enterprises will assume maintenance on the house and will rent the lower floors." He held out the paper. "It's a fair deal for all of us."

She laughed. Seeing his eyes slit with fury, she said, "You must think me a dolt to agree to such an arrangement. Your father has not been the Mission's only benefactor."

"Who else?"

"That, sir, isn't your business." She kept her shoulders square. She could not let him know the truth of her desperation. Why had she spent the money on fabric instead of food? She feared she had let her own hidden yearning to quilt again betray her and the children. "Why do you want to know? So you can intimidate them into halting their philanthropy to the Mission as well?" Turning to the door, she added over her shoulder, "Good day, Mr. Winslow, and good-bye."

Chester scurried to keep up with Sarah, but she said nothing as he held the door for her. Stamping down the steps, she clenched her hands on her empty bag.

Empty! How was she going to manage to feed the children? How could she pay Rachel? Gas was needed for lamps and soap to wash their clothes. She was not sure how she would persuade Mr. Pettigew to grant her more time and still sell her food for the Mission.

She did not pause until she was half a block from the house. Her chest ached as if she had run miles, but it was cramped with the tears she refused to let fall. She stared sightlessly at the elegant brownstones on the far side of the cobbled street.

She would not turn the Mission into a tenement, but she needed another source of money while she and the children finished the quilts and waited for them to sell. As she watched a carriage drive by, she saw the befeathered hat the woman inside wore. She smiled. The Mission's basement rooms, where a millinery shop had been, were empty. She could lease those again. The few dollars that would bring might be enough to keep the Mission open.

Sarah looked for a carriage to take her back to the Mission. No, she could not afford a cab until she found a new way to fund the Mission. Everyone was going to have to do without, and she must, as always, set an example for the children.

The walk back to Second Avenue was longer than she had guessed. The houses became dilapidated and filthy. Dragging her spirits behind her, she tried to guess how she could find someone to rent the cellar rooms.

"Why so glum on such a nice day?" called a voice woven with laughter.

Although Sarah wanted to smile when she saw Benjamin swinging down off Rogue, it was impossible. "I thought you worked in Five Points."

"Rogue and I patrol wherever we're needed. At the moment, it looks as if you need some help."

"I'm just tired." She wanted to add more, but pride kept her silent. Pride? She almost laughed. There was no shame in being destitute. How many times had she told the children that?

"Is the baby still keeping you from sleeping?"

Sarah smiled. "Birdie last night and Innis the night before. Innis is teething."

"Grand name for such a slip of a boy."

"He'll have to grow a lot to grow into it." Her smile wavered. To grow, the children needed food.

He lowered his voice. "How is Conlan?"

"Not good." She sighed. "I'm sorry, Benjamin, but he was hysterical this morning when I touched the quilt. The poor child fears I'm going to take it from him."

"If you did—"

"He would go mad."

"A child that young?"

"Who has seen his mother lying in her own blood."

He put his hand on her shoulder, then stroked down her arm. "I'm sorry, Sarah. I know you're dealing with this every day."

"But Captain Potter wants that quilt."

With a rueful smile, he nodded. "I'm dealing with *that* every day."

"As soon as it's possible, you'll have it."

"If I could just examine it . . ."

She shook her head. "Not today. Let me try again with him this evening. When he's sleepy just before bed, he needs less coaxing to let me close to him."

Heat sparked in his eyes as his arm slipped around her waist. "I'd need no coaxing to let you close to me then, sweetheart."

The sounds along the street, the clatter of wheels on stone and voices, were swallowed by the thunder of her heartbeat when he drew her up against him. She should not be standing with him like this in public, but she could not push herself away. Gazing up into his shadowy eyes, she wondered if she dared to explore the passions within them, if she could ever find her way out of their succulent web. Or if she would want to.

Her mouth hungered for his on it. She wanted his arms enfolding her as their breaths mingled in a fiery wind. And his fingers . . . She yearned for their touch lilting across her, creating a song that came from the depths of her heart.

"Stop looking at me like that," he whispered, "or you may have to call a policeman to stop me from kissing you."

"Would kissing me be breaking any law?"

"None that I know of." He brushed her lips with his. When she moaned as he drew back, he tapped her nose. "What happened to the Sarah Granger who must think of propriety first?"

"I got rid of her for the afternoon." She laughed tightly, her happiness fading. "What good will she do me now?"

"What's wrong, Sarah?" All humor left his face.

"Money. What else?" She shook her head. "Prices go up by the hour, and my benefactors are nervous about the war, so they aren't making donations."

"I had no idea." He looped Rogue's reins around his wrist and held out his other arm to her.

"I don't know how much longer I can keep the Mission from closing. The children are doing what they can."

"With their sewing?"

She nodded. "But they still are a long way from completing their first project. I need to have money this week or next at the latest. Maybe if I could rent the rooms in the cellar, it would help."

"To a family?"

"No, for a shop." She raised her chin again as she had when she faced the younger Mr. Winslow. "I will not turn the Mission into a tenement."

"I can mention to a few folks who might be interested that you're looking for someone to rent the rooms."

"Would you do that?" Putting her hand on his arm, she smiled. "Thank you, Benjamin."

He put his hand over her fingers to keep them on his sleeve as he said, "Let me walk you back to the Mission."

When she followed his glance toward the steps of a brick row house, she saw four young men watching them intently. Then she realized their gazes were focused on her. One of them licked his lips and made a crude gesture. Hating the heat that climbed her cheeks, she lowered her eyes as she heard their coarse laughter.

"I don't usually walk through this neighborhood," she whispered.

"Don't do it again. If—"

"Hey, copper!" called one of the men.

Sarah flinched at the derogatory nickname. The policemen's copper badges gave the Irish a way to taunt them. Benjamin's hand grew taut over hers.

"Hey, copper! Got yourself a pretty drab whore!"

Laughter raced through the narrow street. Hearing footsteps, she glanced over her shoulder. Shouting insults must not offer enough amusement for the bored men. She bit her lip to silence her gasp of dismay.

Benjamin released Rogue's reins and reached for his nightstick. "Don't stop," he hissed under his breath. "Just keep walking. No matter what."

"Benjamin—"

"Just keep walking."

She tried to obey, but her arm was seized in a painful vise. She fought to jerk her elbow away, but the grip was too tight. Benjamin shouted something. She had no time to realize what as she was spun to face one of the grinning men. The odor of whiskey reeked from him.

"Let me go!" she cried.

"You can do better than a copper, dearie," he said, tugging her close to him. His coat was a deep black, reminding her incongruously of Lorne, and it had been stitched together along the sleeve.

She did not care if he wore cloth of gold or rags. She did not want him touching her. "Let me go!"

He shrieked as a blur flashed between them, striking his arm. Pulling away a half step, she saw Benjamin raise his nightstick again. His face was as emotionless as the portraits in the Winslow mansion.

The man whirled her in front of him and growled, "You'll have to hit her first, copper."

"So that's how you boys play here?" Benjamin's eyes shifted to watch the four men. "Hiding behind a lady's skirts?"

Sarah screamed as she was shoved away. She hit the cobbles hard. Pain ricocheted up her arm, but she ignored it. Fighting her petticoats, she scrambled to her feet. She could not let Benjamin fight four men alone. Raising her clasped fists, she struck one of the men in the back. He collapsed to the sidewalk. She cried out a warning and saw Benjamin duck beneath a wild swing. He hit another man, who fell facedown on the street. The other two men exchanged a fearful look and fled.

Benjamin wiped blood from his lip and frowned at the men on the ground. "What happened to him?"

"I hit him."

His eyes widened as he chuckled. "*You* hit him? Sarah, you are a constant surprise." When he pulled a handkerchief from under his coat, he dabbed it against his lip. He poked the senseless men with the toe of his boot. "Let's go, Sarah."

"You're just going to leave them here?"

"They don't have anything worth stealing, and there's no sense in taking them to the precinct station when room is needed for real criminals." He smiled without mirth. "Welcome to my life in glorious New York City, Sarah."

She walked away with him, but could not resist looking back. One man slowly sat and reached over to shake his comrade awake. "How can you be so nonchalant about all this?"

"Because if things keep going as they are," he said grimly as he glanced behind them to see the men coming to their feet, "we're going to remember these as the good old days."

7

BENJAMIN YAWNED AS HE knocked on the door. The echo of the church bells chiming the hour vanished into the distance across the river. Nine o'clock. He wondered why it seemed as if he had been working for a week without any rest. Maybe because he had. With an ironic grin, he realized he had slept no more than four hours any day during the past week. If he had a lick of sense, he would head to bed. Instead, he was stopping at the Second Avenue Mission for Needy Children.

"You have to keep your personal feelings out of this." Captain Potter's voice rang through his head more loudly than the church bells.

He knew the captain was right. Every hour Sarah delayed handing over the quilt brought the chance of another murder.

"If you can't get that quilt, I'll send someone over to the Mission who will."

His jaw worked as Captain Potter's parting words lashed at him. This was his investigation! He had discovered the victim, and he had garnered the only tidbits of information they had. Which was not much, he had to admit. No one had turned up anything else to help them. Only that blasted quilt, which might be as much of a dead end as everything else had been. Or it might provide the very clue to pinpoint the murderer.

When he knocked a second time, more impatiently, the door opened. Ruthie peered around it. Her eyes crinkled in a smile. "Won't you come in, Sergeant McCauley?"

"Good evening, Ruthie." He gave her a smile, but clasped his hands behind his back to keep the girl from seeing how they clenched. Was Sarah trying to cause even more trouble for herself by letting this child answer the door? If someone else had been calling, the whole street might be in an uproar now.

"Sarah's in the parlor."

"With the other children?" He undid the top button on his coat collar.

"Just with Birdie and Conlan." She looked past him. "Did you bring Rogue?"

His smile became genuine. "He should be asleep by now at the stable behind the police station."

"Can you bring him next time?"

"I'll try."

She grinned and hurried up the stairs, trailed by patched fabric that flapped behind her. She must be doing some repairs to the children's clothing. Or was Sarah taking in mending to help pay the children's expenses?

He could hear the children chattering as well as Rachel Nevins's harried voice. No wonder Ruthie had answered the door. Miss Nevins must be busy putting the younger ones to bed on this hot evening when the late sunset teased them to stay awake.

Benjamin put his hat on the peg by the door. Then he shrugged off his coat. Wiping the back of his neck, he hoped the heat would break at least for a day or two. Otherwise it was going to be a long summer, especially if tempers grew as heated as the weather.

He paused by the door and smiled. Sarah had her back to him. Where had she gotten the well-made cradle she was rocking with one foot as she sat on the dilapidated sofa? She was talking to Conlan, who sat an arm's length from her. Her hand moved, and he realized she was sewing. Whatever she was making held the little boy's attention completely. Conlan's head bobbed in motion with the needle.

"See? I'm making a flower," Sarah said to the little boy. Holding out the fabric she was working on, she asked, "Isn't it pretty?"

Benjamin grasped the door frame as her motion turned her in profile to him. Something seized him in the gut when he stared, enthralled, at the enticing curves above her full skirt. His palms itched with the yearning to cup her breasts, which had been so pliant against his chest. When she leaned toward the little boy, he imagined her tilting over him, her hair falling free across her, her head thrown back as he explored every inch of her skin before delving within her to release the passions she could not conceal. Need tightened across him.

"Benjamin, this is a pleasant surprise."

Her lyrical voice threatened to unleash the longing he was fighting to control. Forcing his fingers to ease their death grip on the door, he wondered if she would say the same thing if he revealed what he was thinking. Would she find it pleasant or a surprise or admit that her own fantasies unfolded in the same direction?

"Am I interrupting?" That was an idiotic question. Of course he was interrupting, just as his few hours of sleep were interrupted with heated dreams of holding her.

Sarah's foot continued to rock the cradle as she glanced from the little boy back to him. Folding the cloth on her lap, she motioned toward the chair. "Come in, Benjamin."

When she frowned as he walked toward the chair, he forced a grin and rubbed his lower back as if it ached. "Long day."

"You look as if you've strained every muscle."

"Just a few are bothering me at the moment."

"Do you want me to have Rachel chip some ice off the block to put on them?"

He could not keep from grinning. "No, thanks." Even ice would not cool him down, when the very tilt of her chin was enough to fire him up. Sitting, he asked, "What are you doing?"

She held up what she had been sewing. The fabric had been stitched together in a daisy pattern, and she was quilting it with easy curves that brought to mind her own. He struggled not to think about that as he took the square. The stitches were tiny and perfect, and each petal was the identical size. He suspected that only a very skilled seamstress could manage that.

"I was showing Conlan," she said while he looked at her work, "how I have been teaching the children to make quilts."

"You've been teaching the children to *quilt*?" A queasy sense of disquiet raced through his stomach.

"When they aren't busy with other things." She ran her fingers along the fabric, and he imagined them touching him as lightly. "I quilted as a child, and I enjoyed it so much. I thought this would be a skill the children should have as well." She glanced at Conlan. "I know it's not as pretty as *his* quilt, with all its nice colors."

"No . . . No, it isn't," he added hastily when she frowned at him. He tried to clear his mind of the snares of desire, so he could help her in trying to reach the child, but the simple touch of her fingers when she took the cloth back riveted him.

When she turned to the little boy, he fought not to scowl. He should not be annoyed, because she was trying to help him, too. But the help he wanted from her right now was in assisting him to draw the pins out of her hair as he pulled her into his arms. How could she be so unaware of the sparks that bolted along his skin whenever it brushed hers?

"Will you rock the cradle, Benjamin?" she asked as she spread the cloth out on the cushion between her and Conlan.

"Sure."

She did not look at him as she pointed to the center of the material. "See? This is red just like on your quilt, Conlan. And, this is blue." Her voice remained even as she said, "Not so quickly, Benjamin. Rock the cradle more slowly."

He feared he would explode when she put her hand on his knee. Rocking slowly was what he wanted to do, but with her, and when the only quilt they had to think about was the one beneath them on a bed.

When Benjamin clamped his hand over hers, pinning it to his leg, Sarah halted in midword. She turned to meet his blazing eyes. His fingers stroked hers in rhythm with the motion of his leg as he rocked the cradle, one finger slipping beneath her hand to tantalize her palm. The sensation was wildly enticing, urging her to toss aside all thoughts but of him. His other hand drifted up her arm and over her shoulder. When she tipped toward him, wanting more, his lips parted in an eager grin.

Smaller fingers covered hers on the fabric piece. When Benjamin's gaze tore from hers to look past her, his eyes grew wide. She blinked, trying to gather her thoughts.

"Sarah!" The intensity in Benjamin's voice freed her from the fascination.

She moved only her head as she glanced back at Conlan, who slid to rest his head against her arm. He held his rolled quilt in one arm, but his other hand caressed the quilt square she had sewn.

Making no sudden moves that might send the child fleeing back into his fear, Sarah slid her hand out from beneath Benjamin's. She ignored the pulse of dismay that the magic was gone again. Conlan needed her now.

She picked up the closer end of the quilt square. "Would you like to have this, Conlan?"

He gazed up at her, his thumb in his mouth again.

"It is just the perfect size for a little baby, don't you think?" She held out her hands as she had before. "Would you like to hold it while you're my baby?"

"Amazing," murmured Benjamin as Conlan wiggled into her arms.

She handed the fabric square to the little boy, who held it on top of his quilt as he nestled against her as he had before. Keeping her voice low, she said, "He needs to be a baby now. Maybe it makes him believe he's safe."

"He is safe with you."

"I wish he could believe that." She smiled. "He did not recognize you without your uniform coat, so maybe that's why he's able to relax."

"I'll have to remember that when I bring Rogue back to give the children more rides." His lips grew straight. "Sarah, you can't have the Brown children answering the door. It's too dangerous to keep reminding your neighbors about them living here."

"They aren't supposed to answer the door."

"Ruthie let me in."

She sighed. With Doreen gone and the extra children, she and Rachel could not watch each child all the time. "Thank you for telling me, Benjamin. I'll speak to the children and Rachel. We don't need any more trouble."

"You've had more trouble?"

Nothing but you making me want to forget everything but your kisses. She glanced down at Conlan, needing to escape the honest disquiet in Benjamin's eyes when she could not be so candid with him. "Things have been quiet here."

"I'm glad it's quiet one place in the city."

The frustration in his voice drew her eyes up again. Seeing the lines ground into his face by the sun and too many hours of work, she asked, "What's going on?"

"Don't look so distressed, Sarah." He chuckled. "Just the usual. First, the ragman's horse bolted on Twenty-eighth Street. It nearly ran down Mr. Costello in front of his store. There was a huge family argument on Thirtieth Street, and we had to keep the wife from raising a lump on her drunk husband's head."

She laughed. "I'm not so sure you should have stopped her. It probably would have made her feel better, and he's going to have a headache in the morning anyhow."

"I considered that, but they were causing quite a racket." As if on cue, Birdie began to cry. He reached to scoop up the baby. "Where did you get the nice cradle, Sarah?"

"Mother had it shipped here when I wrote to her about Birdie sleeping in a drawer."

"It's your family's cradle? Here?"

"This is my family, Benjamin, as much as my parents are." When Birdie kept crying, she asked, "Do you want me to take her?"

"No, you've got your arms full already." He grinned. "And I'm not so inept with babies." He shifted Birdie, and her cries eased. "In fact, I've helped deliver two or three myself."

"You have?"

"Part of keeping the peace." He arched a brow. "I don't have any trouble with them when they're this size. It's when they're bigger that they become problems."

"Maybe you should give up patrolling the streets to become a nursemaid," came Rachel's cool voice from the doorway. Not giving him a chance to reply, she turned to Sarah. "I'll take these two and put them to bed now."

Kissing Conlan on the forehead, Sarah hoped he would react. He only slid off her lap and walked slowly to where Rachel stood. Tears filled her eyes as she wondered if she would ever be able to reach the outspoken little boy he had been.

"I'll take the baby, Sergeant," Rachel continued and held out her hands.

"Rachel," Sarah said, "I can—"

"No, *you* stay here." Her genteel shudder made it clear that she had no interest in spending even an extra second in Benjamin's company.

"Rachel, there's no need for that tone."

"No?" She took Conlan's hand and walked out of the room.

Benjamin said quietly, "Don't push her."

"She's being unreasonable."

"She only wants to protect you."

"From you?"

He grinned. "You needn't sound so incredulous."

"I am." Sarah smiled as she stood. "If you just got off duty, you must be hungry."

"No, I had a bite to eat at the station, but I could use some lemonade if you have any left."

The sound of Conlan's slow steps up the stairs disappeared as Sarah led the way into the kitchen. Without Doreen O'Brien here, the dishes were stacked, waiting to be washed. Tonight's supper had been soup . . . again. The children had grimaced, and she had let them think they were having soup for the third time in two days simply because Doreen had left. She did not want them to guess that there had been no money for other food. Along with the cradle had come some cash from a collection at Reverend Granger's church. If she was careful, it would buy them enough food for another few weeks. Then . . .

Her fingers trembled as she took the pitcher from the icebox and lifted a platter of cookies from beneath the bread box. She could not think of the future when she had enough to worry about with this week's task of trying to find new benefactors for the Mission.

She put the pitcher on the table. Stretching high on her tiptoes, she tried to grasp a plate from the top shelf.

"Allow me, Sarah."

"Thank you." She started to move, but Benjamin stood behind her. As he collected the plate she wanted, his rock-hard body brushed her. Time became meaningless, for she was swept back to the moment when his fingers had covered hers on his knee. All the sensation, all the wanting surged through her.

"Here you go."

Her breath burst from her when he placed the plate in her hands. "Thank you," she murmured.

He stroked her shoulders. Closing her eyes, she wanted to melt into the pleasure of his touch. His fingers moved from her shoulder to glide along her jaw. She yearned to touch him. She started to face him, but he kept her against him. Resting her head back against his chest, she let a sigh of pleasure ooze from her lips when his fingertips crossed her cheek.

"So soft you are," he murmured in her ear.

She was about to reply when she saw a motion at the

back porch window. She pulled away and raced to the door. She swung it open. No one stood on the small porch.

"What is it?"

She closed the door. "I thought I saw someone."

"On the back porch?" He reached for the doorknob, but she kept her hand on it.

"No, don't go out there. I think the sight of you scared whoever it was away."

"If whoever it was is afraid of the police," he growled, "then you should be afraid of them."

She put her hands on his arms. "You know that isn't true. The Mission is here to serve those who need it."

"Sarah, there are murderers on these streets. You've witnessed them yourself. Maybe they know that."

"Hungry children come here, and I give them what I can."

"But you didn't see children the night that woman was murdered down by the church."

"I told you I couldn't see well enough through the storm to see anything but that they were grown men and a woman."

He pounced on her words. "A woman? You didn't mention that before!"

"I didn't remember it until now." She put her fingers to her temples. "I should have remembered it, but when you arrived with that dying woman, I forgot."

He smiled wryly. "It doesn't matter. The man who was shot is dead and unmourned. Perhaps it was as simple as Father Tynan tried to convince me. Just one drunk Irishman against another."

"No!" When she saw his eyebrows lower over his narrowed eyes, she stumbled on, "He was running, and they ambushed him."

"But you saw nothing to identify them?"

"I'm sorry, Benjamin. I don't remember anything else."

"If you do, you must tell me right away."

Searching his face, Sarah saw his strong emotions. "You believe this is connected with the trouble at the docks, don't you?"

"Yes." He poured two glasses of lemonade. "And to Conlan's mother's murder."

"How?"

"If I knew the answer to that, I might have the murderer under arrest." He handed her a glass. "I may be wrong. I hope I am, and that this is the end of it, but . . ."

He did not finish. He did not need to. Some instinct made Benjamin suspect there were other brutal murders being plotted in Five Points.

Putting the glass back on the table, she whispered, "Can't you stop this?"

"There aren't enough policemen to patrol the streets as they should be patrolled. With the high taxes to pay for the war, the mayor's office doesn't want to raise them again to pay for more policemen." He picked up his glass of lemonade and drained it. "How about a walk?"

"Now? It must be after ten."

"I have to report at midnight, so I won't have any sleep tonight anyhow."

"Benjamin, you just got off duty."

He shrugged, then grinned around a yawn. "Such is the life of a policeman. We have less than fifteen hundred men to patrol all of New York."

"That's ridiculous!"

"And how about you, Miss Granger of the Second Avenue Mission for Needy Children? How often have you worked without sleep?"

"That's different," she asserted.

His hand on her arm drew her closer. "Is it, sweetheart? This Mission is your obsession just as the work I do on the streets is mine. I think you and I are very, very much alike."

Sarah knew she should fire back a sharp answer. As she stared up into his eyes, she could not form a single thought, except to savor the sound of his voice calling her *sweetheart*. It had been far too long since anyone had called her anything but Sarah or Miss Granger.

When his hand slid behind her nape, she quivered. A warmth spread from his fingers. Her hands rose. She

wanted his strong body beneath her fingertips. She
wanted—

She turned away and went to the door to the hall. When
she realized Benjamin had not moved, she glanced over her
shoulder. "Well?"

A smile twisted his lips, but the embers continued to
glow in his eyes. "Well what?"

"Aren't we going for a walk?"

"If you want to."

"Yes, I do." She did not dare to remain in this shadowed
kitchen. From here it was too easy to imagine him holding
her in her office on the settee, or in her bedroom on the—
She halted that thought.

He held the door, and she went to pull her bonnet from
its peg. When she reached for her black cloak, he said,
"You don't need that. It's still hot outside, and, if you wear
it, I could lose you in the dark between street lamps."

"How about you in that dark uniform, Sergeant Mc-
Cauley?" she asked as he drew on his coat.

He seized her arms and tugged her closer. When she
gasped at the craving ricocheting through her, he grinned
fiercely. "I wear dark colors so I can leap from the shadows
to pounce on unsuspecting criminals."

"I'm not a criminal."

He chuckled as he released her. "No, you're not. I can't
imagine you as anything but the angelic Miss Granger."
Taking her hand, he raised it to his lips. He smiled as she
sighed with pleasure. In a husky whisper, he added, "Or
maybe I can imagine you as something else."

"Benjamin, if we're going . . ." She did not want him to
see the answering desire in her eyes.

He reached past her to open the door. When he swung it
aside, his hand settled in the center of her back. His fingers
slid around her as they walked out the door. He turned to
close the heavy door, and she stared at his silhouette, which
eclipsed the peeling paint. She fought residual shivers of anticipation for his touch. When he offered his arm, she put her
hand on it. Beneath the rough texture of his coat, she sensed
the power coiled to explode.

"Going out so late?" called a voice from the other side of the avenue.

Sarah saw Mrs. Clyne looking out her window. The plump woman, whose thinning hair was a white cloud around her lined face, never seemed far from her perch by the second-floor window. Sarah often paused to listen to the old woman's gossip. More accurate and up-to-date than even the *New York Times*, Mrs. Clyne kept an eye on the street from her aerie.

Benjamin tipped his cap. "Up so late yourself?" he teased. "How will you rise in the morning?"

"Soon 'twill be morning, Sergeant McCauley." She chuckled; the sound was like a rusty hinge. "Taking Miss Granger for a turn?"

"She needs to get out of the Mission now and again, don't you think? Want to come along, Mrs. Clyne?"

She laughed. "When I was a lass, no good-looking laddie asked an old woman along on a turn. Get on with ye!"

Beneath the umbrella of Mrs. Clyne's infectious laughter, Sarah walked with Benjamin toward the corner. When they were out of earshot, she said, "Now everyone will know we were out tonight."

"And that bothers you?"

"No." She smiled. "If I'd cared about what folks thought, I never would have come here in the first place."

"Your family didn't want you to come here?"

"It's too lovely a night to discuss disagreeable things." She glanced along the street and took a deep breath. *Or to linger in the pain of the past.* She had thought she had left her past behind her when she came to New York City, but it was returning, piece by piece, to become part of the pattern of her life once more. Not just the cradle, but the pleasure of watching her needle slide in and out of fabric with a sound so soft that she heard it more with her fingers than with her ears.

The heat was easing, taking with it the worst of the odors from the open sewers. Although the city was never silent, its tempo had slowed. The windows were gray eyes in the black face of each building. The reed-thin sound of a baby crying broke the quiet. Only the stars, which shone more brightly than the fitful streetlights, seemed real.

Suddenly Benjamin swore under his breath. When she looked at him in astonishment, he said, "I should have guessed they'd be out already."

"Who?"

His smile was macabre in the darkness. "Don't ask any questions now." He raised his voice. "Liam, what are you doing so far from Worth Street?"

She grasped the rickety newel post of a row house as she saw someone creeping through the shadows. She did not fear the streets during the day, but night brought all the beasts from their lairs.

"Sergeant McCauley?" called back the man. "I didn't know you came up here. I— Oh!" His stare pierced the darkness.

"Don't say anything," Benjamin ordered quietly before raising his voice again. "Are you going to stand there and shout all night, Liam? If so, I'm going to have to arrest you for disturbing the peace."

Liam edged closer, but kept more than an arm's length between them. "I wasn't going to cause any trouble, Sergeant."

"Just help yourself to a few things?"

"Things folks throw out." He rocked uneasily from one foot to the other.

Sarah recognized his stance. She had seen it on other young men in Five Points. He was scared. She hoped his fear would not convince him to do something stupid.

"Or leave out," Benjamin said with a taut chuckle.

"Sergeant—"

He raised his hand. "I'm not interested in listening to your excuses. I want you to take a message to Mick for me."

"Which Mick?"

"You know which Mick." He laughed, but tension ran through his arm under Sarah's fingers. "The leader of your ragtag gang. Tell him I want to talk to him tonight. Usual place."

"I don't carry messages."

"That's your decision, but think how Mick's going to feel when he discovers you didn't tell him."

The young man muttered something, then ran down the street toward Five Points.

"Do you think he'll tell Mick?" Sarah asked.

Benjamin put his finger to her lips. "Forget that name. Forget everything you just heard and saw."

"You don't need to be so melodramatic."

"I'm not being melodramatic. I just don't want you getting involved in something you don't need to be involved in."

"You sound like Father Tynan."

"I know." He pushed her glasses up on her nose. "I think we've walked far enough for tonight."

Sarah considered asking another question, but it would be useless. He would not tell her anything more. Keeping the streets quiet was his job, not hers.

She recognized the sound as they approached the front steps of the Mission. Too many times before she had heard the weak cry of an abandoned baby.

"Sarah?" Benjamin called as she rushed to the steps.

She gathered up the baby, which was wrapped in rags. Looking both ways along the street, she saw something move in the shadows near the church. "There, Benjamin!"

He ran toward St. John's while she opened the door. Taking the baby out to the kitchen, she set him on the table. She peeled back the rags and moaned. The baby had not even been washed. He could be no more than a few hours old and was so small, his heartbeat could be seen through his emaciated chest.

Glad that the water in the bucket by the door was still warm from the day's heat, she dipped a cloth into it and began to clean the baby. He wailed, sounding more like a kitten than a child.

Swaddling him in other cloths, she rushed to the laundry basket to see if she could find a gown small enough for him. She thought she had one, but was horrified to see how big it was when she slipped him into it. She wrapped him in a blanket, not wanting him to be chilled, and held him close to her heart as she warmed some milk.

He was almost too weak to suck, but she squeezed some drops into his mouth, watching that they did not fall back out. His feeble crying eased as the door opened from the hall. She turned with an expectant look.

Benjamin shook his head. "I didn't see a sign of anyone. Father Tynan told me to tell you that he would keep looking, because I need to head up to the precinct station and get Rogue. Father Tynan said he would let you know if he finds anyone."

"If the mother has slipped away, she won't be found now."

"I know." He sighed and pushed his cap back on his forehead to wipe away gleaming sweat. "I have to go. I'd like to stay and help you . . ."

She smiled. "I appreciate that. Rachel will help me. She works miracles with babies." Her smile fell away as she looked down at the baby's wizened face. "And we may need a miracle to save this one."

"While you're ordering a miracle, get one or two for me," he said.

"Be careful tonight."

"I'm always careful."

"More than ever."

He kissed her gently, taking care not to bump the baby. "You need to be, too." His voice darkened as he glanced toward the back door. "More than ever, especially if those miracles don't come soon."

8

"YOU NEED TO REST." Rachel gave Sarah a not too gentle shove out of the smallest bedroom. "I'll watch Quigley."

Sarah wanted to argue, but she could not. She had been caring for the little baby, without a break, for—how long had it been? Two days? Three? More? It had been at least two days since Father Tynan came to the house to baptize the child, whom she assumed was Irish. He had a saint's name that was longer than he was, but the children called him "Wiggly Quigley."

She wished he would wiggle more. He continued to fight to live, but she wondered if it was a battle he could win. He was so little, and his heart throbbed so hard against his narrow chest.

As she came down the stairs, she looked about for the children, then remembered Rachel had sent them out to play in the tiny backyard. They no longer could play out front, because the Brown children were ridiculed and insulted.

She paused when she saw someone in the parlor. Going in, she smiled. "Fiona, I thought you'd be outside playing with Ruthie."

"Someone needed to sit with Conlan." She glanced at the boy, who was staring at the wall.

"Has he—?"

"He hasn't done anything." Fiona scowled. "Isn't he getting tired of doing nothing?"

Sarah chuckled. "It sounds as if you are. Go out and play. I'll watch Conlan."

"Rachel said you were going to rest."

"I can rest with Conlan."

Fiona jumped to her feet and wrinkled her nose. "He never makes any noise, so you should be able to rest all you want."

As the girl ran out to join the other children, Sarah sighed. Each time she thought she had made some progress with Conlan, he retreated again, afraid to trust again.

Just like me.

She froze at the thought. No, that was not true. Not any longer. Right after Giles had died, she had wanted to as well, sure her life was over and that she could never be happy again. She had put aside everything that made her happy, fearing that happiness would bring only more sorrow. She had stopped singing, and she had stopped dancing. And she had stopped quilting. Any hint of glee seemed a betrayal of the love she had for Giles. He was dead, never to be happy again. How could she, who survived, rejoice when she was surrounded by grief? That unhappiness had become a habit.

Then, she had come to the Mission and opened her heart to all the children here. She had to help Conlan do the same.

Sitting beside him on the sofa, she smiled. "Is that the corner of the square I sewed for you that I see sticking out of your quilt?"

He looked up at her.

"Right there," she said, pointing to the square. "Did you bake it into your quilt like the four-and-twenty blackbirds were baked into a pie?"

She held her breath as he unrolled his quilt and drew out the wrinkled square. He put it on the cushion between them.

Stroking the flower she had made out of slips of material left over from the other pieces, he continued to suck his thumb.

She picked up the square and drew her needle from the waistband of her apron where she kept it as she had years ago. Contentment, unlike any she had known in all that time, swelled over her as she began to create a swirling pattern of quilting over and around the flower. It was as if dozens of butterflies swarmed around the petals.

He reached out to touch her stitches, and she turned it so he could see it. *Be happy!* she wanted to cry. *Dare to be happy.* It was advice she needed as well, but she was learning it was possible as she rediscovered her quilting and discovered passion in Benjamin's touch.

Trying to hide her excitement, she began to babble about how she had decided to make the flower because she missed her mother's garden. She was glad, for once, that he did not look at her, because she did not want him to see her staring at the quilt.

She set the daisy square on the sofa so he could examine it more closely. She looked past it to his quilt. She stumbled over her words as she discovered what was odd about the quilt pattern in Conlan's quilt. Not only had the quilting been done with black thread, an odd choice for a child's quilt, but the pattern was undeniably supposed to be a bird's feather. The work was intricate and far too sophisticated for something that would be used in a nursery.

Black wings sewn into a quilt with blackbirds around its edges. It had to be unique in all of New York City. With it, the police could start asking questions to trace the children's route the day their mother was killed.

Her words faltered as Conlan gathered up the square and stuck it back within his quilt, holding it close again. If she told Benjamin about this discovery—which might have far less significance than she guessed—he would be even more impatient to take the quilt to his captain. That might completely destroy any chance of drawing Conlan out of his pain.

As she held the little boy on her lap, she wondered how

difficult it would be to keep this truth from Benjamin. He was always honest with her . . . and she had lied to him so often. This would be just one more.

∞

"AND HERE HE IS." Leaning against the post separating Rogue's stall from the next, Benjamin laughed as Sarah stretched to pat the horse's nose. "You don't have to talk to him as sweetly as you do to the children. Rogue's accustomed to much harsher language."

Taking a deep breath of the thick odor of oats and manure, he smiled. Sarah did not shy away from this part of his world, this part that once had been his whole world. When his father had been able to buy the livery, the family had escaped from the rat-infested tenement to move into one of the rooms that now held carriages. It had seemed like a vast improvement, and he had enjoyed waking to the scent of horses each morning.

Now this was the life he loved. Rogue was his partner, imperturbable on the street and strong enough to work long hours. Together, they were struggling to keep the anger boiling through Five Points from exploding.

He leaned his elbow on the stall door. It might all be for naught, if the draft were held this summer. That would divide the city as nothing else had. Already he had been snarled at in the slums because the poor Irish believed he could afford the three hundred dollars to pay someone else to serve in his place if his name were drawn in the draft. Others had asked him if he would be excluded because he was a policeman. He wondered if they would have tried to sign up if he had said yes.

Why didn't they hold the draft lottery and get it over with before the summer's worst heat smothered the city? Maybe the governor and the mayor were hoping for some glorious victory to put an end to the war or get everyone excited about it again. He could tell anyone who asked that it was too late for that now. The poor Irish were tired of the war that had taken their livelihoods and their lives.

"The children are hoping you'll visit them again soon, Rogue," he heard Sarah say.

Sarah Granger . . . She was a complication he had not expected now. He enjoyed admiring the softly feminine profile of her body, but there was nothing soft about her uncompromising conviction that she could reform the world, one child at a time. The combination of strength and gentleness made her unique and, he feared, vulnerable. He dreaded what could happen to her and her optimistic dreams if the unease whispering along the streets became a roar.

"I bet you enjoyed the children, too, didn't you, Rogue?" she continued. "They all wanted to feed you the carrots they were supposed to be eating for supper."

"So that was why they were so eager to feed him."

Sarah chuckled as she turned to Benjamin. "One thing I've discovered about children is that they're always thinking about finding a way to get out of doing something they don't want to do."

"Just let me know when you're serving carrots again, and I'll bring him around."

She smiled as she continued to stroke Rogue's nose. She had not been able to stop smiling for the past day, because Quigley was doing better with every passing hour. He was able to suck about an ounce of goat's milk before falling asleep from exhaustion. The frantic beat of his heart had eased. Maybe he had simply been frightened.

Yet when Benjamin had invited her to visit the stable behind precinct headquarters at East Fifty-ninth Street and Third Avenue, she had hesitated. Not because of the baby, but because of the secret of the pattern sewn into Conlan's quilt. She was awash with guilt each time she saw Benjamin's smile. If he knew . . . And he would know, just as soon as she could safely take the quilt from the little boy. As soon as she could. That was the promise she had made to herself and to him.

"Sarah, is something wrong?"

At his quiet question, she wanted to shout out the truth. Instead she slowly faced him, her gaze moving along his dark coat. The copper buttons shone in the dull light sifting through the dusty stable.

"Things are going better than usual at the Mission," she said. That was the truth. "The children's sewing may bring in some money soon. Mr. Pettigew is interested in having some of their work for sale at his store on the corner."

He took a step closer. "I wasn't talking about the Mission, but about you. You seem on edge." His hand rested on the stall as he moved even nearer.

She discovered she was caught between the unyielding stall door and his hardened body. He closed the distance between them to less than a finger's breadth. Each breath stroked her against him, sending hot pulses through her. She grasped his sleeves as her heart began to beat even more feverishly than the baby's. When his arms moved around her, she needed no other invitation to tip her mouth beneath his.

Losing herself in the spiraling sensations, she let her fingers roam along his back. Even through his thick coat, she could sense his reaction to her tentative touch, for his muscles moved smoothly, urging her to be more brazen. She gasped as his mouth left hers to explore the length of her neck, following her bonnet ribbons. The flicks of his tongue along her skin sent her down into an eddy of desire.

"How sweet you taste, sweetheart," he murmured in the second before his mouth found hers again.

Her fingers curved up over his nape and into his hair as his caress across her back enticed her into surrendering to the ever-escalating pleasure. Whispering wordlessly against her ear, he sampled its downy curve as he held her against the stable door.

Sarah sidestepped away from him and the stall. Clutching another stall door as she fought to support her wobbly knees, she stared at the floor, littered with hay. Her breathing rasped, swift and eager, in her ears. She should not be in a stable kissing Benjamin as she dreamed of giving him her heart and herself. Had she lost her mind? The answer to that was easy. Yes, she had.

His hand settled on her shoulder. "Sarah?"

She could not fault him for being baffled. One moment, she had been as eager as one of the harlots in the brothels in Five Points. The next, she had pulled away like a frightened child. How could she explain to him that when she was in his arms she was, for the first time in longer than she could recall, unsure of her judgment?

"Sarah?"

She adjusted her glasses. "I'm sorry."

"For what?" His eyes twinkled like the dust motes dancing in the dusty sunbeam. "For kissing me or for stopping?"

"I shouldn't be kissing you here."

"Tell me where." He draped one elbow over the stall behind her, again imprisoning her between his hard flesh and the door. "Tell me where I should kiss you, Sarah, and I would gladly do so." His finger ran along her cheek. "Do you want me to kiss you here?"

"That's not what I mean."

"Or perhaps you want me to kiss you here." His fingertip brushed her lips.

She bit her lower one to silence her gasp of pleasure before saying, "Benjamin, you aren't listening to me."

"Of course I'm listening to you." He leaned toward her so she could not escape from the dark fires in his eyes. "Perhaps you want me to kiss you here."

Her eyes closed as his finger trailed down her neck and up around her ear, where the heat left by his breath had not cooled. "Benjamin . . ."

"Or could it be here?" His finger slid down between her breasts before uncurling across one.

The craving became a void deep within her. With a soft moan, she pulled his mouth down over hers. She must kiss him. She must share these incredible, indescribable sensations with him. She must—

She must stop!

Turning her head away, she whispered, "Benjamin, no more."

He did not release her. When she stared up at his taut face, she waited for his rage to explode. Giles had been furious, cursing at her and raising his hand, although he had not struck her, the one time she had dared to gainsay him. Benjamin's passions were even stronger.

He bent and kissed her cheek. "Is that what you wish from me?" he whispered as he stepped back. "Is that all you want us to share?"

She stared at him. She had thought he would be furious. He *was* furious, she could see that when she looked up at him, but he was hurt as well. How much more betrayed would he be if he discovered the many secrets she held in her shattered heart?

"What I want," she said, "and what I should do are—"

"Two different things. I know that, but answer my question."

"Benjamin, I'm—"

"Will you answer my question? I know you're Miss Granger of the Second Avenue Mission for Needy Children. I know your behavior must be exemplary, but do you want nothing more from me than a chaste kiss?"

Her hands settled on the sleeves covering his sturdy arms. "I want more. I shouldn't, but I do. I want you to hold me and kiss me and kiss me and kiss me until I can't focus my eyes."

"And where do you want me to kiss you, Miss Granger?"

"Everywhere," she breathed. "Here in the stables. In the parlor at the Mission. Everywhere."

Laughing, he bent to brush his lips against hers. It fired the flame deep within her, and she sighed with unbridled longing. At the sound, he pulled her against him again. The bell of her skirts struck the door before swirling around his legs. His finger stroked her cheek when he whispered her name as his mouth sought hers.

The clearing of a throat froze Sarah in his arms. She tried to clear her dazzled eyes. Past her pounding pulse, she heard Benjamin speak to an emaciated man with sunken cheeks. A walrus mustache overwhelmed the rest of his face. Skeleton-thin, the man's bones protruded from his wrists, which reached too far out of his sleeves. When she saw the insignia of a Metropolitan Police captain on his surprisingly broad shoulders, the heat of embarrassment climbed up her cheeks. She hoped the dim light and her bonnet would conceal her blush.

Benjamin chuckled, and his hand in the center of her back brought her forward. Her eyes widened as his closed in a lazy wink. She fought the urge to laugh as she realized how silly she was acting. Trying to hide that Benjamin had been kissing her was about as futile as trying to conceal Ruthie's and Mason's skin color beneath rice powder, which had been one of Rachel's suggestions.

The thin man's smile broadened, tilting his thick mustache at a seemingly impossible angle. "McCauley, do I take this surprising appearance at headquarters during your off-duty time as a sign of your interest in working today?"

"Certainly not, sir. Not after twenty hours on yesterday."

The man chuckled. "Only twenty? You're slacking off."

"I'll try to remedy that after I get a week or two of sleep. Captain Potter, I'd like you to meet Miss Sarah Granger." Benjamin nodded toward the man, then added, "Sarah, my commanding officer, Captain Milo Potter."

Bowing over her hand, Captain Potter murmured, "My pleasure, Miss Granger."

"And to meet you, Captain, is indeed an honor." She smiled. "I'm delighted to meet the man who leads those keeping order on our streets."

A grin appeared beneath his bushy mustache. "I'm glad to hear that testimonial, Miss Granger. As McCauley can tell you, we're more accustomed to insults than praises."

"She's seen that," Benjamin said with an ironic tone.

"I'm sure." Captain Potter eyed her up and down. "Forgive me for staring, Miss Granger, but you seem familiar."

Benjamin answered, "Sarah is the director of the Second Avenue Mission for Needy Children."

"Ah, now I know where I have heard your name." Captain Potter smiled. "We were called to the Mission when a window was found broken in the back of the house. In the kitchen, I believe."

Sarah hid her astonishment. Rachel must have reported the broken window, although Sarah had told her to forget the incident. "Yes, it was in the kitchen."

"I trust you found the window repaired to your satisfaction."

"Yes." She had not suspected the police department had played any part in the repair. Seeing Benjamin's abrupt frown, she did not give him a chance to ask any questions she did not want to answer, especially in front of Captain Potter. "Should I thank you, Captain Potter, for your kind favor to us?"

"I'm glad to hear that you consider it a favor, Miss Granger, because I would like to ask you for a favor in return."

"Of course."

"McCauley has, as I know you know well, been investigating the murder of a young woman who left behind two children you are caring for."

Sarah clenched her hands in the full folds of her skirt. She knew where this was leading. If Benjamin had brought her here to give his captain a chance to insist that she turn over Conlan's quilt to the police, she had misjudged him. She had not guessed he would put her into such a discomfiting position.

When Captain Potter opened his mouth to continue, she said, "I am sure Sergeant McCauley, as I know *you* know well, has expressed your interest in seeing the quilt that was found with the children. You will when it is safe to allow that."

"Safe? Miss Granger, do you have any idea how much danger you and the Mission may be in?"

"Yes." She walked toward the door of the stable.

Behind her, she heard Captain Potter say, "McCauley— Say, where are you going?"

Sarah flinched when a hand brushed her back, then the sweet warmth told her it was Benjamin's. As she was about to speak to him, he gave her such a vicious scowl she understood why the rowdy-boys on the street respected him. He held out his arm in a clear command.

She put her hand on it and said nothing as they walked across the paved courtyard between the stables and the precinct headquarters. When they reached the sidewalk, she waited for Benjamin to chide her for speaking so to his captain. Instead, he remained silent.

"Benjamin, if you brought me here only to—"

He stopped in midstep. He ignored the curses of passersby who had to walk around them on the narrow sidewalk. A man grabbed his arm, then blanched as he saw the copper badge that identified the Metropolitan Police. He scurried away, to the reprimand of his flustered wife.

Benjamin drew Sarah under an awning over the door of a produce market. The shadows could not disguise his taut lips. "That was a very, very interesting exchange you had with Captain Potter."

"I told you that you could have the quilt when—"

"Not about the quilt." He grasped her shoulders. "Why didn't you tell me that you'd had a prowler?"

"It wasn't that important. Nothing was missing except a loaf of bread."

"You can devise a better lie than that!"

"You don't believe me?"

"Why should I? You're lying, aren't you?"

Pulling away, she walked toward the streetcar that had stopped near the corner. When Benjamin's hand on her arm halted her, she glared up at him. The hazy sunshine glittered off his cap's brim, but it was not as piercing as his rage.

"I thought you trusted me, Sarah!"

"I do trust you." If only she could explain . . . but that was impossible. Some secrets had to remain secrets to protect those who had a place in her heart. "You must trust me."

The clang of the streetcar bell halted his next question. With his hand on her arm, he guided her aboard the crowded vehicle. She noted how the people moved aside. They were not frightened of Benjamin, as some of the people along Second Avenue were, but his uniform obviously daunted them. After he had greeted the car driver by name and paid a nickel for each of their fares, he sat her on one of the unpadded benches.

With a jerk, the vehicle started. She held on to the edge of the open window as they bounced along the uneven street. A finger beneath her chin brought her to look at Benjamin.

Softly, he ordered, "Tell me, sweetheart."

"Not here."

"Nonsense," he said with a laugh. "No one's paying attention to us. Come on, Sarah. It can't be that horrible, can it?"

She took a deep breath to steady her voice. The temptation to tell him the truth became stronger, but she remembered the smile on Lorne's face. She could not risk Lorne being discovered in New York City now. Maybe he had taken her advice and gone back South. No, he had never been sensible. He had always depended on Giles for advice, and he must now be adrift without his brother.

"Sarah?" Benjamin's forehead was rutted with concern.

Her fingers longed to smooth out those lines, but she locked them together in her lap. "It really was nothing. The man made a mistake coming into the Mission, and he won't do it again."

"How do you know?"

"Because I know him."

His lips eased into a smile. "I should have guessed that you were trying to protect someone." His finger ran along her cheek as his voice lowered to a husky whisper, "That's one of the things I love about you."

"Love?" she choked. He must not love her! She did not want to have his heart ache with grief as hers had when Giles had died. Then she had promised herself that she would never leave her heart so unguarded again. She would allow only those who were passing through her life to hold a place in it.

"Don't bristle up like a porcupine!" He laughed. "I guess I should have chosen my words more carefully." Again his voice dropped to an intriguing hush. "Maybe it's because I keep finding myself thinking of making love with you."

"Benjamin!"

Heads turned at her sharp gasp, and she heard the low buzz throughout the carriage.

In a whisper, she said, "You shouldn't say things like that."

"Why not? It's the truth." His eyes slitted. "I figure if I want you to be truthful with me, I should be the same with you." His finger curved under her chin, and he brought her face up so she could not hide beneath the brim of her bonnet. "I know you well enough to know that you'd have mentioned the broken window if you weren't trying to protect someone. I'm not your enemy, Sarah."

"I know that." She wanted to close her eyes and let the thrill of his touch sweep away all thoughts. Then she could revel in this delight. "And neither was the person who broke the window."

"All right." He searched her face, and she hoped he would see nothing to convince him that she was lying. She was not lying. She just was not being completely truthful. "I'll accept your tale under one condition."

"Which is?" She had not lowered her defenses, although they had wavered when he touched her.

"If you need help, sweetheart, you will not hesitate to ask me."

She smiled. "That's easy to promise."

"Is it? You haven't asked me for help before."

"I haven't needed it."

He started to say something, then clamped his mouth shut. With a sigh, he nodded. "Just answer me truthfully about this. Whoever broke that window, will he hurt you or anyone at the Mission?"

"No!"

At her vehemence, he smiled. She was sure he would ask another question, but he only put his arm along the top of the bench. The scintillating fire of his touch burned through her gown, but she did not let it tempt her to soften against his sleeve. If she did, she might not be able to keep the rest of the truth imprisoned in her heart, which wanted to open to his.

The silence became a chasm between them during the ride south along Third Avenue. When they reached a corner not far from the Mission, he handed her down. He offered his arm again as they walked to Second Avenue. She wanted to say something, but she was not sure what.

At the door of the Mission, Benjamin said only, "Have a pleasant evening, Sarah." His kiss on her cheek offered no more passion than one of the children's kisses they gave her before going to bed each night.

Had she destroyed the joy she had found with him? Maybe, but she had no more idea how to bridge the abyss between them than she knew how to help Conlan.

She stood on the stoop and watched him walk away. The jaunty bounce was gone from his step. She had hurt him. She had not meant to, but she would hurt him worse if she let him inveigle his way more deeply into her heart.

Tears stung her eyes, but she ignored them as she entered the Mission. When she saw Rachel coming out of the kitchen, wiping her hands on her stained apron, Sarah forced a smile back onto her lips.

"Sarah, are you all right?" Rachel asked. "What did he do now to hurt you?"

"I'm fine." Lying was becoming easier. "Thank you."

"You aren't fine as long as you welcome *him* here. Folks along the avenue don't like you spending so much time with a copper."

"I asked you not to call him that."

Rachel's chin jutted in a fury as fiery as her hair. "It's better than what other people around here call him. You've got to tell him to stay away."

"Benjamin wouldn't do anything to hurt me or the Mission."

"Maybe not intentionally." She folded her arms in front of her. "If he weren't a copper—"

"Rachel!"

Her laugh had a harsh sound. "Stop being naïve, Sarah! You've got to persuade him to stay away from here instead of inviting him back again and again. Our neighbors don't want him around here, and if you keep welcoming him at our front door they won't want us here either. You've seen what they do to their enemies."

"I'm not their enemy!" She flinched as she heard the

echo of Benjamin's voice in her head. *I'm not your enemy, Sarah.* "Neither is he!" Pulling off her bonnet, she set it on its peg so hard the straw creaked.

"No?" Rachel slapped a calling card in Sarah's hand. "Look at this."

" 'Miss Stapleton's Dresses for Discriminating Ladies,' " she read aloud. "What does this have to do with Benjamin?"

"Miss Stapleton came to look at the rooms in the cellar. She was interested in opening another shop here and was anxious to sign a lease—until she heard your name."

Sarah tossed the card onto a table in the parlor. "She has no reason to like or dislike me. We've never met."

"But she's heard of you. She's heard of you and *him*!"

"If that's how she feels, she can go to perdition!"

"Sarah!"

She flung out her hands. "What do you expect me to say? That other people sharing your prejudice against Benjamin makes it all right? It's not all right. He's trying to protect us and everyone on his patrols. What does he get in return? Distrust and insults! I've heard all I want to about this."

"Listen to yourself. You're defending him with the fervor of a woman in love."

"Benjamin is my friend." *Or he was.* "I don't turn folks away from the Mission door because of prejudice."

"Then you're endangering the Mission. You're endangering every child here." Rachel put her hands on Sarah's arms. "Folks are upset enough about the Brown children being here. They think you have Benjamin coming here to keep anyone from hurting them."

"That's absurd."

"Is it? Think about what you are doing. We need the money from renting the rooms downstairs, but how can we rent them when *he* comes here all the time?"

She whispered, "You're asking me to make a choice between Benjamin and the Mission."

"Because that could be what it might come to, Sarah."

9

AS THE BACK DOOR opened, Sarah looked up from where she was trying to convince Quigley to drink a little more milk. "Doreen!" She set down the bottle and put her other hand on Conlan's head. She guided him by her side while she stood and walked around the kitchen table. He now clung to her skirt as tightly as to his quilt.

Doreen O'Brien eased her swollen body through the door, but did not take more than a single step into the kitchen. She glanced at Conlan and away, avoiding meeting Sarah's eyes. Her clothes were stained with sweat, and her hair was falling out of its bun to hang limply around her face. "I was wondering if you could use help, Sarah."

"Ruthie and Mason Brown are still here."

"I know." She rubbed her distended belly. "I don't like cooking for *them*, but I need work. I'd like to come back here."

"And you'll cook for all the children?"

She continued to stare at the floor. "As long as I don't have to eat with *them*."

Sarah almost laughed. The venom in Doreen's voice matched Rachel's when she spoke of Benjamin. This was ridiculous! They all needed to depend on each other when

things were so uneasy on the street. Anything could deto-
nate the anger that simmered beneath the fake smiles. Here,
in the Mission, they had to be honest with one another.

Then why aren't you being honest with Benjamin?

She ignored that question, as she had each time it had
taunted her the past two days. She could not get it out of
her mind any more than she could Rachel's comment this
morning. *Can we depend on the police to protect us if the
hatred is aimed at us?*

"Doreen, we need your help in the kitchen." She reached
for the bottle on the table. "With three babies in the house,
neither Rachel nor I have time to keep up with the work
here."

"So I see." Her nose wrinkled as she ran her finger along
the counter by the dry sink. "This could use a good scrubbing."

"I agree. Can you start today?"

"Don't have any other place to go." She picked up a
cloth and dunked it into the bucket by the door. "Still about
a month before my babe is supposed to be born. I'll stay
that long."

"You can stay longer, if you'd like."

"Maybe. Maybe not."

Sarah was tempted to add something else, but Doreen
turned her back on her to begin work. With Conlan in tow,
she went into the parlor. She held the bottle to Quigley's
mouth, and he took a suck on it. She smiled. Maybe everything was not wrong, after all. This was the life she had
made for herself, one where she had been safe from grief
by keeping herself too busy to think about the past or the
future. Here, there was only now.

As she watched the baby struggle to drink more and she
smiled down at Conlan, whose head was resting on her
knee, she tried to persuade herself that being safe was
everything she wanted. Maybe it was, but Benjamin's
kisses had divulged that was not all she needed.

∞

PEACE AND QUIET . . .

Sarah smiled as she looked down at the baby in the cradle. At last, Birdie was asleep. She had been almost impossible to console this evening. Had she known that Rachel was over on Staten Island visiting her family, so that Sarah had the job of putting all the children to bed by herself?

The needle pricked her finger, and she looked back at her sewing. Fiona had managed to finish the top for this small quilt. It was only large enough for a young child, but they needed to give something to Mr. Pettigew to sell without delay. He was trying to be kind, but she knew he needed money almost as much as the Mission did. No one was wealthy along Second Avenue.

Relaxing in her chair, she used the same swirling pattern that she had quilted into Conlan's daisy square. It was almost musical, the rise and fall of the pattern across the material, an unbroken melody with no beginning or end. She smiled. Her mother had always spoken of quilting and music with identical delight. Maybe that was why the two were intertwined in her mind.

She knew she would never be able to give up this quiet joy again. Working on the quilt was allowing her to open her heart enough to savor the small happinesses she shared with the children. Food might be scarce and the same day after day, but they were together and none of them were starving.

Laughing softly, she looked at the other quilt top waiting for her to begin work on it. Fiona and Ruthie had challenged each other to see who finished piecing their quilt tops first. As she watched them work side by side, she was able to share in their young pride and enjoyment.

The two girls had been helpful tonight tucking the younger ones in bed, but the other children had not been as cooperative as Sarah had hoped. Her smile faded. Finding someone else to replace Rachel was going to be difficult, but Rachel would not return to the Mission once she was married.

Sarah continued rocking as Birdie went to sleep. Sitting

in her bedroom, dressed in her wrapper because it was cooler than her dress, she fought her heart, which begged her to jump out of this chair and seek out Benjamin wherever he was patrolling. She wanted to apologize for not being honest with him as he put his strong arms around her. Her hand clenched on the arm of the chair as she imagined his lips on hers, powerful and promising even more potent rapture. His wind-roughened face would brush her as his mouth swept moist flame across her skin.

With a sigh, she looked down at Birdie and whispered, "Why does it have to be so hard when it should be so easy?"

"It's always that way, Sarah."

Her head jerked up at the familiar voice. No, not again! Looking toward the door, she saw the lamplight glow off black hair. She drew her wrapper more tightly around her as she stood. "Lorne!"

He smiled. Although he again wore black coat and trousers, as when he had last called, his shirt beneath his waistcoat was a brilliant white. How could he wear that when he must have skulked through the dark streets to get here? Or had he?

"How did you get in here?" she asked as he continued to grin at her.

"I see you still are quilting."

"Yes. How did you—"

He picked up one end of the quilt she was working on. Rubbing it between his fingers, he said, "Giles used to say he couldn't figure out why you spent so much time quilting."

"I like making pretty things."

"But sewing made your fingers rough." He took her hand and kneaded it as he had the quilt. "Of course, that's not all that makes your hands rough now, is it? You work like a scullery maid around here."

She pulled her hand away. "You haven't answered my question. How did you get in here?"

"The back door wasn't locked."

She started to argue that of course it was locked, that it

was always locked. Then she realized Doreen might have forgotten to secure it before she went to bed.

"You need to leave," she said quietly.

"Before I have a chance to see your pretty quilt?" He smiled. "Don't be rude, Sarah."

"I'm not the one sneaking into someone else's house."

"No, you are only living here with a bunch of children that aren't your own, making quilts for them out scraps of cloth you can beg from the rag-seller."

She shook her head. "I'm teaching the children to quilt in hopes that we might be able to sell some of the quilts or trade them for the things we need."

"I see you haven't changed. You always were trying to do for the less fortunate with your quilts." He took her hand and raised her fingers to his lips. "It's been far too long, Sarah."

She pulled her hand away, staring at him in disbelief. "You were here just a few—"

"Of course! Of course!" Shuffling his feet, he pointed to the rocking chair. "May I?"

She wondered why Lorne was acting uneasy. Last time, he had acted as if he were the master of the Mission. "What are you doing here again?"

"Can't an old friend stop in and see how you are doing?"

"You've already done that."

His childish grin irritated her. With his visits, he could jeopardize the Mission and all its work. All *her* work! Rachel's warning resonated through her mind. Her assistant could not guess that Benjamin was less dangerous to the children than Lorne Fontaine.

Lorne never had been sensible like his brother. He would not pause to think about the consequences of his call. He just would visit if he decided he wanted to. Why couldn't he be more like Giles, who had carefully thought out every detail of even the most mundane task?

"I thought you might have had second thoughts about what we talked about last time," he said.

"I don't know what you mean."

He pulled at the hem of his long black coat so it did not

bunch under him. "About coming South with me."

"I—We never talked about that!"

"Of course we did." He rose and draped a companionable arm over her shoulder. "Remember? I told you that you shouldn't be here when trouble is coming."

She stepped away from him. "You'd like trouble to come here, wouldn't you?"

"You know where my sympathies lie."

"I never thought you were like this." She bit back a sob. "Giles wouldn't recognize you as a rabble-rouser!"

His smile disappeared. "Is that so? And what would he think of you living like this?"

"We discussed that last time you called. I think you should go, Lorne. Don't come back." She pointed at the door. "Go, please."

He kissed her on the cheek. "Don't be angry, Sarah. I just want to be sure you aren't hurt when—"

"When what?"

"Get out of New York before it's too late. Go back to West Point or, better yet, head north beyond Albany." Putting his hand on the doorknob, he added, "Don't be a fool. Giles told me so often how he admired your intelligence. Are you going to prove him wrong?"

Sarah did not answer as he left. With a sigh, she dropped to the rocker. Nothing made sense any longer, and she feared it never would again.

∞

BENJAMIN EDGED AROUND THE door and slipped into the public house. Without his uniform, he doubted if he would be noticed by its patrons. He kept his coat buttoned so it would not reveal the pistol he wore beneath it.

Captain Potter would be furious to discover Benjamin had a gun with him. The policemen were not authorized except in an emergency to carry weapons other than nightsticks, but he would be a fool to come in here without a gun.

His fingers opened and closed. He grinned wryly. He

wished he could have brought his nightstick, too. In the past few years, he had learned it could be a good weapon in a situation like this, but he would have to do without it tonight. He did not want anyone to recognize him as a member of the Metropolitan Police.

The room was thick with the stench of unwashed bodies and spilled whiskey. The fiddle music sounded like someone strangling a mating cat. It could not drown out the raucous conversation. As he pushed through the crowd toward a table in the far corner, he ignored the drunken curses fired at him.

A hand settled on his arm, and he glanced at an emaciated woman who could not be much older than the children at Sarah's mission. She gave him a calculated smile. "Are you new off the ship, laddie?"

"I've been around New York for a while," he said, making no attempt to copy her lush Irish accent. He had worked too hard at ridding himself of his own.

Her gaze slipped along him, and he guessed she was trying to appraise the value of his clothes and, more importantly, the gold in his pockets. Although he was dressed as poorly as the other men in the tavern, she must have noticed that he did not reek with a month's sweat.

"Going to stay a while?" She ran a hand along his chest, crumpling his shirt. "Want to stay with me?"

"Why not?" Benjamin slipped his arm around her skinny shoulders and drew her hand away before she discovered the pistol. He wandered through the crowded room. He did not listen to her chatter as he eavesdropped on the conversations around him. He learned nothing new.

The Irish huddling in these slums wanted the life they had dreamed of. They believed it was their due, and that everyone else, including the government, was part of a conspiracy to keep them from getting it. Drunken threats of what they would do were ones he had heard before. They found both comfort and courage in their whiskey, but, as long as it remained talk, he paid it no mind.

When the woman's arm slipped around his waist, he drew it away. He wanted to keep his money in his pocket.

Glancing at her, he sighed. This bedraggled kitten should be living with her family or in a place like the Second Avenue Mission for Needy Children. Sarah offered her children a future better than whoring in this public house.

Sarah. He wished he was holding her. He tried to imagine her in a place like this. His grin vanished as he realized she probably had visited more than one of these taverns alone.

He wondered if anyone could convince Sarah to be more cautious. As adamant as she was, nothing deterred her from trying to save her small part of the city. He admired her perseverance, but it could prove deadly here in Five Points.

He gave the young woman a companionable squeeze and a whispered order. He released her as he continued toward the table where five men were playing cards. A bearded man looked up as he approached. In a nonchalant tone, Benjamin asked, "How are you doing, Mick?"

The bearded man dropped his cards and started to put his hand beneath the table. When Benjamin tapped his coat to reveal the outline of the pistol beneath it, Mick rested his wrists on the table.

"What do you want, McCauley?" he asked.

"A little whiskey and a lot of answers."

Mick grinned, his broken teeth creating a strange pattern in his beard. "Sit down. We can get you the first. Not so sure about the second."

"Private."

Mick hooked his thumb toward the door. "See you later, boys."

Benjamin smiled coolly at the men who eyed him as they edged away. He recognized all of them, except one dark-haired man who had his collar turned up to hide his face even though the night was hot. The man glanced back at him, and Benjamin saw the pale line of a scar across his cheek. Mick must have recruited some new lads.

Only when he saw them walk out did he sit on the chair that gave him a view of the whole tavern. He did not need one of Mick's rowdy-boys sneaking up on him. Keeping his hand near his pistol, he focused his smile on Mick.

"Don't trust me, McCauley?"

"Should I?" He nodded to the young woman as she set a bottle of whiskey and two glasses in front of him. Pressing a coin into her hand, he poured a generous serving in each glass and shoved one toward Mick.

"*I* wouldn't trust me," said the bearded man as he downed half the glass. "I sure as hell don't trust you."

Lifting his glass, Benjamin took a cautious sip. He knew Paddy Sheehan distilled this so-called whiskey out back. It had a kick as potent as gunpowder. "Mick, I don't want to have to drag you and your lads before Captain Potter. If I don't get some answers about this murderer I'm trying to run to ground, you're going to give me no other choice."

"Don't know nothing."

"About—"

"Whatever murder you're investigating." He grinned. "Lots of them lately."

"Too many."

Mick shrugged. "The city was getting too crowded anyhow. A few less folks won't matter."

"It will matter to you when your boys are the target."

"My boys?" He sat straighter. "What have you heard?"

"Enough to know it's worth your while to tell me what you know about the murders up by St. John's on Second Avenue and the one over on Mulberry."

"What one on Mulberry?"

"A woman. Young. Nicely dressed."

Mick waved his hand, dismissing the subject. Grabbing the bottle, he poured more into his glass. "You asked me about her the last time we talked. Said I didn't know anything about that, and I don't know anything about the murders up by St. John's."

"Captain Potter's going to find that as hard to believe as I do. Mick Fitzwilliam knows everything that's going on in Five Points. I've heard you brag about that."

Mick reached for the bottle. "Listen, McCauley, I don't want to be the next with a hole in my head. I don't talk about them, and they leave me alone."

"I don't want *them*. Not now. I want the name of the man in charge."

"Don't know it."

Benjamin resisted the temptation to grab Mick by the lapels and shake him until he realized that the police were trying to protect even the rowdy-boys like Mick and his lads. "You know they won't put up with you much longer. They want all of Five Points."

"They want all of New York."

"But they're going to start with Five Points." He smiled. "Where will that leave you?"

Mick started to shoot back a reply, then hesitated. Watching him closely, Benjamin saw fear in his eyes. Weeks ago, the young man had been even more cocky. That had changed with this new gang who preferred murder to pranks.

Rubbing his finger against the glass, Mick murmured, "I don't know his real name, McCauley. My boys have been trying to find out, but the only thing I've learned is that his boys call him General Feich."

"His boys? Who are they?"

"O'Connor from Anthony Street and Hartman from around there, too."

Benjamin stood. "I'll talk to them. Maybe they'll see sense before you all end up with holes in your hides."

"McCauley—"

"I won't say where I heard their names." He pushed the bottle toward Mick. "If you hear something else, look me up."

"At the Second Avenue Mission?" Mick laughed as he leaned back in his seat, once again the self-assured rogue. "Hear that you and Miss Granger are keeping company. You're wasting your time. No one's gotten more than a smile from her. Except those kids of hers. She'd do anything for them."

"We're not here to talk about Miss Granger and the Mission."

"I hear she's got the lasses and laddies working hard on a new project."

"Mick—"

"Selling quilts, of all things."

He fought to keep his face serene. Any other reaction might cause trouble for Sarah. Quilts? She was selling the children's quilts? She must be mad. If this General Feich connected her with quilting, he might connect her with the quilt that Conlan had and suspect she knew more than she did about the murder. She was endangering herself and those children. "Let me know what you hear, Mick."

Pushing his way out of the reeking building, Benjamin scanned the street in both directions. The first stars were vanishing into the gray before dawn splattered light across the sky. He strode away from the tavern, and a smile slipped along his lips. He would let Sarah know about her foolishness as soon as he completed one more errand in Five Points. O'Connor and Hartman were due a visit from the Metropolitan Police as soon as he was in uniform.

∞

SARAH SLAMMED THE DOOR. How dare he! She took a deep breath as she turned to see Rachel regarding her, wide-eyed.

"Sarah, I can't believe you asked that man to leave."

"*That man* wanted to buy the Mission's building and put our children to work sewing for the army." She stroked Conlan's hair as she tried to restrain her fury. How dare Averill Winslow come here and try to force her into selling the Mission to him! And how dare he come here just when she was trying to get the children fed! She hoped his ears stung with her sharp reply, and that he would tell his coachman to lay on the whip to return him to his fancy mansion and never bring him back here. She tried another steadying breath before asking, "How is Quigley?"

"Not good."

Sarah sighed. Maybe she had overreacted to Mr. Winslow's offer because she had had no sleep last night. After Lorne's visit—thankfully *after* his visit—Rachel had alerted her that the baby seemed sick. Every effort Sarah

had made to get Quigley to eat had been for naught. He
did not look at any of them when they held him or changed
him. If Sarah did not know better, she would have guessed
that he was willing himself to death. She wished she could
find the infant's mother. Perhaps that would ease Quigley's
pain, but she feared it was too late.

"I just wanted you to know." Rachel rubbed her eyes and
yawned. "I'll let you know if there's any change. One way
or the other."

"Good." She struggled to smile as she looked down at
Conlan. "I promised Conlan that I would finish up another
quilt square for him before he goes to bed tonight." This
smile was easy because she could not silence the throb of
joy at the thought of spending a few hours quilting. First
she would do Conlan's square, then she would try to finish
Fiona's quilt. Ruthie's was already done and on display at
Mr. Pettigew's shop. He had been pleased with the work
and offered her another week to pay for the fabric as well
as advancing her credit for another week's worth of food
for the children.

"Sarah—"

"Let me know." She did not want to get into another
disagreement with Rachel about the amount of time she was
spending with Conlan. If there was any chance the little
boy might speak again, she must keep trying to reach him.

Sarah sat with Conlan on the settee in her office. Each
evening, she did this. Sewing a different square, each with
another flower on it, while she talked to him about any
amusing events in the Mission and around the neighborhood. Some evenings, she had to strain to come up with
tidings that were not grim.

"And this is how they go together," she said, picking up
one of the squares he had piled beside him.

He regarded her with fright.

"No, no," she said to soothe him. "Look, I'm just sewing
them together to make a quilt like yours." She smiled. "It's
not as pretty as yours, but I think it will be nice when it's
finished." She paused as she was pushing the needle, which
was curved from use, through the layers of fabric. Reaching

out, she touched Conlan's quilt. "This one isn't finished. Would you like me to do the stitching to finish it all up so it will be pretty?"

She waited, not sure what his reaction would be. He trusted her as much as he trusted anyone now, and he allowed her to touch his quilt. Nothing more.

He stared at her, unblinking. She wanted to draw him into her arms and tell him that she understood how hard it was to open a broken heart. The fabric bunched beneath her fingers. Had she shut herself off as completely as Conlan? Yes, she talked to those around her, but she shied away from any topic that might touch her battered heart. Only Benjamin's kisses had reached through to it, and she pushed him away with half-truths. To let him closer . . .

She gasped when Conlan placed one end of his quilt in her hands. Too late, she realized she had no black thread with her. She could not chance going to get some now. She must use this opportunity to reach the little boy.

"See the feathers in here?" she asked as she ran her fingers along the small section of the quilt. Dipping her needle through the fabric, she smiled. "They were black feathers. Now these will be white feathers."

She kept talking until Conlan fell asleep. She knotted off the thread and let the quilt fall back across his lap. Tucking it around him, she smiled. He had watched every stitch intently. More than once, she had seen him open his mouth as if to speak. She must keep sewing on this quilt until he broke through the pain holding him prisoner.

"He's letting you hold his quilt?"

Sarah glanced over her shoulder. "Benjamin! I didn't hear you come in."

"No one did." He drew off his coat and tossed it over the back of her chair. "I knocked, but no one answered. Father Tynan told me the latest foundling is ailing, and I thought I'd stop in to see how the lad is doing."

"Not very good."

When he did not answer, she glanced at him, curious about his unusual reticence. He regarded her without expression. She rose and put her hand on his arm. His shirt was matted to his skin with perspiration. "Would you like something cold to drink?"

"I'd like to see that quilt."

"No."

"Sarah—"

"Benjamin, be patient. He's beginning to let me touch it."

He smiled. "Good. Have you seen anything remarkable about it?"

"The blackbirds—"

"Anything else?"

"The pattern of quilting is a bit odd. It's a feathery pattern."

"To go along with the birds?"

"I suspect so."

Shaking his head, he rubbed the back of his neck. "Maybe you've been right all along. Maybe there isn't anything about the quilt that will help us solve this murder."

Sarah put her hand on his arm again. She hated his defeated tone. What had happened to steal his customary optimism? When he turned away, she said quietly, "You never answered me. Would you like something cool to drink?"

"That might not be a bad idea. It's been as hot as the blazes out there today."

"Have you been on duty all day?"

"Most of it."

"Why don't we go out to the kitchen? I think Doreen made some iced tea earlier."

Again he did not answer. What was bothering him? It could not be another report of a broken window here, for Lorne had left no sign of his most recent call. Something else was disturbing Benjamin.

In the kitchen, he sat at the table as she took two glasses from the shelf. She placed them on the table before going to the icebox and pulling out the pitcher.

"I hear you're having high-classed callers," Benjamin said abruptly.

She stirred the tea, but her shoulders stiffened. Could Mr. Winslow's visit be what was upsetting him? Pouring iced tea into the glasses, she said, "I bet Mrs. Clyne could hardly wait to tell you that."

"Actually it was Mr. Pettigew down on the corner." He folded his arms on the table. "So your caller's arrival was witnessed by the whole neighborhood?"

"It appears so." Handing him a glass, she smiled. "It isn't often they have a tidbit of gossip about me. Why destroy their fun?"

His auburn eyebrows underlined his creased forehead. When she turned to put the pitcher in the icebox, he seized her wrist. "Who was it, Sarah?"

She gasped as the tea splashed on her arm and his hand. "Benjamin! Look what you made me do!"

Instead of answering, he drew her down on the bench beside him. "Who was it? I don't want you getting into more trouble than usual."

"My benefactors wish to keep their identities secret."

"Then Winslow shouldn't have driven down Second Avenue in that fancy carriage."

"You know him?"

"Of him. Averill Winslow has aspirations of becoming mayor or governor or maybe even president. He doesn't hide that fact from anyone." He laughed sharply as he took a sip of tea. "He must have known that fancy getup couldn't go unrecognized."

"I promised Mr. Winslow I wouldn't reveal his identity."

"The older or the younger?"

"The older."

"Watch your step with his son."

"Don't worry. I doubt if I'll ever see him again. He wants to buy this building and put the children to work for him. I told him no."

"He wants the building? Why?"

"I have no idea." Sarah looked around the kitchen, which, like the rest of the house, needed paint and new curtains. "He must believe he can make a profit with it."

"Or he thinks he can control you."

"Me? Why should he care about me?"

"You denied him what he wants. Now he's going to be more determined to obtain the Mission."

"I won't sell it to him!" She smiled. "I have been working with the children on a way to earn money, so we don't have to be dependent on him."

"By making and selling quilts?"

"Yes."

He grasped her by the shoulders. "Are you out of your mind?"

"What?" She arched her shoulders, trying to break his hold on her, but he refused to release her.

"You mustn't do anything that will help anyone to connect the Mission with quilts as long as Conlan's quilt is here." Pain burned in his eyes. "You could have told me, so I wouldn't have had to hear this on the street when it might already be too late to protect you."

"I told you all about it."

He shook his head. "You said the children sewed and were learning to quilt. You said nothing of selling those quilts."

Sarah was ready to retort, but saw the truth in his eyes. She had been so sure he knew what they were doing. He had been here often enough when the children were sitting on the floor sewing. Then she realized that, every time, his attention had been more on her and Conlan's quilt. Just as hers had been riveted on Benjamin, so she had not noticed until now how she had failed to explain all she had planned.

"Not telling you was not intentional," she whispered.

"This is." His fingers tightened on her shoulders as he bent toward her. "Sarah, you have to stop the quilting. Now. Today. No more."

"Mr. Pettigew has a quilt there that Ruthie made."

He groaned. "You must get it back right away. Tell him whatever you want, but not the truth. Maybe it's not too late to keep the word from spreading."

"I can't ask for it back. Selling the quilts is the only way I can pay off Mr. Pettigew and keep getting food for the children."

"Sarah—"

"Benjamin, I put the last of my money into the project. I can't stop now."

"You must."

This time, when she drew back, he let her go. She wondered if she had ever felt more alone. Tears burned in her throat. "Benjamin, if I do that, the children will starve."

"You could sell the house to Winslow."

She shook her head vehemently. "No, I won't do that. I told him that."

"Publicly?"

"I didn't whisper it in his ear." She laughed. "I'm surprised Mr. Pettigew didn't hear me from down on his corner."

Instead of smiling, he took a deep drink of tea. "Whispering in his ear might have been better. If you denounced Winslow publicly, he is sure to think he's been shamed."

"I'm not afraid of Averill Winslow."

"I know that. You're afraid of only two things. The truth and me."

"You?" She stood and went to the counter. Setting her glass on it, she laughed coldly. "I assure you, Sergeant McCauley, that you don't frighten me."

He took her hands and brought her sharply against him. When she gasped, he whispered, "But you *are* frightened of this." He did not allow her to escape his lips.

She meant to push him away. She intended to keep him from wooing her with sweet madness, but her body betrayed her, and she softened against him. As her lips parted to release her eager breath, his tongue stabbed at hers. Trembling when his mouth etched a flame along her neck, she tasted the dusty flavor of his ear.

A thrill surged along her fingers when she discovered his shirt had come out of his trousers. Her fingers slipped upward along his strong sinews, and she delighted in his hot, sticky skin. Held between the cupboard and his unyielding body, she moaned as his leg rubbed hers. No amount of material between their skin could lessen this pleasure. When he drew away, she opened her eyes to see passion glazing his.

"That," he whispered, "is what you're frightened of."

"No, I want you to kiss me, Benjamin."

"Only kiss you?" His hand cupped her cheek. "I have tomorrow night off. I'd like to spend it with you."

"Benjamin—"

"Sarah!" Rachel's shout careened into the kitchen as she raced down the back stairs. "Sarah, Quigley's worse!"

"I'll be right there." She turned to Benjamin. "It's the baby. I—"

"Go!" he urged.

Glancing from his strained face to where Rachel had disappeared up the stairs, she did not hesitate. The yearnings of her heart must never prevent her from doing what she had promised to do.

And, God forgive her, going to help the baby now kept her from having to answer Benjamin and her heart, which were asking for the same thing.

A chance to savor love.

10

SARAH KEPT HER ARM around Rachel's shaking shoulders that shook as her friend sobbed. Watching Father Tynan speak a final blessing over the tiny body in the small box in the dining room, she wished she could weep, too. It might relieve the bands of grief tightening around her chest. She looked across the room to where Doreen huddled in a chair. The young woman did not look up as the priest put his hand on her head before crossing the room to where Sarah stood.

"Thank you, Father," she whispered. "Quigley was so sickly the children never became too attached to him, so that should ease their loss."

"But not yours?"

"I don't lose graciously."

His smile was sad. "I suspected that. If you ever wish to speak of your loss, I would be glad to listen."

"Thank you." Sarah was tempted to tell him that she had come to terms with her grief long ago. She would not acknowledge it, and it would not plague her. A sigh bubbled into her throat. She was only fooling herself if she thought she had reached a truce with the pain of losing Giles. A few months ago, she was sure she had, but, since Benjamin came into her life, she was no longer certain. Her heart longed to touch his. She could not let that happen, because that would leave her defenseless once more.

While Rachel gathered the children to take them outside to play, Sarah walked with the priest to the door. The parlor clock clanged, and she counted along to discover it was already eleven o'clock.

She glanced around, amazed, when she realized Conlan was not clinging to her skirts. Seeing him huddling in a corner by the stairs, she held out her hands to him. He ran to her, throwing himself into them so hard, he almost knocked her to the floor.

"I have some letters to write and all other sorts of boring tasks." She stood. "Would you rather go out and play with the other children?"

He shook his head and slipped his hand into hers.

Sarah struggled not to let her startled gasp escape. He had not spoken with words, but he was beginning to respond to her. Maybe, just maybe, she had been right to coddle him, even though both Benjamin and Rachel had been frustrated by her attempts to reach the little boy.

"All right," she said, glad to smile. She refused to look toward the dining room. Father Tynan would send someone for Quigley's small coffin within the hour. Maybe it was better that Conlan did not witness that. "How would you like to go with me to see Mrs. Clyne? I've heard she is in need of some company."

Her hope that he would nod disappeared when he held on to her hand and his quilt and stared across the foyer.

"I'd like to show Mrs. Clyne the sewing I've done on your quilt. She laughed yesterday when I told her about the white feathers I was adding to your black ones."

He continued to look at the stairs.

Bending again, she whispered in his ear, "Mrs. Clyne loves babies."

He looked up at her. She hoped that was anticipation she saw glowing in his eyes, not just unshed tears.

Giving him a jaunty smile, she picked up her bonnet. She managed to tie it under her chin without letting go of his hand. She did not want to lose this fragile connection between them. Maybe Mrs. Clyne's kindness would touch the little boy and tear down a bit more of the wall surrounding him.

She was running out of ideas on how to reach him, and Benjamin was running out of patience with her refusal to give him the quilt to take to his captain. She was beginning to wonder if she would ever be able to coax Conlan to part with it.

∞

SARAH RUBBED HER TIRED eyes and stared across her office. She folded her arms on her desk, being careful not to strike the open bottle of ink. Leaning her head back, she stared at the ceiling. So often she had sat here while she traced the lines of cracked plaster and considered the future of the Mission.

She should not be angry at Doreen. She should be pleased that the young woman had come to her instead of leaving again. But maybe it would be better if she had left, because a woman who complained about children should not be working in a foundling home. Doreen avoided the children, scowling when they entered the kitchen and yelling after them if they said more than a word to her. Her latest complaint was about the noise the children made during the night when they went up and down the back stairs near her room to use the privy in the back yard.

It was a small problem, but Sarah had too many other problems, both big and small. The Mission had always demanded every ounce of her, and she had been happy to sacrifice her time to make a home for the children. Then she had met Benjamin. Everything became more complicated. His kisses teased her into dreaming of more. Not just more kisses, but more of the mind-melting touch that overpowered her with longings she had not guessed existed.

She kneaded her aching forehead, and the pain slid away to settle in her temples. She could not leave. If she resigned as director, she guessed the Mission's board would sell the building to Averill Winslow. He would put his plans into action, and the children's lives would become as horrible as what they had left in Five Points. Admitting defeat left a bitter taste in her mouth, but the thought of continuing to fight this battle she might never win daunted her.

She pushed aside her accounting book and took a clean piece of paper from the drawer. She picked up her pen and dipped it into the ink bottle. With her pen poised over the paper, she tried to compose her thoughts. She began to write, the words coming swiftly as she released her pain onto the paper.

The words faded away, and she stood. Going to the settee, she reached for the bag where she kept the quilt tops that Ruthie and Fiona continued to piece together with more and more skill. She drew her feet up under her, allowing her skirt to bunch oddly. She took the needle from out of her waistband and began to quilt. What had been a sanctuary in the past had become a sanctuary once more, even though she knew it was ironic that the one person who wanted her to halt this was the very same person who had inspired her to try to grasp for joy once more.

Benjamin . . . His arms were the sweetest haven she could imagine, but she feared she would never know that again. She had thought he would call when he heard of the baby's death. Instead, the day had passed without him coming to the Mission's door. Maybe he was so disgusted with her refusal to heed his advice that he was staying away.

When her door opened, she did not pause. "Unless it's important, please come back later."

The door closed quietly. When fingers stroked her tight shoulders, she lowered her needle and looked back to discover her sorrow reflected in Benjamin's eyes.

"Father Tynan sent for me," he said simply.

"That wasn't necessary."

He sat on the corner of her desk. "Don't you understand, sweetheart? I know you can take care of yourself all by yourself, but you don't have to joust dragons alone."

"What are you talking about?"

He did not let her avoid his gaze, which cut through her.

She feared he could see the pain dammed in the shadowed depths of her soul. He stood, bringing her to her feet and up to his chest as she shivered. Caressing her rigid back, he whispered, "I understand, you know."

"Understand what?"

"How you are hurting inside right now because the baby died." He leaned his cheek against her hair. "Since I joined the Metropolitan Police, I've seen people who shouldn't have died die. I've tried to save people, and I couldn't. Sometimes, death simply has no meaning."

She drew away. "I know that."

"You did all you could for that baby. More than most folks would have done."

"I know that, too, but that doesn't ease the pain of losing Quigley."

His lips tightened. "Nothing eases the pain. Nothing hardens you enough. I wouldn't want to work with a policeman who was unmoved by death." He took a deep breath and released it through clenched teeth. "Sarah, you should think about taking these children and leaving New York City right away."

"I've thought of it."

"Then pack up and leave."

She turned to gaze out the window. "I'm not sure any other place would be any better for my children."

"It couldn't be worse."

"It could be. Our neighbors here are barely accepting of Ruthie and Mason being here. Elsewhere . . ." She shrugged.

She waited for him to answer. Looking up at the stars scattered across the sky like sugar crystals, she watched as lights went out in the house across the street. She had not realized it was so late already. A yawn teased the back of her throat where tears slowed every breath.

She turned. "Benjamin, if—" Her eyes widened when she saw what he held in his hand. The page she had been writing on! "You shouldn't be reading that!"

"It's addressed to me."

"Maybe, but you shouldn't be reading it." She reached for it, but he held it out of reach.

"Why not? It starts, 'My dearest Benjamin.' Someone else?"

"No, of course not." Sarah leaned against the desk as she realized she could fool neither him nor herself any longer. She had been pouring out her sorrow to him on this page, but she had not intended for him to read it. The words that stuck in her throat like her tears had been so easy to put on paper.

"Then, may I read it?"

She nodded. Maybe it would be for the best, because she was tired of keeping all these secrets hidden. If she could trust him with this one, maybe she would be able to trust him with the others in her heart.

" 'My dearest Benjamin,' " he read aloud, " 'if only you were here to close the wound that cuts clear through me. I'm tired. Tired of the struggle for something I can't name. But you never falter in your belief that your efforts are helping those who need help. What keeps you going when you see the dying around you? What gives the dream new life when it withers?' " He paused. "There's more."

"I know. I wrote it."

He brushed her cheek with the back of his fingers. The motion was so honest, so gentle, so much what she needed that she almost lost the battle to keep the tears in her eyes. Searching his face, she saw his pain. She ached to ease it, but, unlike with the children, his anguish would not be cured with a kiss. He wanted more, and so did she.

"You won't give up, Sarah."

"Sometimes I want to."

"So do I."

"You never show it."

He smiled wearily. "Maybe not, but I think often enough about whether my work here and in Five Points makes any difference."

"It does!" She lowered her voice as he raised a single brow. "It has to me."

Again his fingers curved along her cheek. "We are very

much alike. Blaring our horns at the walls in hopes that
they will tumble down and everything will be better." His
finger curled under her chin, tilting her face toward him.
"Sometimes we chip away at the mortar. Sometimes, we
don't see anything but stone."

"Sometimes I wish my heart was made of stone."

"That would make a few things easier."

"I thought I could save him, Benjamin." She blinked
back the tears that were flooding her eyes. "I thought he
would defeat the odds against him."

"He did. For a while with your help." His smile was as
tender as his touch. "But even you can't work miracles all
the time. Is Conlan doing any better?"

Benjamin swore silently when Sarah pulled away, her
eyes growing hard so the tears in them glistened like fac-
eted diamonds. That accursed quilt! She thought he was
asking about the boy because he wanted the quilt. He did
want the quilt, but he was concerned with how the child
was faring.

"He's very much the same," she whispered, her back to
him. "Clinging to me and saying nothing."

He bit back his next question. He could not ask about
the quilt now. Then she would be right to be furious at him.
One child had died here. Another was deeply hurt. All of
them were in danger. He could not fault her for thinking
first of the children.

But he could not think of anything but her. Watching
how the lamplight glistened in her ebony hair, highlighting
it with a glow as blue as her eyes, he wanted to loosen it,
bury his face in it, and breathe in its enticing perfume . . .
her enticing perfume. He fought to keep his gaze on her
hair instead of letting it admire those curves he had touched
just long enough so his fantasies taunted him every waking
hour and turned into delicious dreams that left him thrash-
ing and sweaty when he woke.

He grazed her neck with his lips. A quiver raced along
her, but she did not turn. When his mouth moved along her
swift pulse, her fingers closed into fists. He smiled when
her eyes closed and her head slanted back toward him, ex-

posing her beguiling throat. Tracing a path across it, he slowly brought her to face him and into his arms. He relished the flavor of her luscious skin as he captured her lips.

His arms tightened around her as he fought his craving to lean her back on that lumpy settee and find every bit of rapture waiting for him along her. When her hands slid up his back, drawing her breasts up against his chest, he moaned into her mouth. She swayed, and he knew she was as enthralled by this passion as he was.

When she drew back, her breathing uneven and her eyes glazed with desire, he halted her fingers from reaching for the buttons on the front of his coat. "I'm on duty, sweetheart. Shall I come back when I'm off duty?"

"When?"

Her breathless voice stirred something exquisitely agonizing deep within him. "In about twelve hours or so."

The bright glow in her eyes faded. "Twelve hours?"

He nodded.

"No," she whispered. "Go home and get some sleep."

"I'd rather sleep with you." His arm around her waist pulled her to him again. "No, let me be honest. I'd rather have you keep me awake."

"Twelve hours from now you'd have a houseful of children ready to keep you awake."

"We don't need that many chaperones."

She shook her head.

Smiling, he asked, "Why don't I try to get back here when they're asleep, you're awake, and I'm not on duty?"

"I'd like that."

He kissed her quickly, not daring to hold her any longer, for he might not be able to let her go until he had made each one of those taunting fantasies come true. Picking up the page from the desk, he folded it and put it under his coat.

"Benjamin, that—"

"Is addressed to me."

She dampened her lips with the tip of her tongue, which he wished was slipping along him instead. "I'm not sure I really meant for you to read it."

"You never do anything without a reason." He glanced at the door. "I've got to get back out on patrol." He edged her face with his hands. "I need you more than you can know. I've seen hell tonight. I'd love to discover heaven with you."

"Hell? What happened?"

"Nothing different." He sighed as he stroked her shoulders. "Here it's possible to believe that what's happening on the streets is nothing but a nightmare."

Her eyes grew wide again. "Has there been another murder?"

"Two." He turned away and kneaded his forehead. "Two people who are dead because of me. General Feich apparently doesn't like me asking about him."

Sarah sat on the settee. "General Feich? Who is he? Union or Confederate?"

"General Feich leads no army but his own here in the streets. He's the leader of an Irish gang that's been killing off its rivals in Five Points. I spoke to two people in a tenement on Worth Street a few days ago, and now both of them are dead. Their bodies were left where Rogue and I patrol, so I could stumble over them."

"Who?"

He shook his head. "No one you know. An Irish rowdy-boy named Tom and one of the prostitutes who worked for Paddy Sheehan at his public house." Brushing her hair back, he whispered, "My sweet Sarah, they died because they dared to trust a Metropolitan Police officer. I won't risk you."

"I'm willing to take that risk."

Kneeling in front of her, he folded her fingers between hers. "I know you are, and I know that, even though I should, I can't walk out that door and never come back."

"Come back when you can, Benjamin."

"If I can."

"Don't say that. You said we're alike, and we'll keep fighting as long as there's breath in our bodies to save those who need us."

"Or we win the battle," he answered with a grim smile. "Along with everything we desire."

11

THE CHILDREN OF THE Second Avenue Mission for Needy Children were subdued as they walked in single file out of St. John's Catholic Church. Sarah carried Conlan propped on her waist and held the hands of two more children. Looking back, she saw the line following in close order.

No one called a greeting as they walked to the Mission. Sarah saw her neighbors peering from their windows or around their doors, but they respected the children's grief.

A stranger stood on the steps of the Mission. The skinny man's light brown hair was topped by a bedraggled silk hat that matched his dreary black frock coat. He turned to tip his hat to her as she climbed the steps. When he saw the group of children behind her, his mouth grew as round as his eyes. His voice cracked as he asked, "Do I have the honor of speaking to Miss Granger?"

"Yes. May I help you?"

"I understand you have some rooms to rent."

Sarah opened the door. Letting the children scurry past them, she set Conlan on the floor. He grasped her skirt, but she peeled his fingers off and put his hand in Rachel's. She held her breath, but he went with Rachel. She smiled. Even

a few days ago, he would have screamed in despair at being
parted from her. This was another good sign.

Remembering the man was waiting for her to answer,
she motioned toward the door under the stairs. "The rooms
are in the cellar, Mr. . . . ?"

"Sawyer Everett," he said with a shy smile. "Dr. Sawyer
Everett, I should say."

"Dr. Everett, having you here would be a godsend. The
children are always getting ill or attempting to break some
bone or another."

He chafed one bony hand against the other. "To be honest, I'm a new doctor without much training. I thought I'd
start here where people need me."

"There's a big need along Second Avenue." Opening the
cellar door, she lit the lamp and went down the narrow
stairs. "There's a door to the street, but I've kept it locked.
Although the few furnishings aren't much, I didn't want
them stolen."

Light sifted through the dusty window in the main room.
It was empty except for a broken settee. She led him into
the small kitchen, where a cast-iron stove took up most of
the floor. When she saw him frowning at the paint peeling
from the ceiling around the gas lamp, she sighed. She
would have redone the rooms if she had had the money,
but every penny was needed to feed the children.

"I trust I can paint these rooms," he said.

"Of course, but—"

"At my expense?" Dr. Everett smiled again. "You are
not asking a lot for the rent, and these rooms are much
bigger than I expected."

"You can move in as soon as you wish."

"I would, except there is no secured closet for my medical supplies."

Sarah nodded. He might not be experienced as a doctor,
but he was smart enough to know how valuable his medicines and bandaging would be. Thieves would leave him
nothing if he did not lock it up.

"I have a closet upstairs in my office that locks. I keep
my own medical supplies in there so the children can't

touch them. If that's not too inconvenient, you can use it, too."

He smiled as he offered his hand. "You have a tenant, Miss Granger."

Sarah smiled as she shook his hand. "The pump is in the back and—"

"Miss Granger, if I'm not being too forward, I noticed several of your children looked to be about eight years of age."

"Yes, and a few older than that."

"Would some of them be interested in a job here?"

Sarah forced her shoulders not to stiffen. She should have talked more to this young doctor, found out more about him and his opinions, before welcoming him into her house. Mr. Winslow had wanted to put her children to work. She had refused him, and she would Dr. Everett.

"They are very young to be working," she said coolly.

"I thought they might like some money for candy at the neighborhood store. I can't pay much, but I'd be glad for the help painting."

"Painting? You want them to help with that?"

He stared at her. "What did you think? In surgery?"

She laughed. "Forgive me, Dr. Everett. You are the unfortunate focus of my anger at someone else who wanted to hire my children to work in a sweatshop in order to pay for their food."

"I don't blame you for being angry at that."

"I shall ask the older children if they are interested in helping you, although you may come to regret this offer. When I had two of the girls help me whitewash the kitchen, I believe they had more on them and the floors than on the walls."

He looked down at the worn carpet. "It can only help here."

Listening to him talk about what changes he would make and when he would open his office, she walked with him up the stairs to show him the storage closet behind the door in her office. She bid him a good day and smiled as she closed the door behind him.

The Mission might be one step further from destitution. It lurked, ready to pounce on them, but a thin doctor with a longing to help the residents of Second Avenue might keep the Mission alive and well a while longer.

∞

BENJAMIN CLOSED THE DOOR behind him, making sure it made no sound. He did not want to interrupt the game being played in the parlor. Slanting back against the door, he listened to the childish voices chiming in to join the verses of a silly song. He recognized the tune. It was "London Bridge Is Falling Down." The words were different.

"The frog in the pond is hopping 'round,
Hopping 'round, hopping 'round.
The frog in the pond is hopping 'round,
All through the day-o."

The younger children were jumping around the room in time with the words. When they began to sing about the cat on the stoop meowing, they giggled as they imitated the sound.

In the midst of the game, Sarah sat in a battered chair and sang along with the children even as her needle flew through the fabric as she worked on another of those blasted quilts. She hugged a little girl who flung her arms around her. She laughed when one of the boys crawled around like a slithering snake hissing in time with the words.

Joy glowed on her face, sanding away the lines of fatigue and worry. For the first time, he was seeing the young woman she would have been if she had not come to New York City, a young woman whose only cares were which beau she would allow to escort her to the church social. Her sapphire eyes glistened with laughter, and her smile revealed how deeply she cared for every child in the room.

When the children sang about a butterfly flitting about, she took Conlan's hand in hers and flapped it like the other children were doing. Benjamin stood straighter when he saw a smile on the little boy's face. He had not thought it possible, but Conlan was responding to Sarah.

But then how could he not? Benjamin almost laughed aloud at the thought. *He* certainly reacted every time she was near. Watching her graceful motions, he wanted her slender fingertips brushing him and her smile beneath his mouth.

"Sergeant McCauley!" A boy ran toward him.

Ruffling Skelly's hair, he smiled. "How are you doing, lad?"

The singing faded as the children swarmed around him like a busy hill of ants. When he told them that he had ridden here on Rogue, they pushed to look out the window at the horse. Their excitement over his horse had amazed him until he had realized that the children walked whenever they left the Mission. Sarah could not afford to pay for all of them to ride.

A glare sliced into his back, and he turned to see Rachel Nevins glowering at him. He did not smile either, for he suspected that would distress her more.

"Come along, children," she said in a voice so sharp it could have cut through glass. "It's time for bed."

"But Sergeant McCauley—"

"Did not come to give you rides at this time of night." She herded the children toward the stairs, pausing only long enough to say, "Sergeant McCauley, please consider the hour before your next call. It doesn't do to get the children this excited just before bed."

His eyes were caught by Sarah's as she came to stand in the doorway. With a laugh, he lifted her off her feet. He twirled her until her wide skirts brushed the wall.

The children crowed with delight. Fiona and Ruthie began to sing another verse of their song, this one about Sarah's skirt going 'round. The other children joined in as he set her back on her feet.

She gave him a wry grin before walking back to the door. Holding out her hand, she drew Conlan out into the hall. She put his hand in Miss Nevins's.

"Up the stairs with Rachel," she said with a smile. "Sleep well."

A chorus of good nights came in reply as the children went up the stairs.

"You have them well trained," he said.

"Or they have Rachel and me well trained." She laughed, then her eyes narrowed. "It's been a lot longer than twelve hours since you left."

"Did you think I wasn't coming back?"

"I hoped you were safe."

He smiled. "Don't worry, Sarah. If something happens to me, Captain Potter would let you know."

"When he came to get Conlan's quilt?"

He glanced toward the stairs and the sound of the children on the upper floor. "He seems to be doing much better."

"Better, yes. Much, no." She sighed. "He no longer ignores everyone, and he will go with Rachel as well as me, but he still has not spoken a single word."

"And he still needs his quilt."

"Yes. Just have patience, Benjamin. He's getting better. I know you need—"

He grasped her arms and tugged her against him. Pressing his mouth over hers, he sampled her soft breath. His exhaustion melted away as she pressed closer. Raising his head, he tapped her glasses. "These get in the way, sweetheart. Every time I want to kiss you, I have to steer my nose around them."

"If I take them off, I can't see across my office."

"Take them off."

She laughed. "I hope the children aren't eavesdropping and heard that comment."

"Where can we go where it's private?"

He must have betrayed himself in some way, because she whispered, "Benjamin, has there been more trouble?"

"Not here, sweetheart." Glancing along the hallway, he said, "Someplace private."

"How about the roof? There's a place where Rachel and I sit sometimes."

Benjamin nodded and motioned for her to lead the way. He wanted to enjoy the flutter of her skirts up the stairs as he left the problems of the streets behind them. But his concerns followed them as she gathered her skirts and went with him up the stairs.

"Leave this door open," Sarah said as she put one foot on the first riser of the narrow upper stairs. "We don't have any lamps up here."

He stepped past her and opened the door on the small landing at the top. The chipped glass knob turned easily, but the hinges screeched. Taking Sarah's arm, he went out onto the flat roof.

Benjamin started to warn her to be careful, then paused as he watched her gaze up at the moon, which was shining more brightly than the street lamps below. No one was more cautious than Sarah. The only thing she had done to flout common sense was not give him Conlan's quilt. Patience, she had urged. He hoped what he had to tell her would make her see that the time for patience was gone.

"Sarah?" When she turned, his heart flip-flopped. He cursed silently at it. For five years, he had devoted his life to the Metropolitan Police force. If he was lucky and his name did not come up in the conscription lottery, he planned to spend many more years as a policeman. He had no place in his life for Sarah.

"What's wrong?"

"The same that's been wrong since summer began."

"Is telling me that why you wanted to be alone where no one else could eavesdrop?" She laughed. "Benjamin, I know you're worried about the Irish gangs, but they've left the Mission alone."

His fingertip teased her downy cheek. "I have only an hour before I have to be back on duty, and I wanted to spend it with you."

"Benjamin, you're working again tonight? You're going to kill yourself at this rate."

"Unless General Feich's men kill me first. They're getting rid of the other Irish gangs with an efficiency that's frightening."

"You don't know who this man is?"

"I've heard he's a disgruntled veteran. I've heard he's a Confederate spy. I've heard he's a runaway slave. He's been described as having black hair, blond hair, and no hair at all. No one knows."

Sarah went to the railing and leaned her arms on the top. "When I stand up here and look at the stars, I can't believe that any fighting is going on. I love the city at night. With the lamps sparkling along the streets, it's as if we're part of a parade of fireflies."

"It's not lovely." He stood beside her. Her fragrant perfume teased him, but he fought its enticement. He had to tell her what he must before he had to return to his patrol in Five Points. "Can't you sense the fear boiling on the streets?"

She shivered as she continued to stare at the broken line of the roofs. It amazed him how the navy and gray shadows intermingled, for colors were not enemies in the night. "I try to ignore it."

"Why?"

"I'm afraid to acknowledge that Ruffin was correct."

He turned his gaze from the glitter of the river to look at her. "Ruffin? Who's that?"

"Edmund Ruffin. He wrote a tract predicting that the unemployment caused by the loss of Southern markets would lead to widespread rioting in the North. When the cities burned, the United States Army would be decimated by street armies. In the aftermath, a truce would be worked out to the advantage of the South."

"How did you read something like that?"

"I found a copy."

"Where?"

"I don't remember."

He took her shoulders and brought her to face him. "That sounds like regret, Sarah."

"It is. I hate the idea of this rebellion. I had hoped President Lincoln would have settled it peacefully."

"No one forced any state to secede or to fire on our army."

She wrapped her arms around herself. "You make it sound so simple, Benjamin."

"It is."

"Maybe you're right. Or maybe Governor Seymour is right to protest the draft."

He placed his elbow on the wooden railing, but kept his hand on her arm. "Seymour is the worst of the Copperheads. Even if he supports the right of the Confederacy to exist, he should keep that opinion private."

"He'd argue that states have the right to follow their own path." When he glared at her, she held up her hands. "That's his opinion, not mine."

He drew off his coat and tossed it over the railing. "And what's your opinion?"

"I want the dying to stop." She hesitated, then whispered, "Have you had any luck finding out anything about Birdie and Conlan's mother?"

"None."

Sarah stared up at the stars again when Benjamin did not add anything else. He did not need to. So often he had told her he must have the quilt, that it might give him a way to identify the children and their dead mother.

"It's so hot when summer has just begun," she said to fill the silence.

She could not read his shadowed expression as he sighed. "A rainy summer with chilly days might be this city's salvation, although nothing is going to cool heads if the draft continues to hang over all of ours."

"Maybe the Rebellion will be over soon."

"It won't. Lee will keep fighting to the last man."

She looked up at him. "Don't you ever doubt your opinions?"

"Seldom." He slipped his arm around her waist and brought her closer. As the firm length of his legs pressed through her skirt, she put her hand up and gently guided his lips to hers.

There was nothing gentle about his kiss. As her hands clenched on his shoulders, she was swept away by the power of his longing. She gasped for the breath he stole from her and quivered at the touch of his tongue along the slick surface of her lips.

"Enough talking about politics," she whispered. When he nibbled her earlobe, she urged, "Let's go somewhere more private."

He released her and jammed his hands in his pockets. "I've put off telling you this too long already."

Iciness ate at her heart. "What?"

"I'm not coming back to the Mission again."

"Benjamin, if you don't want to—"

He gripped her arms. She stared up into his face, which was hardened by the anger she could sense along his tense body. "I've told you how much I want you! I want you so badly I can't sleep. Every bit of me aches to be touching you. I can think of nothing but holding you and discovering the pleasures beneath your clothes. But, even more, I want to keep you alive. Do you know how tormenting it is to hear you offer me my heart's desire when I have to refuse?"

"I'm willing to risk—"

"The children and the Mission, too?" When she hesitated, his hands gently moved along her arms in a slow caress.

He wanted to shake some sense into her head, because she had not listened to him about the quilts. He had seen Ruthie's quilt in Mr. Pettigew's store. The quilting that Sarah had done was so beautiful that the quilt was a topic of much discussion among her neighbors. Faith, if one of them discovered Ruthie Brown had done the work, there would be the devil to pay.

"Sweetheart," he continued, "I can't ask you to choose between the Mission and me."

As the echo of her own words heckled her, she whispered, "Why are you doing as I asked now?"

"I won't have you murdered, too."

She took a deep breath, trying to pay no attention to how her body moved against his with the simple motion. Impossible! She wanted him touching her, driving her mad with desire. "Benjamin, I'm safe here."

"Are you?" His thumbs beneath her chin tilted her face back. "Is this the life you want? A man who wants you, but who can give you nothing but heartache? You deserve better than waiting for a man who, with the upcoming draft, might never come back to you."

"Don't say that!"

"I won't do that to you!" he continued as if she had not spoken. "If you will get me the quilt, I'll leave."

"The quilt?" She stared at him in astonishment. "How can you think of taking Conlan's quilt when he's just beginning to trust me?" Her laugh was whetted with her pain. "And he trusts me more than you do."

"With the quilt out of here, you should be safe."

"And you'll have no reason to call, right?"

Even in the dim light, she could see his jaw working. He pushed past her and opened the door. She thought he intended to storm through it and down the stairs, but he held it for her to go first. She walked with her hand on the wall. The dim light oozing up from the lower hallway was weak.

Listening to Benjamin's boots behind her, she did not pause until she reached the foyer. She asked, "Will I see you again?"

"I'm sure. The Mission is part of my patrol now." He slipped his arms into his coat, but did not button it. "Good night."

She put her hands on his strong arms. Stepping forward so she could lean against his chest, she whispered, "Benjamin, don't leave me forever." She drew his arms around her. "Benjamin . . ." His name dissolved into a sigh when his fingers slid along her waist.

Hearing his desperate moan, she clung to him as his hand rose along her bodice to caress her breast. He pressed her to the wall. When she slipped her fingers along his shirt, loosening the buttons, the warm hair across his chest brushed them. She wanted to discover his heart surging with the power of the passion aching within her.

His mouth branded his desire into her lips. As her hair cascaded around them, she did not notice the clatter of her hairpins falling to the floor. He twisted his fingers in it, holding her even closer. Wanting more of the excruciating ecstasy, she reached to lower his coat along his arms.

Sarah gasped as he cursed and pulled away and said, "I have to leave."

"Now who's scared?" she cried.

"You're right I'm scared. For you!"

"For me? Or of me? Of what you and I could share? You kiss me, then fling me aside like yesterday's casualty lists. If . . ." Again her voice faded as fury blazed in his eyes.

"You think I'd do that to you?"

"Aren't you?"

"Maybe."

"Maybe?" she choked.

"The Rebellion—"

"The Rebellion provides a convenient excuse, doesn't it? You're wrong, Benjamin McCauley. If all you want is a woman to tumble, then I'm glad you're leaving!"

His face flushed red, then paled. Reaching for the door, he slammed it behind him.

Sarah stared at the door and fought back tears. If she ran after him, nothing would change. By safeguarding her, Benjamin was breaking her heart anew.

She heard Rogue's hoofs on the cobbles as she walked into her office. She hurried toward her bedroom. Maybe if she could sleep, she could forget this new pain.

She groped for the lamp. As she lit it, she heard a scratch. Before she could turn, an arm snaked around her waist. A hand clamped over her mouth. She shrieked against it, fearing the danger that Benjamin had warned about had found her.

12

A LAUGH AGAINST SARAH'S neck sent chills rippling
along her. She gasped when the hand over her mouth jerked
her back against a hard form. Benjamin was out of earshot
by now. She closed her eyes, praying that her captor would
not harm the children.

"Hush, Sarah," whispered a familiar voice.

Pulling away, she whirled to see Lorne's grin. "Are you
mad? You scared a year off my life!"

"You walked right by me. I thought you'd seen me."

"Why should I be looking for you?" She adjusted her
glasses, frowning at his insolent shrug. "You must have
seen Benjamin's horse out front! If he knew you were
here—"

"He doesn't know I was eavesdropping on your surprisingly loud parting with the honorable Sergeant McCauley."
With his shoulder against the wall, he rested his boot on
her footboard. She flushed at the suggestion of intimacy.
When he began to smile, her embarrassment became anger
again. His eyes narrowed as she brushed her disheveled
clothes back into place. "It appears more may have happened than I guessed."

"My life isn't your concern."

"It concerns me that Sarah Granger is allowing some low-class police sergeant to paw her. Is this what you want? To oversee a houseful of orphans and have a copper pant over you?"

Avoiding him by picking up the quilt top Fiona had finished just this morning, she wondered what had changed Lorne. He never used to taunt her like this. Her fingers clenched. Tonight, when her lips were still warm from Benjamin's kisses, she did not want to remember that.

He grinned when she did not retort and scratched his cheek.

"Is your scar bothering you?" she asked.

"It's hot tonight. Sometimes the skin's uncomfortable."

"Why are you back here spying on me?"

"Not spying, my dear. Just a friendly call." He took the quilt top and shook it out on the bed. "I'd heard that you'd given up quilting when Giles died."

"You saw me quilting when you were here last. You should go now."

He ignored her as he ran his fingers along her work. "Perfect as always, Sarah." His eyes narrowed when he looked at her. "Does this mean that you're done mourning Giles?"

"Of course not! That sadness will be a part of me forever, but only a part of me. By quilting, I can remember the good times when Giles sat beside me as I quilted."

"So this is a memorial to him?"

"No, it's my way of grasping for the future. I'm happy when I quilt, Lorne, and it's a way to earn money for my children."

"Your children? Where are they?"

"Asleep. I trust you will remember that when you leave. I don't want you disturbing them at this hour."

"You didn't seem averse to having your copper call on you this late in the evening."

"Benjamin has been concerned about us. He checks here frequently."

His ebony eyebrows reached for the curl dipping across his forehead. "What a valiant hero!"

"Stop it, Lorne! Benjamin is—he's my friend."

"A friend?" He put his hand on her arm and brought her around the end of the bed. "I didn't think you'd let a friend hold you as he did."

She jerked her arm away. "What do you want? I don't know what you have planned, but keep it away from the Mission."

His eyes became slits. "How—?"

"You warned me yourself! Don't you remember? Last time you were here."

"Yes, yes."

"Please go, and don't come back."

His gaze swept along her as his lips curled. "You've changed."

"You have, too." She glanced at his black sleeve, where the stitching reminded her how everything was different. "You're an enemy to the country I hold dear."

"As dear as you held Giles?"

Her defiance faded. "I don't want to talk about Giles. He's dead."

"How long did you mourn him? Is McCauley just your latest caller?"

Swallowing roughly, she whispered, "I'll mourn him for the rest of my life." She squared her shoulders. "But I don't want any part in what you're doing."

When he put his hands on her shoulders, she looked up at the face that was so much like Giles's. "All right, my dear. If that's the way you want it."

"That's the way I want it."

"And this is the way I want it." He trapped her face between his hands and fiercely kissed her. She gasped, stunned. When she tried to turn away, he laughed. "You weren't reluctant to kiss McCauley."

"I don't want you kissing me!"

"You *have* changed." With another laugh, he forced her mouth beneath his again. "I never thought you'd let yourself be seduced by a low-class Irish copper."

She wiped the back of her hand against her mouth. "Get out, or I'll call Benjamin here to deal with you."

His eyes narrowed once more. "Before the summer is over you may be sorry you said that."

"What do you mean?" Suddenly she was afraid.

"You'll learn soon enough."

She called a question after him, but he rushed out through her office and vanished into the shadows. She did not bother to chase after him. When the front door opened and then closed, her shoulders sagged.

This man from her past and Benjamin were intricately bound together in a way that might spell disaster for all of them. She had no idea how to save both of them without betraying one of them.

∽

"NOT SO QUICKLY, RUTHIE." Sarah smiled. "This isn't a race to see who can finish first." She bent over the child to see how she was doing with her third quilt top. Running her finger along the even stitches, she said, "That is beautiful work."

The girl's needle darted through the cloth with obvious skill. "Mama taught me how to sew from the time I could hold a needle. Told me that, even if my clothes were made of castoffs, they could look as pretty as any fine gown worn on Fifth Avenue." Her sadness fell away as she grinned and wiggled her needle. "But I like this quilting."

"You need to be certain you have sewn all the layers together." She took the girl's fingers in hers and showed her how to dip into the cloth with the needle. This was the first time that Ruthie and Fiona were doing more than piecing the tops together, and they were as enthusiastic and competitive about quilting as they were about everything.

"Oh, I see." Ruthie giggled. "This is going to be so pretty."

Fiona, who was never far from Ruthie, peered over her friend's shoulder. "I like that paisley cloth, Sarah. Do you have any more?"

"Look in the scrap bag over there."

As Fiona, with Ruthie following, went over to the bag

where Sarah had stored the quilt pieces, Sarah's smile broadened. She had not been sure if the older girls were ready for this next step, but they loved it. Just as she did. It was a wonderful way to spend a rainy day.

She glanced at where Conlan sat with his quilt on the settee. He was too young to sew, but he was watching the older children intensely. Bafflement drew lines in his forehead as he looked from what they were doing to the squares Sarah had made for him. He fingered his quilt, letting it fall open as he did so seldom.

She took a step toward him, hoping to get a better look at the quilt, but whirled as she heard a shriek behind her. In horror, she saw Mason clutching his knee. Blood flowed past the needle in his skin. He must have knelt on it.

Calling for Rachel to come and watch the children, Sarah scooped him up and rushed toward the cellar stairs. She hoped Dr. Everett was in.

She stared around the cellar. The main room was filled with furniture that was in better condition than what was in the Mission. Two settees covered the holes in the plaster walls. A drooping fern was set in a sunlit corner. Beyond it, through the door to another room, she could see a desk and an examination chair. The door of a glass case was ajar, and boxes of supplies sat on the floor in front of it. The caustic scent of cleaning fluid stripped away the damp odor.

"Miss Granger?" the thin doctor asked. He did not give her a chance to answer. Taking Mason, he carried him into the other room and set him on the chair. He patted the little boy's shoulder and smiled, but his words were for Sarah. "I thought I'd heard a cry."

"Mason hurt himself. Can you get the needle out?"

"Yes." He opened a drawer and pulled out several instruments.

Sarah glanced at Mason, expecting him to shriek again at the sight of these horrible-looking tools. Instead he peered at them with curiosity.

"Miss Granger," the doctor said, "you may be more comfortable if you sit at my desk."

"Thank you." She understood his offer as the order it was. He did not want her in the way while he tended to Mason. Groping for the chair, she sat heavily as he bent over the little boy.

Dr. Everett said, "This is going to hurt a bit, Mason, but it will be quick."

"I'm brave!"

"I know that." He reached for what looked like a pliers. With quick efficiency, he plucked the needle out of the boy's leg and bandaged it. "Keep it clean, Mason, and come down to have the bandage changed every night before you go to bed."

Sarah stood and put her hand on Mason's shoulder. "Thank you so much, Dr. Everett. How much do—?"

"May I speak with you alone?" he asked, his tone abruptly stern.

"Yes. Yes, of course." She motioned for Mason to wait in the other room.

As soon as the little boy walked out, Dr. Everett closed the door. "Miss Granger, I wanted to speak with you privately about Mason."

"I appreciate you tending to him. There are so few doctors who would tend to him and his sister, even in an emergency."

"Miss Granger, you're misunderstanding me." His smile returned. He rubbed his hands together. "I am delighted to help Mason or any of your children, although I hope the need does not arise often. What I wanted to discuss with you was if you would consider, in lieu of payment, allowing Mason to help me one or two afternoons a week."

"Mason? You want Mason to help you?" She paused, then said, "Dr. Everett, forgive my surprise. There's been much trouble since Ruthie and Mason came here to live."

"Trouble?" His light brown hair fell into his eyes. "He seems like a good youngster. Intelligent, too—he asked me dozens of questions when he was here helping the older children paint these rooms. He has a real aptitude for science. I would like to teach him while he helps around here, but I wanted to ask you first."

"If Mason is interested—and, judging from how he looked at your instruments, I'm sure he is—I'll be glad to let him come down here for a few hours each week. No more. He's still a child and needs to play."

The distant opening of a door was followed by the shout of her name down the stairs. Dr. Everett smiled. "It sounds as if you are always busy, Miss Granger."

"Always." She smiled as she went with him out to where Mason was peeking into the glass case at the medicines. She held out her hand to Mason.

With a reluctant look back at the case, he slipped his hand in hers. She thanked Dr. Everett again and went to the stairs. Just as she put her foot on the first riser, the street door opened.

"Sawyer? I heard you were setting up shop here. I—" Benjamin glanced at her as he set a bag on the floor. "Good afternoon, Sarah."

"You know Miss Granger, Benjamin?" asked the doctor.

"Yes, we know each other."

When Dr. Everett continued in a cheerful tone, she guessed he was unaware of the tension. "When did you start patrolling around here, Benjamin?"

"I'll leave you to chat," Sarah said. "Good day, gentlemen."

She rushed Mason up the stairs, her skirts swishing behind her. The last time Benjamin had been here, she had embarrassed herself by throwing herself at him.

Rachel was waiting for her. "I saw Sergeant McCauley arrive. Where is he?"

"He wasn't coming to see me."

"Yes, I was," came his deep voice from behind her. Sarah turned to see Benjamin at the top of the stairwell. "We need to talk."

"We can go to my office," she said as Rachel walked away.

"You may not want to be so gracious when you see what's in here."

The hated thump of fear twisted in her stomach. What was in the bag? Her eyes widened as he upended it and a trio of quilts fell out. The three quilts she had taken to Mr. Pettigew earlier in the week!

"I didn't buy them, if that's what you're thinking," he said.

"I wasn't thinking that."

"I persuaded Mr. Pettigew to give them back."

"How?"

"I had a few dollars I could spare."

"Benjamin, you shouldn't—"

He put his finger to her lips. "There's no sense in arguing about this. What's done is done. Mr. Pettigew is not expecting more quilts from you, but he will let you continue to buy groceries until the end of next month."

Her shoulders sagged as she bent to gather up the pretty quilts. "And then what? I'll have to return these to him."

"Maybe by then it won't be a problem."

"You've found out who—"

This time, he silenced her with a heated kiss. She rocked back on her heels when he released her. "I told you that we need to talk." He caught her hand between his and drew her toward him. "Not here. Not now. How about tomorrow? I thought we could take the children and see how the work's coming on the construction of the new sections of Central Park."

"To Central Park? That's almost two miles from here."

"I can get a wagon from the police department. It would give the children an outing, and you and I could have a chance to talk."

"Is it all right? I mean—" She faltered, torn between her delight and her fear. The fear won. "Benjamin, we'll be very visible to your enemies. I thought you wanted to stay away from me and the Mission."

"I did, but . . ." He trailed off, looking toward the parlor.

She turned to see Fiona and Ruthie standing there, grinning. She guessed they had heard Benjamin's invitation.

"Trust me," he murmured so low that the words would not reach past her ears.

She let herself fall into the deep pools of his eyes, which glittered with desire. Those bright sparks should be skim-

ming across her skin, setting it afire. She wanted him as
her lover, as the one she loved. The days he had been away
had been long and empty. Somehow, he had become as
much a part of her life as the beat of her heart, which
longed to belong to him.

"Yes," she heard herself whisper.

When he smiled, touching her cheek lightly before leaving, she was not sure if she had been agreeing to go to
Central Park tomorrow or to admit her love for him.

∽

"FOR ME?"

Sarah held her breath as she reached out and took the quilt
Conlan held out to her. He watched her with eyes that were
too solemn for his age. Slowly she unrolled it. She smiled as
the quilt squares she had made for him fell out. When he
pointed at the area that was not yet finished, she went to her
desk and got a needle and thread from the bottom drawer.

Sitting on the floor beside Conlan, she threaded the needle and easily followed the pattern someone—had it been
his mother?—had begun. He sat beside her and rested his
head on the quilt in her lap. She resisted bending and kissing his doughy cheek. She must not do anything to chase
him back into his terror, for she could never guess how he
would react. Her head turned as she heard a moan.

Doreen leaned against the door with her hands pressed
to her stomach. "It hurts, Sarah," she whispered.

"Is it the baby?"

"It feels like it must be." Her face wrinkled with pain.
"It hurts."

Sarah looked down at Conlan on the quilt. Taking two
more quick stitches, she broke the thread. The last feather
in the pattern had a few less stitches than the others, but it
could not be helped.

When she discovered the little boy was asleep, she gathered up him and the quilt and set them on the settee. The
sagging cushions surrounded him in a gentle embrace.

Drawing the quilt over him, she straightened to put the thread and needle on her desk. She froze when she saw the odd expression on Doreen's face.

"Are you all right?" Sarah asked. "Has the pain returned already?"

"That little boy—" She winced as she tried to move.

"You must have seen him with the quilt when the children have their meals. He got attached to it after Birdie came with it to the Mission."

"The baby?"

"Yes, it's hers." She smiled. "He finally trusts me enough to let me finish it for him. I've never seen a quilt like it, with those crows and the feather pattern in the quilting."

"There are feathers on that quilt?"

"Do you recognize it?" She had not considered that the answer to Conlan and Birdie's mother's name might be right here in her kitchen.

Doreen glanced at her, then clenched her eyes closed as she gripped the door frame.

Sarah sent Skelly running for Rachel as she put her arm around Doreen. Slowly they climbed the stairs. Doreen faltered and moaned again as they reached the second floor. Murmuring encouragement, Sarah steered her along the hall. She wished she could put Doreen in one of the children's rooms, but she did not want to frighten the youngsters.

When Doreen was in her bed, Sarah touched Doreen's distended stomach. The firmness of the contraction passed, and Doreen sagged against the mattress.

Hearing footfalls, she turned. "Rachel! Will you get Dr. Everett?"

"He's not here," Rachel answered, her eyes wide.

"All right." She sighed as she glanced at the bed. "Tell the children to keep an eye out for him. We may need him."

"Sarah!" shrieked Doreen.

She hurried to the bed, but the contraction was easing even before she reached it. She began to smile. This was erratic and might be nothing more than false labor. Quietly she asked, "Do you want us to contact your family?"

"No." Doreen clasped her wrist. "I don't want them here. Not now."

Sarah nodded, relenting because, as the afternoon passed, no more contractions tormented Doreen. Sarah gave her a dose of laudanum so she could rest.

With Rachel's help, Sarah prepared supper for the children. She soothed the youngsters' complaints about the same bread and meat that they had had at midday by promising them a long story before bedtime.

The children resisted going to sleep, even after two stories. They seemed to sense the tension that had gripped the house this afternoon. When she finally could bid Rachel good night and go down the stairs, the clock was chiming midnight. She groaned. Not only would the children be crotchety tomorrow, but she wanted to sleep until her body no longer ached with fatigue.

The first floor was wrapped in a blanket of dusk. Papers crowded on her desk, but she did not pause. No wonder the children did not want to sleep. It was impossibly hot tonight. No clouds obscured the stars, so it would be as uncomfortable tomorrow. Maybe an afternoon thundershower would ease the heat.

Wiping sweat from under her bun, she loosened her hair as she went into her bedroom. She shook it out and pulled off her chemisette and skirt. She folded them and set them on the rocking chair, then drew on her thin wrapper.

A soft sound came from her office. She stiffened. Was Lorne back? Dear God, she hoped not!

She looked into her office carefully. Maybe it was Rachel. Another chill slid icily along her back. That would mean Doreen's labor had started again.

Her eyes widened when they met Benjamin's. He said nothing as he crossed her office and paused in the doorway. Something flickered in his eyes as he stared at her, but his face could have been carved of the same wood as the door.

"I was going by on my way back to the precinct station, and I saw the lights on in here," he said softly.

"It's been a long day. We thought Doreen's baby was coming this afternoon. That got the children all excited, so

it's taken a long time to get them quieted and to sleep."
She edged past him. "If you'd like some iced tea to cool
off—"

"Iced tea isn't going to cool me off." He spun her back
to him. Hunger blazed in his eyes as his hands slipped to
her waist.

"No!" she gasped with a laugh.

He growled against her ear, "Sarah, I won't—"

"No!" She clawed at his hands. More laughter rippled
from her, and she struggled to cry, "Stop! That tickles!"

He released her, and she pulled off her glasses. The
lenses were spotted with her tears.

Taking them, he folded the glasses carefully and put
them on her desk. "Maybe I should just leave. It's a long
walk back to the station."

"Walk?" She glanced toward the window. "Aren't you
riding Rogue?"

"No."

When she saw the anguish etching lines into his face,
she put her hand against his cheek to turn his face toward
her. She gasped as he caught her by the waist and tugged
her close again. His mouth over hers silenced her.

Tasting the dregs of bitter agony on his lips, she drew
back enough to whisper, "Benjamin, what is it?"

He released her and leaned one hand on the door. Gazing
into the glow of the lamp at the end of the street, he murmured, "They must have been lying in wait for us."

"They? The members of that general's gang?"

"They led me on a wild chase," he continued without
looking at her. "Then they scurried like the rats they are
down an alley that was too narrow for Rogue. I was afraid
it was a trap, so I left him on the street. By the time I was
halfway down that alley, I heard their laughter. Then gunfire."

Sarah put her hands over her mouth to silence her cry of
denial.

"They could have killed me, too," he whispered, "but
they didn't."

She wrapped her arms around him. With her cheek

against his back, she said, "They want you to suffer, Benjamin."

"Why?" He stepped away as he slammed his fist against the molding. "If I could just figure that out, I'd be able to stop them. General Feich's boys have been killing off their enemies with cool precision, so, if he wanted me dead, I'd be dead. He wants me alive. Why?"

"I don't know, but I'm glad you're still alive." When he faced her, she looked up into his tortured eyes. She put her fingers over his heart's strong, even beat. To think of it silenced . . . No, she could not stand that thought. "Benjamin, ask Captain Potter to transfer you away from this madman."

He smiled sadly as he brushed her hair back from her face. "My job is to find this madman and stop him. I can't shirk that responsibility any more than you can shirk off your responsibilities here at the Mission."

"You could be killed!"

"I could, but that's something I accepted when I pinned that copper badge onto my coat." He stroked her shoulders. "Sarah, people die every day. They die without making a mark on the lives around them. I don't want to be that way. I want to live my life doing what I know is right for me and for the city."

"Why do you have to be so selfless?"

"Why do you?"

She smiled. "As you've said, we aren't that different. We want the same things."

"Yes, we do. We want the same thing tonight."

She had no time to react to the sudden intensity in his voice. His mouth claimed hers as he tugged her against him. Through her thin wrapper, the hard angles of his body offered the hint of the rapture she could discover in his arms. He knelt, bringing her with him. Wanting to tell him that her bed was only a few feet away in the other room, she could not speak as his tongue pursued pleasure in her mouth.

He leaned her back on the floor as his ravenous lips

tasted every inch of her face. Holding her to the worn carpet, he captured her lips again.

She laughed and pulled away. From the settee, she pulled
the quilt she had been working on. She looked at him and
could not look away as he took it from her and smoothed
it across the carpet. When he held out his arms to her, she
let him draw her against him. This was perfect, for quilting
had helped her put her past in the past just as Benjamin
had. With quilting, she had found contentment and happiness. With Benjamin, she sought complete rapture.

She lifted her arms to encircle his shoulders. When she
touched him, the longing within her escalated into madness.
She did not care if they were on her office floor, in her
bed, or in the middle of Second Avenue. All she cared
about was claiming a share of this delight.

She tightened her arms around him as his lips sought
along her neck. When he opened her wrapper and pushed
it aside, she gasped as his heated breath seared her. The
gasp became a moan as his tongue found the curve of her
breast above her chemise.

She slid his heavy coat off his shoulders, and he tossed
it across the room. Her fingers rose to the buttons on his
shirt. As his shirt gaped open, her fingers spread across his
skin, which was softened so slightly by the hair shadowing
it. She longed to discover every inch of him.

Her breath was ragged as he sat and pulled her up against
him. She leaned on him, wanting his strength against her.
His whisper of her name sent fiery shivers along every inch
of her. Tonight, for as long as she could, she needed to
forget everything but joy, the joy she could find only in his
arms.

When her wrapper dropped to the floor behind her, she
slid her arms up across his back. With a husky laugh, he
drew them away and edged the strap of her chemise along
her right arm. He held her gaze with his. In his eyes, she
could see the promise of passion. All the bonds of grief
snapped inside her, freeing her heart to soar as he lowered
the other strap. Her chemise gaped, and he teased the warm
valley between her breasts. Each touch of his tongue against

her skin burned through her with dazzling pleasure. He reached behind her to loosen the ties of her chemise. Peeling it away, he tossed it aside.

Her skin tingled as his gaze moved across it. She stared at his face and wanted so desperately to tell him of the yearnings of her heart. No words formed in her muddled mind. As he moaned and pulled her to him, she brought his mouth over hers. She gasped when her skin touched his. She was caught in the midst of her most precious dreams, and she wanted nothing but more of this sweet, sensual sensation.

He ignored her soft denial as his mouth moved from hers. She was glad he had when, with his hands on the waistband of her pantalets, his tongue explored her breast, as each breath pushed her against his mouth.

She eased his shirt from his shoulders before sweeping her fingers up through his thick hair. When she swayed with the power of his teasing kisses as he unleashed her rapture, his mouth moved in a slow, sinuous motion to the tip of her breast. An involuntary moan escaped from her lips as he lowered her pantalets, caressing her legs.

He pressed her back against the floor as his tongue flicked along her abdomen. Her heart hammered with the tempo of each touch. He laughed lowly as she clung to him. Standing, he removed the rest of his clothes. Through blurred eyes, she watched as he kicked aside the discarded clothes. Her hands reached out to him in invitation. When she started to speak, his mouth covered hers, silencing her. His arm became an unyielding pillow as his naked body stretched over hers.

She stared at his face, which showcased the escalating need that surged from where every inch of her came into contact with him. As she wrapped her arms around his broad shoulders, she whispered, "Kiss me . . . please." She wanted even their mouths melded together.

"From top to bottom."

Again he silenced her with the heated demand of his lips. His hands swept along her until she writhed beneath him, the craving uncontrollable. When his fingers caressed the tender skin along her legs, she stroked him as boldly. His eager reaction showed her how much she wanted to explore him. The varied textures of his male body urged her to leave no part of him untouched.

She moaned his name when he found the most fierce fires within her. Each movement was a separate ecstasy. Clutching his shoulders, she arched toward him as her breath exploded from her in incredible delight.

With a groan, he claimed her lips as he had her body and rolled her onto her back. She gasped in unfettered passion as he found a welcome within her. The sparks of his touch wove together to create a heat that burned outward, unstoppable, unquenchable. Every motion added to the increasing intensity. At the moment when she feared she could tolerate no more of the wild ecstasy, a whirlwind captured her, twisting her away from everything but the man she loved. Holding on to him, she surrendered to the glory when he shuddered, and they lost themselves in the love they had denied themselves too long.

∞

BENJAMIN OPENED HIS EYES, drowsy with a lethargy that urged him to go back to sleep. He did not move. Slowly he became aware of the scratchy carpet beneath him. He shifted, and a quilt moved with him. Seeking into his memories, he tried to recall how he had to come to be lying on a quilt on the floor.

When hair tickled his chin, he smiled. He looked down at Sarah. Her cheek was pressed to his chest, her arm thrown across him. He admired her supple body, which still was molded against him. In slumber, her face had softened to reveal the innocent determination that gave her the strength to keep the Mission running.

Fury flooded him. Fury and pain and grief. How much longer would she be allowed to live? General Feich's rowdy-boys had executed Rogue tonight. Would Sarah be the next target?

He had not been honest with her. He had not stopped in

for a cool drink. He had stopped here because he wanted
to reassure himself that she was still alive. As soon as he
returned to the precinct station, he would tell Captain Potter
about the changes on the street. The Mission must be kept
under constant surveillance.

With a sigh, he knew the captain would not be able to
help. The city had too few policemen, and none of them
could be pulled from their customary patrols to stand guard
on the Mission.

Slowly Benjamin lifted Sarah's arm off his chest and
rose to cross the floor, following the silver path of the
moonlight. Stepping over her discarded wrapper, he smiled
as he recalled her fevered reaction to his caresses. Had she
ever imagined that they would become lovers on the floor
of her office? He had imagined making love with her here
and in her bedroom and on the roof and in the parlor
and . . . everywhere. He half turned to look at her shadowed
silhouette on the carpet. So easy it would be to draw her
back into his arms and wake her with the kisses that would
lead again to the succulent satisfaction.

With a sigh, Benjamin knew he must let her sleep while
she could. They had found an escape for too short a time.
If she could be free of it for a few more minutes, he must
let her sleep.

Even as he thought that, the muscles along him tightened.
One sample of her whetted his appetite for more. His smile
vanished. He was a fool. He should have left the Mission
and never come back. If his enemies knew that Sarah was
his lover, they might be even more determined to destroy
her.

His fingers fisted on the carved window molding. His
life had been so simple until Sarah came into it. Enjoying
his work, he had been sure nothing could halt him from
stopping any criminals who committed their crimes where
he patrolled. Then he had met this woman with wondrous
dreams of her own.

He leaned his forehead against the glass and looked at
the moonlit street. He was traveling a road toward disaster.
His allies in Five Points were being exterminated. Each

death was a warning of the death that waited for him if he did not give up trying to capture General Feich. He could not, but he risked the woman who had given him herself, even though she knew the danger of loving a man who must not love her.

Benjamin started when warm lips caressed his shoulder. Lost in his thoughts, he had not heard Sarah's soft footfalls. He faced her as she draped the quilt over his shoulders. He smiled when he saw she wore the wrapper, which outlined her luscious curves. Unable to halt himself, he ran a finger along the neckline that dipped across her breasts. When she quivered, he whispered, "Chilly?"

"No." Her arms rose to his shoulders.

"I am. Why don't you warm me, sweetheart?"

When he loosened the ties of her wrapper, she smiled. His arms encircled her and, as his mouth explored the contours of her face, her eyes closed in eager desire. It had been stupid to seduce her once, insanity to allow it to happen again. He did not care. He wanted her more than he ever had.

When she turned toward the bedroom door, he scooped her into his arms. Her smile sent his pulse thundering in his ears. He placed her on her bed. As he drew her beneath him, he did not think again of the consequences of sweet love in a city filled with hate. For now, for tonight when her soft skin was against his, nothing else mattered.

13

THREADING HER WAY THROUGH the excited children, Sarah picked her bonnet up off the peg in the foyer. Sunshine streamed through the open door. She smiled when she saw the children crowding in the doorway, watching for Benjamin and the wagon.

Benjamin . . . She paused in midstep as she savored the memory of what they had shared. She tingled when she imagined him touching her so enticingly again. The powerful man who daunted bullies on the street had offered her a passion as potent. As Skelly pushed past her to look out the door, she wished this day could be just hers and Benjamin's. It would be a day for her and for him and for the Second Avenue Mission for Needy Children and for the Metropolitan Police force. What they did was an inseparable part of them.

"Here comes Sergeant McCauley!" shouted Fiona, who was tall enough to look over the other children.

"Slowly, slowly," Sarah said as she tried to stem the flood of children rushing down the steps toward the street. "If someone gets hurt, we won't be able to go."

"Are you sure you don't want me to go with you?" Rachel frowned when the children milled around Benjamin, welcoming him to the Mission.

Sarah did not reply as she stared at him. Instead of his woolen uniform, he wore a light gray frock coat. Beneath it, his striped trousers led her eyes from his shining boots to the quiet dignity of his black vest. He looked so different from Sergeant McCauley, but one thing had not changed. Her fingers longed to touch him as he wrapped his arms around her.

She looked down at her funereal gown. Maybe it was time to put mourning behind her. Giles had been dead for so long, and, for the first time, she wanted to be frivolous.

"Sarah?"

At Rachel's impatient question, Sarah hurried to say, "I'm sure. You are going home to spend the day with your family and your fiancé. You've been working without a break for almost two weeks."

"You're leaving Doreen here alone?"

"She should be fine. Dr. Everett is downstairs if she needs someone." She looked back at where Benjamin was lifting the children into the back of the wagon. They squealed with happiness. "The children need this outing."

"Be careful, Sarah."

"We will."

"No." Rachel took her by the shoulders. "*You* be careful. Being seen with *him* could cause all sorts of problems."

Sarah shrugged off her assistant's hands. Although she wanted to ask why Rachel continued to distrust Benjamin, she did not. This day should be wonderful, not filled with suspicion and hate like other days were.

"Have a good time with your family," she said with a smile that was as stiff as her shoulders. She picked up Birdie's basket, which held both babies. She had tucked her sewing kit in one corner along with more scraps of material in case the children needed some quiet activity after running about in the sun. Taking Conlan's hand, she hurried down the steps. She did not look back at Rachel's frown.

Benjamin lifted the last of the children into the back of the wagon. His smile as he set the basket on the seat and

put Conlan in the back with the other children could have
melted the block of ice in the icebox. It sent delicious anticipation swirling through her when he held out his hand
to her. When he took her hand to assist her into the wagon,
quivers flowed along her as his lips had.

With a laugh, he grasped her at the waist and lifted her
onto the seat. "Your shoe may be unbuttoned, sweetheart."

"My shoe?" She bent forward to check it.

He caught her chin in his hand as his mouth covered
hers. His kiss was swift, but seared away the grief binding
her heart, freeing it to fill with happiness.

"I like using some subterfuge to kiss you," he whispered.

She ran her fingers along his cheek. "You are the devil
himself, Benjamin McCauley."

"So I've been told."

"Help me down."

"Down?" His eyes widened.

"Down." When he set her on the sidewalk, she smiled.
"Watch the children. I forgot something. I'll be back in just
a moment."

Benjamin chuckled as Sarah ran up the steps and back
into the Mission. Hearing a cry from the basket, he climbed
into the wagon and lifted out Innis. He rocked the baby
boy as he looked at the Mission and dampened the guilt
that had haunted him since he had spoken to Captain Potter
at the end of his shift this morning.

The captain had shared his concerns about the escalating
unrest. Copperheads and Confederate spies were using the
newspapers to pass their encoded messages. Whispers,
which could be heard outside any Irish public house as well
as in some taverns on the better side of the city, hinted at
trouble if the draft were actually held.

When he had mentioned the tract that Sarah spoke of
during their conversation on the Mission's roof, Benjamin
had been astounded to discover his captain was familiar
with it.

"Traitorous balderdash," Captain Potter said.

"But others may believe it."

"Those who are being stirred up can't read. We can't

stop it from being read to them." He had tapped his pen on
his desk. "What we need to do is listen and observe. Why
don't you do that?"

Although he wished he did not have to involve Sarah
and her children, this was the easiest excuse he had to go
out among the city residents and simply listen. He hated
using Sarah to achieve his ends. He put the baby back in
the basket with Birdie. If she had just given him the blasted
quilt, then he could have . . . He knew was lying to himself.
He wanted to take advantage of any chance to see Sarah
again.

He leaned his chin on his hand as he rested his elbow
on the front of the wagon. A wry smile twisted his lips. He
was beginning to suspect it would be easier to stop General
Feich and his bloodthirsty gang than to keep from tugging
Sarah back into his arms. He ached to savor again the ecstasy they had shared last night. When he had left before
dawn, taking care that no one noted his departure, he had
had to fight his own yearning to toss aside caution and
return to her sweetness.

"Let's go!"

At the lyrical sound of Sarah's laugh, he turned to answer
her. His words froze on his tongue. Accustomed as he was
to seeing her wearing black, he was stunned by the vision
she was when dressed in a pink silk summer frock. His
gaze followed the narrow, vertical stripes along the bodice,
which closed with a single row of pearl buttons. At her
slender waist, the gown billowed out over wide hoops and
crinolines that rustled as she moved down the steps and
closer to him. When she put her hand on his arm, the
sleeves, which were gathered on her upper arm before nar-
rowing to a white cuff at her wrists, brushed against his
shirt.

"Is something wrong?" she teased, her eyes glittering like
warm jewels behind her gold-rimmed glasses. "You needn't
look so astounded!"

Hearing the children's reaction behind him, he laughed.
"I'm not the only one who is surprised to see how pretty
you look in that gown." He bent toward her and whispered,

"I'm the only one who knows how beautiful you look out of it."

"Benjamin . . ." Her voice faded into a sigh as his hands splayed along her back, pulling her soft breasts up against him.

His own heart leaped at the sensation of her delectable curves. Without his thick coat, he could enjoy them more, but not as much as if they were alone and he held her skin to his. He fought the urge to forgo the trip to Central Park and spend the day with her in her bed. Lowering his hand to her waist, he chuckled when she flinched and moved it. "I forgot you're ticklish, sweetheart."

"Did you, or do you like to tickle me?"

"Such a shrewish comment." He smiled at the children. "Don't you think she should be nicer to me?"

Fiona folded her arms on the side of the wagon. Her face was serious. "You shouldn't tickle her."

Sarah smiled. This was the Benjamin who had touched her heart. He handed her into the wagon. She drew Ruthie's poke bonnet forward and tugged on the brim of Mason's floppy hat. She did not want to draw attention to the Brown children.

"Look out!" Skelly called.

With a laugh, Benjamin caught a makeshift ball that sailed toward them. He bounced the tightly bound rags in his hand as a boy raced down the street.

"Good hit." He tossed the ball to the grinning boy. "Why don't you take your friends over to where the building burned on Forty-seventh Street? The empty lot will give you plenty of room to play the ball."

The lad tipped his cap to Sarah before racing off, the buttons on his knickerbockers loosened to leave them flapping about his knees.

As the boys disappeared down an alley, Benjamin swung up onto the seat. "What happens to them? They're so innocent, so full of life now. In a few years, they'll be bemoaning the fact that they haven't been offered a fair deal as they flood their sorrows with cheap whiskey."

"Not today," she whispered. "Let's think only of good

things. I want to pretend—" She laughed. "I don't know what I want to pretend. I just want us to enjoy today."

He swept his wide-brimmed hat off as if it had a fancy plume on it. "Lady fair, it shall be as you wish."

"You'd make a very dashing knight," she said as the children giggled. She slipped her arm through his.

He winked at her and then at the youngsters. "Just practicing for the time when Mayor Opdyke petitions the governor to promote me from Sergeant McCauley to Lord McCauley."

"Which should be any day now."

"Undoubtedly." He picked up the reins. "Ready, sweetheart?"

"Let's go!"

Over his shoulder, he asked, "Are you ready?"

A chorus of young voices called, "Yes!"

When Sarah waved to Mrs. Clyne, who was stretching at an uncomfortable angle to see them drive away, Benjamin laughed. By the time they returned, the block would be buzzing with the news of Miss Granger and her children going for a ride with Sergeant McCauley. That should send a message to those who wanted to cause trouble that he was watching this house.

"I'm glad you changed your mind about coming back to the Mission," Sarah said softly.

Could she hear his thoughts? No, it was nothing more than that she, too, was able to judge the temper of the street.

He held the reins with one hand while his other arm settled behind her on the seat. "I realized that staying away might prove more dangerous for you." His fingers brushed her waist as his voice lowered. "I realized that staying away would be impossible for me when I want to hold you again."

Sarah wanted to rest her head on his shoulder, but turned at the children's yelps from the back. Warning the children to sit down so they were not bumped out of the wagon, she gave Mason's hat another tug. Bringing the Brown children with her was an invitation to trouble, but she would not leave them behind when the other youngsters were enjoying this treat.

Picking up Birdie, she cradled the fussy baby, holding a blanket over her face to keep the sun out of her eyes as they rode north. New York was outgrowing the lower half of Manhattan Island almost as fast as the children outgrew their clothes. Soon it would have to burst into the rocky ridges of the land past Central Park.

The stench of the squatters' town sifted down the street even before they saw the shacks that edged the park. The rickety houses looked ready to fall down the hills of debris at any moment. Pigs and goats and other beasts looked for food in the mud. Broken wagons cluttered the street. As they drove past, catcalls followed them.

"Sit down," Sarah urged, glancing back at the children. She motioned to Fiona, who grabbed Ruthie's arm. A moment later, Ruthie drew her brother next to her. The other children obeyed more slowly.

"We'll be through here quickly," Benjamin said, keeping his voice low.

"I thought Five Points was the worst part of New York."

"It is." He laughed without humor. "This just seems worse because you aren't accustomed to it." He steered around a wagon wheel that had been left in the middle of the street. "If they hadn't built a wall along the edge of the park, these goats and pigs would have ruined it by now."

"I'm surprised the city hasn't moved these folks out of here."

He chuckled. "It's not been from a lack of trying. If the war hadn't come along, City Hall would have cleared this area. Too many men are gone with the war and haven't come back."

"I know." She looked down at Birdie to avoid his curious gaze. How could she believe that she loved him, but still conceal these secrets in her heart?

The road into the park was clogged with carriages, but Benjamin maneuvered the wagon through them. He turned off the main path and took a shortcut along a rose-edged boulevard.

He stopped at the edge of a grove. Jumping down, he held up his hands to help her. "Trust me, Sarah. I won't tickle you."

"I trust your words, but not that twinkle in your eyes," she said as she set Birdie back into the basket where Innis slept.

Laughing, he lifted her to the ground, keeping his hands at her waist. "You're smart not to trust it, sweetheart. *I* don't trust it because it means my thoughts are headed in a very pleasurable direction."

"I hope you can stay for a while after we get back to the Mission," she whispered, stroking his cheek.

"You can be certain of it." Kissing her lightly, he reached up for the basket and called to the children to climb out.

They spilled from the wagon like a litter of puppies and bounded across the grass, the younger ones trying to keep up with the older. The three oldest girls lingered to pet the horse on the nose.

Sarah smiled, glad to see that Missy had overcome her initial jealousy of the friendship between Fiona and Ruthie. Taking the baby's basket from Benjamin, she offered her hand to Conlan. He would not stir far from her side in this strange place.

"I wish," Missy said with a grin, "that you'd brought Rogue, so we could ride."

"That would have been fun," Fiona chimed in.

"Lots of fun," Ruthie added.

Seeing Benjamin's stricken expression before he quickly masked it, Sarah asked, "Why don't you pick some of the clover blossoms, and I'll show you how to make a necklace of them?" She put the basket on the ground and touched his arm as the girls rushed off with shouts. "Benjamin, I'm sorry. I can tell them—"

He drew her hand within his arm before he picked up the basket. "Don't ruin their day." He sighed, then squared his shoulders. "How about sitting over there beneath the trees? This sun is too hot for a man used to the shadows of narrow streets."

She was surprised when he selected a spot near other

picnickers. He went back to get the wagon and tied it to a bush. Sitting beneath a thick maple, she drew Conlan down beside her. She stretched to get some clover blossoms and began to tie the stems together to create a chain. Looping it, she dropped it over his head. He chuckled, surprising her. He had smiled, but not laughed until now.

"That's a pleasant sound," Benjamin said as he walked back to sit with them. He set a small basket on the grass.

"I was just thinking that." She put her arm around Conlan, who cuddled next to her, his thumb in his mouth, his eyes sparkling. "I thought he might be frightened here, but he seems more at ease than I've ever seen him."

"Maybe he recognizes something here."

"Maybe he doesn't." When Benjamin glanced at her, puzzled, she said, "If this is all new to him, there would be nothing to bring forth painful memories. All he can see are the sunshine and the grass and the trees."

He smiled as he opened the small basket. "It would be easier to learn his mother's identity if his reaction were a clue toward something instead of away from something." He drew out a bottle and two cups. Pouring wine into a cup, he handed it to her.

"I don't remember the last time I went on an outing like this."

"Then I'd say it's time you did." He loosened the buttons on his coat and leaned back against the tree.

Benjamin was amazed at how Sarah could oversee the children who were playing on the grass, convince the younger ones to take naps here under the tree, and keep others quiet with making clover blossom chains and quilt squares. At the same time, she tended to bruised knees and hurt feelings and laughed at silly jokes and kept her needle gliding in and out in the pattern of her quilting.

"How do you manage all of this at once?" he asked.

She laughed. "Quilting is something I learned so long ago that it's second nature to me. Like breathing."

"And like being so good with these children."

"Sometimes that takes a bit of thought." She reached for another length of thread. "On days when they are endlessly mischievous, I wonder why I don't spend all my time quilting."

"The children mentioned that you hadn't quilted before Conlan arrived with his."

"No."

He noted the sudden wariness about her. "Can I ask why?"

For a long moment, she did not answer. The swirl of activity swarmed around them, but they might have been alone in this cocoon of silence.

She looked down at her quilting as she said softly, "When I was very young, there was nothing I wanted more than to win the blue ribbon for quilting at the church fair. I entered the first time when I was five. They kindly gave me a pat on the head and an apple while they awarded first place to a master quilter. I vowed then to keep working until I won that ribbon." She smoothed the quilt top across her lap. "It took me eleven years, but I won it just after my sixteenth birthday."

"Certainly you didn't give it up then, when you had worked so hard to get to where you were."

"No." She smiled at him. "I won that blue ribbon for the next three years in a row. By that time, I was designing my own patterns and creating quilts for friends as well as my entries for the fair."

"But you stopped."

She nodded. "When the war came, it seemed wrong to be involved in such frivolous pastimes, so I came here to take care of the children who needed me."

"But now you're quilting again."

"Yes, because we need the quilts to pay our bills." She put her hand on his arm. "Benjamin, will you change your mind on this?"

"I wish I could. If—"

Skelly raced up, calling out a question to Sarah. She went with him to solve whatever problem the children had. He could not pull his gaze from her face, which glowed with happiness each time she hugged one of the children or teased them with a joke of her own. Dressed as she was, he could imagine her on a finer lawn overlooking the Hudson River, enjoying the attentions of beaux who would be vying to bring her dinner. She had left that comfortable life to take care of these children for a reason she had never explained to him.

When she stiffened as she walked toward him, her smile vanishing, he did not have to ask why. All around them, a single subject was being debated over and over. The conscription lottery. No date had been set for it, but that did not matter. The anger continued to boil along, with threats of what would be done if the lottery were held. When she glanced at him, he folded his hands under his head so he could stare up through the sunlight sparkling like green gems through the leaves.

"You can't be surprised everyone's discussing the war and the draft lottery," he said.

"I don't like what I'm hearing. They are so angry."

"It's nothing new." He watched a quartet of young men whose clothes broadcast that they could easily afford three hundred dollars to pay another man to serve in their place. He was not the only one watching them, he noted.

Sarah put her hand on his, and her eyes widened at the tension he could not hide. "Maybe we should go."

"I think we'd better stay." He scowled. Those young dandies should know better than to come here and walk about like princes amid the paupers. They were followed by a trio of servants who were bent nearly double with filled hampers.

Looking past them, he saw how the others in the park had paused in their conversations to watch. This was not good. Empty bottles of beer and whiskey were scattered near the picnickers. A single word could ignite this park, turning it into a battlefield between the poor and their wealthy neighbors.

He heard his name called, and he cursed under his breath. Captain Potter! What was the captain doing here? He looked at the folks scattered around the grass. They all eyed Captain Potter as he walked toward them. If the situation had not been tense, Benjamin might have laughed at the sight of so many people wearing guilty expressions.

"So *this* is why you invited us!" Sarah's voice lashed him.

He swore again, this time louder. Gripping her shoulders, he said, "Don't make stupid assumptions! I invited you to come here to enjoy this day."

"With your captain?"

"I didn't know he—What brings you here, Captain Potter?" he asked as tightly as Sarah had spoken.

Captain Potter put his fingers to the brim of his cap, but he stared past Sarah to where the youngest children were sleeping on the grass. "Is that the quilt?"

She put her hand on the blackbirds edging Conlan's quilt. "Captain Potter, I told you that I would see it sent to you as soon as I could."

"This waiting is absurd. We need the quilt." He reached down.

Benjamin's hand caught his wrist, holding his fingers away from the quilt. "Captain Potter, Miss Granger has told you that she will give you the quilt as soon as she can. That time hasn't come yet."

Sarah was not sure if she or the captain was the more shocked. Gathering up Conlan and his quilt, she held them in her arms. The other children had stopped playing and watched in extraordinary silence. Slowly coming to her feet, she said nothing.

Captain Potter shook off Benjamin's hand. "Don't be a fool, McCauley! Don't you realize that you're risking your job and mine by delaying?"

"Yes." Benjamin's voice held no emotion as he stood.

"Then give me the quilt!"

"No, sir." He locked his hands behind him. "It's not mine to give."

Captain Potter's mouth worked, then he spat, "I want that quilt turned over to me by the beginning of the next shift, or I'll see you off the police force for obstruction of this investigation."

Sarah gasped, horrified. When Benjamin put his hand on her arm, she bit back her furious retort.

"I understand, Captain Potter," he said with the same quiet tranquillity.

"I expect to see that quilt at precinct headquarters at the beginning of the next shift." The captain's mouth twisted again. "We need to get this investigation completed, so we can concentrate on keeping trouble from erupting when the conscription lottery begins next Saturday in the Ninth District."

"Just the Ninth?" Sarah asked, although she wanted to put an end to this conversation. For so many weeks, the threat of the draft had been hanging over the city. The waiting had been excruciating, but she feared the lottery itself would bring more trouble. She looked down at the quilt top. No, she did not want to believe that the past might repeat itself with Benjamin dying this time, taking her joy from her forever.

Captain Potter nodded with a scowl. "The provost marshal general's office hopes that when the lads in Five Points see how smoothly things go above Fortieth Street, they won't cause problems when the drawing begins in the lower wards on the following Monday." He glanced toward where the sun was lowering in the sky. "Maybe by then, we'll have the good news that Lee has been whipped at Gettysburg and is ready to surrender. If the war is over, we won't need the conscription lottery." Shaking himself, he said, "By the beginning of the next shift, McCauley." He strode away.

Sarah dampened her lips. "Benjamin—"

"Hush a moment." He turned to the children and said, "Everyone get in the wagon before I count to ten, and I'll stop for some candy at the store on the corner of Thirty-seventh Street."

They rushed away with shrieks of delight.

Framing her face with his hands, he said, "Sweetheart, I know what you are thinking, but Potter won't kick me off the police force." He laughed tightly. "He needs every man he can find now." He glanced at where the four young men still were enjoying their meal with their servants hovering about them. "And he may not get the chance to make many more decisions."

She shifted Conlan in her arms, glad he had slept through the shouting. "Is he going to be put off the police force?"

"All of us may be." He slipped his arm around her to guide her toward the wagon. "If the governor succeeds in putting his cronies in as police commissioners, it's rumored that every officer and sergeant on the Metropolitan Police force will be dismissed."

"You never mentioned this before."

He shrugged. "Rumors gain credence as they're repeated, so I decided not to repeat them."

A shout rang across the grass.

She whirled to see two men standing and shaking their fists at the rich men, who were about to enjoy fresh fruit and cheese at the end of their meal.

"Don't react, Sarah. They're just blowing off steam right now," Benjamin said quietly. "Just keep going toward the wagon."

"What if it becomes more? What if they do what they threaten when the conscription lottery is held? What will the police do?"

"What we're ordered to do." He did not look at her as the two men sat again and continued to mutter. "Those hotheaded fools should stop and realize that every man in this city has an equal chance of having his name drawn first."

"But not every man in this city has an equal chance of having three hundred dollars to buy his way out of serving." As he picked up the baby's basket, she asked, "Was gauging the disquiet why you asked us to come here?"

"Has anyone ever told you that you're an insightful woman?" He cursed and pushed past her as one of the men who had been shouting swung his fist at the other. "Wait here, Sarah."

Benjamin did not look back to see if she obeyed him. He ran to where the two men were fighting. He swore again when he saw the flash of steel. Ducking beneath a swinging hand, he grabbed one wrist and snapped it against his leg. The knife flew into the grass.

Sarah's scream was his only warning. A streak of lightning raced along his left arm. His right hand struck his assailant. Ignoring the hot pain, he hit the man again. Another knife dropped to the ground as the man collapsed.

He whirled to face the first man, but gasped when he saw Sarah holding the man at bay with her scissors. With her chin high, she poked the scissors at him, herding him back toward a tree.

"Lady, I didn't mean any trouble. Lady, don't—" He looked at Benjamin. "Don't let her slice into me."

"You should have thought about that before you started a fight."

"What's going on here?" called another man.

Benjamin smiled as he recognized the officer hurrying toward the crowd that had gathered to watch the fight. "Dunn, good to see you!"

"McCauley?" The rotund man panted as he came to a halt next to the unconscious man. He grasped Sarah's arm. "All right, honey, put it down."

"She's on my side," Benjamin said with a weak laugh. He drew down her hand that was holding the scissors and said to the man by the tree, "Get your friend and get out of here. Rowdy-boys aren't welcome in Central Park."

As the man scurried away, Sarah called to Fiona. The little girl came running. "Find those strips of material we had left over from making the quilt squares."

"I'll be fine," Benjamin said as Fiona backed away, wide-eyed. "How are you doing, Sarah?"

"Angry! So angry I wanted to smash their heads together. Men are dying in Pennsylvania, and those two are upset over something that can't be that important." Tears filled her eyes. "I tried to stop him from hurting you."

Dunn said, "You need to get that arm taken care of."

"I'm fine." He held out his arm to let Sarah wrap it in brightly colored strips. "When we get back to the Mission, Sawyer can look at it. Thanks, Dunn."

"Thank your friend here. She was a heroine today."

Sarah kept her arm around his waist while they walked to the wagon. The children spouted questions, but she hushed them. They halted, horror on their faces, when Benjamin put the basket in the wagon and bent to wipe blood from his hand onto the grass.

Biting her lip to keep it from quivering, she blinked back tears. He put his finger under her chin to tilt her face toward him.

"Sweetheart, it's over. I'm going to be all right." His grin was ironic. "Just hurts like the devil's dancing on it."

"But—but—"

He drew her against his chest. She threw her arms around him, wanting to touch him, to hear his strong heart beating, to close her eyes to the blood staining his coat. She touched his rough face. Running a finger from his brows to the chameleon shape of his lips, she pressed closer. As his arm tightened around her, his lips grazed hers so gently more tears bubbled into her eyes.

Stroking his back, she hungered to touch him without his coat between them. As his tongue flicked along the pulse line of her throat, she sighed, longing to surrender to this heated passion. He groaned, and she stepped away, afraid she had hurt him again.

She took his face between her hands as he had hers. "I don't want to lose you, too!"

"Too?" When she tried to look away, knowing her despair had made her say too much, he brought her face up so her eyes met his. "Whom do you wear black for, Sarah?"

She whispered, "Giles Fontaine."

"Who's Giles Fontaine?"

"He was my fiancé. He was killed in one of the first battles of the Rebellion."

"I'm sorry, Sarah."

"It's over. Nothing can change that. You asked me why I stopped quilting. Giles is the reason. I was working on the quilt for our wedding bed when I was told of his death. I put my quilt away along with my dreams of happiness."

"I'm so sorry, Sarah."

"I know." This was her chance to be honest with him. Completely honest. To tell him the truth of her past with Giles and tell him her dreams of a future with Benjamin.

"Why have you hidden this from me?"

"I haven't hidden it exactly."

"Just never mentioned it." His brows lowered in a frown. "It makes me curious why. Did he have two heads or beat you once a week?"

"Of course not! Giles Fontaine was a fine man, who stepped forward to do his duty when the time came." If they were not here in Central Park, if the children were not listening, she would have told him the whole truth ... maybe. She did not want him to shun her as her neighbors had when they learned where Giles was bound when he left West Point. A pariah among those she had considered friends, she had come here to New York. Softly, she spoke the one truth she could not keep hidden. "Benjamin, I don't want to lose you, too."

He smiled, startling her anew. "Thanks to you, I'm still alive." Looking past her, he added to the children, "Did you see her save my life? Sarah is quite a heroine, isn't she?"

Skelly cried, "I saw it. She took those scissors and was going to cut the heart right out of that man and—"

"Enough," Sarah said with a laugh. She wanted to thank Benjamin for easing the tension aching in her, but she could not without explaining everything. Not now. Maybe later. Maybe ... "It's time to get back to the Mission."

The children were still chirping like a wagonload of canaries as they drove back to Second Avenue. As Benjamin had promised, he paused to get candy for them.

"You shouldn't have stopped," Sarah said when he winced as he handed her out of the wagon. "Dr. Everett needs to see that arm right away."

"The candy was a reward for them." He smiled. "And I think you deserve a reward, too, for saving me." His arm enfolded her to him.

She delighted in his mouth on hers. Combing her fingers into his hair, she let all her cares vanish. She wanted this moment of delight. His hand slid along her back, and she gasped against his mouth as the yearning erupted through her. She wanted him. She wanted him more than she had before he first taught her the ecstasy of his skin touching hers.

"Sarah!"

Rachel's cry echoed off the building across the street.

Pushing herself out of Benjamin's arms, although she did not want to leave them, she saw the fright on her assistant's face.

Rachel ran down the steps and grabbed Sarah's hands. "Come! Now! Doreen is having her baby!"

Benjamin chuckled. "It sounds as if it's time for you to play the hero again, Sarah. Go ahead, I'll bring the basket in."

Rushing into the Mission with Rachel, Sarah paused to look back to where he was lifting the basket down. Pain lined his face, and she wondered how much of his pain he had kept hidden from her. He should have— As she followed Rachel up the stairs to Doreen's room, she was tempted to laugh and cry at that thought. How could she expect Benjamin to be honest with her about his pain when she had never been honest with him about hers?

She must tell him the truth. She wished she knew how.

14

"THAT HAD TO BE the easiest delivery I've ever seen. He's a fine baby boy. Mrs. O'Brien should be pleased." Dr. Everett wiped his hand across his forehead and smiled sheepishly. "I'm glad for your help, Benjamin, especially when Miss Nevins swooned."

Sarah chuckled as she went to get some lemonade from the icebox. Pouring a glass, she handed it to the doctor. "Rachel is not good in these situations. She can handle scraped knees, but not much more." She filled two more glasses. "She'll do well sitting with Doreen now and keeping the children from peeking in."

"That arm of yours looks as if it's a bit more than a scrape," Dr. Everett said, putting the glass on the table. "Sit down, Benjamin, and let me take a look at it."

"Sarah bandaged it for me." He took the glass she held out to him and drank deeply.

"I thought you looked rather like one of the quilt squares she has the children making. Now, will you sit and let me look at your arm?"

Chuckling, Benjamin pulled out the bench and sat. He took another sip of the lemonade, but Sarah saw him grimace when the doctor began to unwind the material. Dr. Everett frowned and motioned for him to take off his coat. With a muttered curse, Benjamin did.

"I hope this isn't a good shirt," Dr. Everett said, opening his bag.

"My best." He winked at Sarah. "I wouldn't take Sarah and her children for an outing without wearing my very best."

A head peeked past the door. "Do you need help, Dr. Everett?"

Sarah rushed to the door. "Mason—"

"Mason?" asked the doctor. "Just the lad I wanted to see. Will you run downstairs to my office and get the small green box on the third shelf and the light brown bottle on the table in the rear room?"

"Yes, Dr. Everett!" He grinned with pride before he ran back along the hall.

"He's a good lad and a smart one. I would like to apprentice him, but . . ."

"Why not?" asked Sarah as she refilled Benjamin's glass. "I know it's not possible for him to become a doctor now, but he's young and who knows what the world will be like when he's grown?"

"You'll have to excuse her. She's endlessly optimistic," Benjamin said.

She slapped his unhurt arm. "You are hardly one to talk, Sergeant McCauley."

Keeping his arm outstretched so Dr. Everett could cut away his sleeve, he hauled her onto his lap. She laughed and pushed herself away, although she would have liked to stay and rest her cheek against his shoulder.

"Are you two quite done?" Dr. Everett put down his scissors just as the door opened and Mason entered balancing a small box and a large bottle. "Excellent job, Mason."

The little boy grinned, then peered at the long line of dried blood on Benjamin's arm. "That looks bad."

"Come and watch." Dr. Everett opened the box and set it on the table. He handed Sarah the bottle. "If you will open this and pour a small portion in a glass, I would appreciate it."

Benjamin held up his hand. "No whiskey. I have to be on duty in an hour."

"It will hurt without it."

"It hurts already, and I don't need to give Captain Potter another reason to dismiss me."

"Another?" The doctor looked from him to Sarah. When she glanced away, he bent to his task of cleaning and bandaging the wound.

Mason helped, handing him what he needed. The child wore a smile when the doctor ruffled his hair and thanked him. When Benjamin offered to shake his hand, the little boy glowed with pride.

Standing, Benjamin flexed his fingers and said, "Thanks, Sawyer. I need to change into my uniform. Can I use your office, Sarah?"

"Of course." She resisted asking more as he picked up his ruined coat and walked out of the kitchen. Pouring another glass of lemonade, she offered it to Mason. "Thank you, Dr. Everett, for all your help today. If you will tell me what we owe—"

He laughed and waved aside her words. "One good thing about renting your cellar to a doctor is getting free medical help."

"We can't ask that."

"Then invite me up for a glass of this lemonade on hot afternoons." He drained his glass. "I've got some patients to visit, but I should be back before dark if Mrs. O'Brien needs anything. I'm sure that won't be necessary." He smiled at Mason. "Why don't you come downstairs tomorrow morning? I'm sure I can find something to keep you busy and out of Miss Granger's hair."

"Yes, sir!" He squared his narrow shoulders like a soldier.

Sarah's smile wavered at that thought. Mason and Ruthie's father had been killed fighting for the freedom that they still did not have. Surely by the time they were grown, this hatred would go away. She hoped so.

As she walked out of the kitchen with Dr. Everett, a

knock came at the front door. She thanked him again for his help and went to answer it.

In amazement, she stared at Chester. What was the Winslows' butler doing here at the Mission? Although she wanted to ask that question, she said only, "Good afternoon, Chester. Do you wish to come in?"

"No, Miss Granger." He shuddered. "I came only to deliver this message to you."

"You?" She closed her mouth before she could insult him more, but a butler should not be carrying messages.

He held out a folded page.

Taking it, she opened the page and gasped. "But he told me his father was not so ill!" She closed the note and said, "I'm sorry, Chester."

"You must be there on Monday morning for the reading of the will. If you are not present, the bequest will be revoked."

"I've never heard of such a thing!"

Instead of replying, he walked down the steps toward a carriage that was not as fine as Averill Winslow had driven here, but was better than anything else on Second Avenue. She closed the door and, rereading the note, walked into her office.

She faltered as she stared at Benjamin, who was looking down at Conlan who was still asleep atop his quilt on the settee. Benjamin had not pulled on his left sleeve, so it hung empty at his side. Her stomach clenched. Was it because she feared he would be hurt if his name were drawn in the conscription lottery or because he was regarding the quilt with the same expression the children wore when they saw the toys other children had?

He turned toward her with a sigh and whispered, "It would be easier if I could convince him to give it to me." Crossing the room toward her, he drew his coat around to put his arm in it. He winced.

"Let me help," she said as quietly as he had spoken. Helping him slip his arm into his coat, she began to button it.

"I would rather you were unbuttoning me," he said with a shadow of his roguish smile.

"Do you think you can do your patrol tonight?"

"I have to."

She nodded, knowing he had been only half jesting when he had said he could not give Captain Potter another reason for demanding his resignation from the Metropolitan Police force.

"What's this?" he asked, indicating the folded slip of paper she held. "Not one of Sawyer's intolerable powders, I hope."

"No." She followed him out into the front hall. "I just received word that Donald Winslow has died. Also that I'm invited to the reading of his will on Monday."

"The thirteenth?" When she nodded, he put his cap on with a frown. "I don't like the idea of you traveling across the city when the conscription lottery is going on."

"I'll have to depend on you policemen to keep the order."

"I hope you can." His tone was grim, but as he drew her into his arms, his kiss left her breathless. Craving exploded through her as he whispered, "I'll try to be back before dawn."

"Stay safe."

"I have every reason to, sweetheart."

As the door closed behind him, Sarah sank to sit on the bottom stair. Then a shout from upstairs sent her back to work. She would lose herself in working with the children. That had worked after Giles's death to ease her heart, but she feared it would not be enough now if something happened to Benjamin.

∞

BENJAMIN CLIMBED TO THE second floor of a tenement that appeared no different from its neighbors. He ignored the odors of human waste, as inured to it as those who lived in these squalid rooms were. He knocked on a battered door at the far end of the hall. Fragments of plaster rained to the floor.

Mick peeked out and opened the door wide enough to let him enter. Closing it again, he sat at the cluttered table in the tiny room. "General Feich had two more of my boys killed last night, McCauley. You said you'd take care of us."

Benjamin straddled a chair and folded his arms on its back. He winced as he moved his left arm, but said, "We can't find him when we've got no description of him."

"I've told you everything I know!" Panic filled Mick's once cocky voice.

"But you know nothing. Your boys have given me so many different descriptions, General Feich could be anyone in New York." He scowled. "He could be hiding in this building, for all you know."

"I know he's from the South."

"Why didn't you tell me that before?"

"I thought I had." Mick gave a shrug and rose, but Benjamin knew his indifference was only a guise when he demanded, "What kind of life is this? I'm hiding away like a child behind its mother's skirts."

"You must have some lads left."

"Only Finnegan."

"Finnegan? Which one is he?"

"Tall, dark-haired, with that scar on his cheek."

Benjamin nodded. He had seen the man the night he went to Paddy Sheehan's public house to meet Mick. "I'd like to talk with him about why he's still alive when your other lads are dead."

"Do you think he's going to talk to you, or any copper, when you had one meeting with Tom and he's dead? You aren't as sneaky as you think you are."

Benjamin stood. "I know Tom's dead. I found him, remember? That's when I told you to find a hole and get in it. Maybe we should put you back on the street and see if we can lure General Feich out."

"I'm a man, not bait to catch a madman." Fear blanched his face.

"I'll check back with you in a couple of days. If your boys find out anything—"

"What boys?" he demanded bitterly. "Except for Finnegan, they're dead, and I've heard Finnegan's gone over to *him*!"

Without a farewell, Benjamin walked out. He heard the lock being slid into place behind him as he went down the stairs, anxious to get a breath that did not reek of filth.

Somehow, he had to find this General Feich and put a halt to his murders. Who was this man? Before, there had been periodic attacks among the rival Irish gangs, even some on the Germans who lived beyond Five Points, but nothing like this. He scowled. These vicious killings had begun at the same time he had started investigating Conlan's mother's death. If that was not a coincidence, he should get back to the Mission right away and—

He heard a noise in back of him. He started to turn, but pain detonated through his brain. The stairs came up to strike him as blackness swallowed him.

∞

THE THICK SMELL OF heat and dirt became more intense as Sarah climbed the steep stairs in the tenement. This was the address that Rachel had given her. Doreen had mentioned to her assistant having relatives at this address. Although Doreen avoided the children and Rachel loved them, they had one thing in common—their hatred of Benjamin and his visits to the Mission.

She wondered if she should have come here. Doreen seemed so unhappy and often stood at the window as if watching for someone to call. Maybe she hoped her family would visit, but how could they when they might not even know she lived at the Mission? When Sarah had suggested going into Five Points to find Doreen's family, Rachel had agreed wholeheartedly.

Now, Sarah was at the address and this horrible tenement. She had been in others, but never could get accustomed to the pressure of so many people in such a small space. The Mission seemed spacious in comparison.

She gripped the railing and tested each riser before she

put her foot on it. She did not want to fall through a broken step. When she reached the landing, she counted doors until she reached the fifth. She knocked, and the door opened enough for a woman to peer out. She did not speak, but Sarah's eyes widened. It was as if she were seeing Doreen two decades in the future.

"I'm looking for Doreen O'Brien's family," Sarah said quietly.

"Who are you?" asked the woman in a thick Irish brogue.

Dampening her dry lips, she tried to smile. "I'm Miss Granger. I'm the director of the Second Avenue Mission for Needy Children. Doreen O'Brien has been working for me. She recently had her baby, and I'm looking for her family."

"She's my daughter." Her hand tightened on the door. "I'm Mrs. O'Brien."

"O'Brien? Mrs. O'Brien? Doreen told me—"

The white-haired woman sniffed. "That she was married? What other pretty tales did she spin for you?"

"May I come in?" Sarah glanced over her shoulder as other doors along the hall came ajar so the neighbors could listen. "What I have to say should be only for your ears, Mrs. O'Brien."

The woman's flushed face became ashen, and Sarah feared she would slam the door. Instead it opened slowly. "Come in, Miss Granger."

Sarah slipped past the door. More than a half dozen people crowded into the room, but it had furniture. Real furniture, not broken crates and dirty mattresses. Not only were there a stove and an actual bed where several children sat, but a table and pair of chairs stood in the center of the floor. Everything was clean.

When Mrs. O'Brien pointed to a chair, Sarah sat and folded her hands on the tabletop.

"Tea, Miss Granger?"

"That would be lovely." She had refused one time while visiting a family in Five Points, not wanting to use even a bit of the family's meager supplies. She had insulted the family by what they saw as condescension. She had never made that mistake again.

She waited for Mrs. O'Brien to pour. Keeping her gaze on the table, she tried to pretend she did not hear the whispers circulating the room. Finally, Mrs. O'Brien placed the cup before her.

Sarah took a sip before saying, "I'm here about your daughter Doreen. I think she would like her family to visit and see her and her baby."

"A boy or a girl?" Mrs. O'Brien asked.

"A boy."

"What did she name him?" asked a young girl.

"Hush, Bridget!" Mrs. O'Brien ordered. "What does it matter when he can't have his father's name, for the dirty dog did not marry her before he got her with child?"

"Is he here in Five Points?" Sarah asked. "Maybe, if I ask Father O'Leary or Father Tynan to speak with him, he would marry her when he learns he has a son."

"Father O'Leary tried. You're wasting your time, Miss Granger."

"Surely you'll come to see her and the baby."

"Not until she's wed." Mrs. O'Brien tilted her chin higher. "You may tell her that, Miss Granger. Maybe she will heed you better than she did her mother."

"I think she needs you now."

Mrs. O'Brien shook her head. "She doesn't need us. We don't need her."

Battling her confusion, she gasped, "She's been an excellent worker at the Mission. She's a credit to you."

Mrs. O'Brien stood and slapped her hands on the table. Tea splashed from Sarah's cup. "She's no credit to this family! She's a harlot who laid herself down with the first man who looked in her direction. Miss Granger, you clearly are a fine woman, but you're wasting your time here." She folded her arms across the bodice of her apron.

"But, Mrs. O'Brien—"

"Good day, Miss Granger."

Sarah sighed. She must leave if she wanted to have any

chance of coming again to pave the way to a reconciliation. Silence followed her.

As she emerged onto the sidewalk two stories below, she heard her name called. She turned to see Bridget, the girl who had spoken in the O'Brien apartment.

"Miss Granger, Ma would have a conniption if she knew I'm talking to you like this."

Sarah clutched the handrail, and it rocked. "Are you going to come with me to see Doreen?"

"No." Uneasily she twisted her apron in her hands. "Be careful, Miss Granger."

"Careful? Miss O'Brien, I can assure you that your sister is safe. We—"

"Aren't safe." She gulped and lowered her voice. "I've seen you about, Miss Granger. I've seen how you help folks. I don't want you or your children hurt." Bending toward Sarah, she whispered, "Ma doesn't want it known that Doreen's babe was sired by a Johnny Reb named Lorne—"

"Lorne!" she gasped in astonishment. "Are you sure?"

"Sure as I'm standing here."

"Lorne who?" It must be a coincidence. It must be!

The girl screwed up her face. "Forbes? No. Finnegan? No. Maybe it was Fountain."

"Fontaine?" she asked, although her stomach cramped with dismay.

"Could be. She didn't say much other than Lorne this and Lorne that."

When the railing wobbled again, she hoped it would hold her. She was not sure her knees would. "Did you see him?"

"She never brought him around to call. She would sneak out to meet him in the middle of the night." Without another word, she ran into the house and up the stairs.

Sarah stared after her. The story seemed incredible, but she thought of the times she had seen Doreen wandering about the Mission late at night. She had been sure that Doreen had been unable to sleep because of her pregnancy, but now wondered if Doreen had been waiting to meet Lorne.

Lorne!

He had spoken to her three times at the Mission. How many other times had he been there? Each time, he and Doreen had risked the children there.

Numbly Sarah walked along the street. She had thought she could trust Lorne. If he had told her the truth about him and Doreen, she would have . . . She was not sure what she would have done.

She knew what she must do *now*. She had to talk to Doreen and insist on speaking with Lorne. This had to be resolved before the children were put in danger. The situation was too unstable already. With the draft lottery coming up, it would become even more hazardous to have even the hint of Southern sympathy attached to the Mission.

Sarah bumped into someone. Not looking to see who it was, she murmured, "Pardon me."

A hand caught her arm. "Aren't you Miss Granger?"

She stared at the young man. His face was filthy with soot, hiding every feature except his blue eyes. His clothes were black from his cap to his boots. "Yes, I'm Sarah Granger."

"Of the Second Avenue Mission?"

"Yes."

"That copper is your friend?"

Her eyes narrowed. "Do you mean Sergeant McCauley?"

"That's the one."

"Yes, he's my friend." Admitting to that could bring her more trouble here in Five Points, but lying would be stupid. She had always been honest with the people in this slum, and they had come to respect her, however grudgingly, for that.

"You might want to go down Baxter then." He grinned, his eyes still cold.

"Why?"

"I'd hurry if I were you." He turned to walk away.

She grabbed his arm and ran her fingers along his sleeve. As he had shifted, she had seen the stitching on it. The pattern matched the one in Conlan's quilt.

"What are you doing?" he asked.

"Tell me who sewed this!"

He tugged his sleeve out of her hands. His smile grew even colder. "You had better hurry over to Baxter and get McCauley while there's still something left to get."

Sarah choked back a gasp. Turning on her heel, she gathered her full skirt and ran along the street. The young man's laugh followed to taunt her.

Other shouts chased her, but she edged around the rag-man's cart and jumped across the open sewers. A twinge seared her ankle, but she ignored it, limping until the pain eased.

She saw a crowd gathered in front of a tenement that looked even worse than its neighbors. Ducking beneath laundry strung from one side of the street to the other, she pushed her way past the gawkers.

"Benjamin!" she cried when she saw him sitting with a bloody cloth to his head.

"What are you doing here?" he asked, looking up at her.

She could tell he was having trouble focusing his eyes. Bruises were swelling his face. "What happened to you?"

"Guess!"

Not caring what anyone thought, she slipped her arm around him so he could lean on her while he came to his feet. Her knees buckled, and she knew he was hurt worse than he wanted anyone to discern. Forcing herself upright, she tightened her grip on him. The people edged back as she helped him lurch away from the steps.

"Wait," he mumbled.

"For what?"

"I need to get my horse."

She looked both ways along the street. The only horses were hitched to carts. "What color is it?"

"Sable is . . ." He winced. "Black, of course. White on the front legs."

"There's no horse like that here."

He leaned against a cart and scanned the street. His curse resonated through her, but a hint of humor trickled into his strained voice. "What do you think Captain Potter's going to do when he finds out I've lost another horse this week? He'll demote me to checking doors."

Sarah did not reply as she drew his arm around her shoulders again. By the time they reached the end of the first block, she wanted to ask for a chance to catch her breath, because he was leaning on her more heavily with every step. She kept going, though, because she doubted she could have convinced her feet to continue if she stopped.

"Who did this?" she asked.

"I'm not sure, but I'm sure who ordered it. General Feich is trying to take over Five Points."

"Let him have it."

He scowled at her, then groaned. "How can you say that when the conscription lottery is coming up and a single spark could be enough to cause trouble everywhere in the city?"

A shiver sliced along her spine. Was that what General Feich wanted? Was that why he was toying with Benjamin? She feared what would happen when the lottery began. Then General Feich might force a confrontation with Benjamin. Only one, she knew, would survive.

15

BENJAMIN SIGHED WITH RELIEF when Sarah helped him up the last step into the Mission. He was not sure how much farther he could go. His head ached. His face ached. He feared at least a few of his teeth were loose and his nose broken. The quilt Sarah had draped over his shoulders was stained with his blood. He was glad it hid how battered he was. He did not need the rowdy-boys discovering how close they had come to killing him.

When they entered the house, the children swarmed over them with questions. He winced. Their voices were like a thousand pinpricks of pain through his skull.

"Missy, take everyone outside," Sarah said quietly.

"No," he muttered, although he wanted to thank her for keeping her voice to a near whisper. "Too dangerous."

"General Feich would have attacked the Mission long ago if he had any interest in hurting the children."

He could not argue with that. He was not certain if he could argue with anything just now.

After sending Ruthie upstairs with a message to Rachel, Sarah herded him past the children and into her office. She did not let him pause as she guided him to her bedroom.

"Lie down," she whispered.

"You're a bossy woman." He tried to smile. Impossible. He fell back onto the bed, sighing again as the pillows touched the wounds on his head.

"And you're going to listen to me." Pulling off his boots, she set a cool cloth on his forehead. She drew the quilt over him. Even its slight weight sent an ache through him. "Benjamin, how long has it been since you slept?"

"What's today?"

"Wednesday."

"Wednesday already?" he asked with honest surprise. "It's been longer than I'd thought."

She stroked his shoulder. "How long?"

"I think I got some sleep Sunday afternoon."

"That's ridiculous! How can Captain Potter expect you to work every day and every night?"

He smiled. "Sweetheart, you've been keeping me from sleeping, too."

"I won't tonight, because you're in no condition to do anything but sleep."

Slipping his arm around her, Benjamin gave her a roguish leer as he pulled her to lean over him. "Are you so sure of that?"

"I'm sure you're going to rest while I get you something cool to drink." She kissed him lightly and hurried out of the room. When the door closed, a stack of papers beside the bed table scattered across the floor.

Benjamin stared at them. His head throbbed as if his attackers were still beating him. He had to clear away the pain. He had to think what to do next. This had become a disaster. He had learned that when a woman had shaken him awake. She wanted him to find out why shots had been fired on a floor above. He had not needed to check. He knew.

General Feich had found Mick. But why was *he* still alive?

The question haunted him. He had invited General Feich and his rowdy-boys to stop him by daring to try to stop them. Southern insurrectionists were stirring up the public houses. When he had begun to frequent Sheehan's, where they were known to congregate, they had set up in the tenements, where, as long as there was no gambling and no signs of liquor on Sunday, nothing could be done to halt them.

Unable to rest, he rose and tossed the cloth back into the bowl. He caught his reflection in the mirror. The bruises on his face were already darkening to match his uniform. He looked even worse than he felt.

His head threatened to burst when he bent to gather up the papers. When he squatted, the room spun, and he fought to hold on to his senses.

As his eyes focused, he realized one page was a piece of wallpaper. Amazement muted his pain when he saw that, although one side was printed with yellow flowers, the other boldly announced it was the *Daily Citizen* of Vicksburg, Mississippi. Curiosity teased him. Why was Sarah saving this secessionist rag? Why did she have it?

He sat down suddenly when he saw a familiar name amid the list of Confederate casualties since the beginning of the war. The door clicked open, and he stared at Sarah. Horror leaped into her eyes. She closed the door.

"Why didn't you tell me the truth?" he asked.

Benjamin's question freed Sarah from her shock. Putting a pitcher of lemonade on the table, she took the paper from him. "I told you that Giles died fighting in the Rebellion."

"Fighting for the Confederacy!"

She recoiled from his anger. "It was his choice, Benjamin, not mine." She put the page on her dresser. "Please don't tell anyone about this. If anyone found out, the Mission—"

"How can you have the Brown children here when your fiancé fought to keep them in slavery?"

"Giles hated slavery as much as I do!"

"Really, or did he simply tell you that because he knew you wouldn't marry him otherwise?"

"Giles was always honest with me."

"He was honest that he intended to fight for the Confederacy?"

She held onto the headboard to keep from throwing her

arms around him. Would he push her away? She saw the revulsion in his eyes. For her? She should expect this, for she had lied to him since they met. If she told him how she had wanted to be honest, what would he do?

"Benjamin," she whispered, "he's dead! I won't let that part of my life intrude again."

"Won't *let* it?" He stood, but did not touch her. "You're scared! Why?"

She could not say this without being in his arms. She put hers around his shoulders and rested her cheek on his chest. She wanted to tell him everything. She had given him her heart and herself, but now wanted to give him something else precious—the secrets of her past. Why didn't he put his arms around her, too? She did not dare to look up at his face, for she did not want his contempt to be for her.

"A Southern sympathizer named Lorne," she whispered, "has come here several times. I think he wants—I *know* he wants me to help him."

"Does he want to stay here until he can smuggle himself back South?"

"He said nothing about leaving."

Brushing her hair back from her face, he said as gently as he touched her, "Sarah, he can't cause trouble for you or the Mission if you turn him over to the authorities. Let me know when he's going to return, and I'll arrest him."

"No!"

"Sarah, the man is our enemy!"

She hid her face in her hands. How could she explain to anyone, especially Benjamin, who saw few shades of gray, why she could not do what she knew she should—what she must—what would betray all she had once believed would be hers?

"You can't know," she said, her voice trembling on every word, "what it was like around West Point after the secession. Friends were now enemies. Giles had been an instructor at West Point. That was how we met. When he heard General Lee had resigned his commission rather than accept the leadership of the Union forces, he resigned as well. He waited only long enough to ask me to marry him before he left. He was so proud to be made a major."

"Sweetheart, I'm sorry."

"Are you?"

Bringing her to face him, he drew her arms around him again. "For you, because I can't feel anything but loathing for a man who abandoned his country at its hour of greatest need."

"It wasn't easy for him."

"Who is Lorne?" he asked against her hair. "Who is he really?"

"Lorne Fontaine would have been my brother-in-law. He's Giles's twin brother." She dampened her lips as she added, "And he's the father of Doreen's baby."

He muttered a curse, and she had feared he would push her away. Instead, he captured her mouth. She leaned into his kiss, wanting passion to cauterize the wounds in the hidden recesses of her soul. When he pressed her back into the pillows, he lifted her glasses off her nose. He put them on the table as his tongue caressed her eyelids. Each quick stroke left a scintillating spark in its wake until she gasped and pulled his lips to hers.

He groaned. Not with longing, but with agony. He cradled his head in one hand. She rose and reached for the cloth in the bowl.

"No," he said through clenched teeth. "I'm on duty. I must go."

"On duty? You can't go back out there when you're beat up like this. You should be resting."

He chuckled. "If I stay here, I won't rest." With a swift motion, he framed her face with his hands. "Are you in danger from Lorne Fontaine, Sarah?" he asked.

"I—I don't think so." She was no longer positive about anything but her yearning to have Benjamin hold her here in her bed and sweep the rest of the world away with his kisses.

"If ever he makes a threat to you, let me know right away."

"Right away."

His thumb stroked her cheek as he tilted her face toward him. "Sweetheart, General Feich had Mick murdered today."

"Mick?" Her eyes widened. "The leader of the Irish gang?"

"Yes, and it's rumored that this general is connected with the Confederates infiltrating the city."

"Lorne's done nothing to threaten the Mission."

"What if General Feich gets as tired of the Southern sympathizers as he has of the Irish gangs? Do you think the Mission or you will be safe then?"

Fear caressed her with icy fingers. "I don't know."

"Can you leave? Go back to West Point?"

"There's no place there for the children. My father's parsonage is tiny. We have to stay here." Her hand slipped into his.

His fingers closed over hers. "If you had money to go out of the city—"

"That might change things." Her eyes grew wide. "Are you saying that you would not bring the quilts back from Mr. Pettigew's store if I took them there?"

He shook his head. "There may be other ways of sending these children out of the city. I will speak with Father Tynan."

"Benjamin—"

"Just be careful," he whispered.

"Will that be enough?"

"Pray that it is, sweetheart, for there may be nothing else we can do."

∞

"HE NEVER SAYS A single word?" Dr. Everett took two bottles out of the closet in Sarah's office. Closing the door, he locked it and handed Sarah the key as he looked at Conlan, who was sitting on the settee, his arm around his quilt.

"Not a word." She put the key in her pocket. "He does smile occasionally, and he will go with Rachel at bedtime, but most of the day he wants to spend here with me."

"A sight like what he saw would have been enough to drive a grown man insane."

"He's not mad." She smiled to soften the snap of her words, but she would not let anyone, no matter how well-meaning, put Conlan into a lunatic asylum. "He'll speak again. I know he will."

Dr. Everett put his hand on her arm and smiled sadly. "Don't be too disappointed if he doesn't." He wiped his brow. "This hot weather is getting worse. The sun has just come up, and already the streets are baking. Thank goodness the battle in Pennsylvania is over. Those poor men must have been roasted nearly alive in their wool uniforms."

"I wish General Lee had ordered a surrender." She glanced toward the street, which was almost silent in the smothering heat. "Then we wouldn't have to have this draft lottery today."

He nodded. "I thought I should have a few extra supplies ready downstairs. Just in case."

"A good idea. If—"

"Sarah!" Rachel shrieked from upstairs.

"Coming!" she shouted back. She forced a smile for Dr. Everett. "That sounds as if Rachel has seen a spider. She will fight a mouse or even a rat, but spiders terrify her."

He smiled. "Do you want me to take care of it for you?"

"No." Her smile wavered. "Get ready in case there's trouble."

As he went to the cellar door, Sarah let her smile fall away.

Rachel bolted into the office and grasped her hands. "I've looked everywhere, Sarah! They're gone!"

"Gone? Who's gone?"

"Doreen and her baby and—"

"Hell and damna—" Sarah bit off Benjamin's favorite curse. If Doreen had left, then Lorne might not come back. If he did not come back, she would not be able to try—again—to persuade him to leave. If he did not leave . . . No! She did not want to think about things being worse.

Quietly, she said, "If she's gone back to her family in Five Points, she will find no welcome there. Then she'll come back here."

"But—" Rachel's voice broke. She swallowed hard, then whispered, "But she took Birdie with her, too."

"Birdie?"

"Birdie's gone. I don't know where she is. I—"

A primitive scream came from the settee.

Sarah whirled. Dear God! She had forgotten Conlan was sitting there, hearing all this.

Running to the sofa, she dropped to her knees and pulled him into her arms. He was as stiff as a stone, but his heart pounded against her. She whispered soothing words. It did no good, for he remained rigid. Seeing his quilt on the floor, she bent to pick it up. He would not take it. Crouching, he whimpered like a beaten pup.

"Sarah, I didn't mean to . . . I mean . . ."

Sarah stood and gave Rachel a tight smile. "I know you didn't mean to hurt him." Stroking the little boy's tight shoulders, she asked, "When did you see Doreen last?"

"After supper last night."

"I saw her when I checked all the doors were locked." She closed her eyes. "Why would she want Birdie? She has her own baby!"

"She's been paying a lot of attention to Birdie the past few days."

"Has she?" Sarah wondered what else she had missed while being worried about Benjamin. She had not seen him since the attack in Five Points . . . and his discovery of the truth about Giles. Seeing that Conlan's quilt had fallen to the floor again, she picked it up and put it on his lap.

He shrieked.

She pulled it back, wide-eyed. What once had comforted him now horrified him. Had he gone mad, as Dr. Everett feared?

As Rachel knelt, trying to comfort him, Sarah saw some of the children clustered in the doorway. She folded the quilt over her arm as she rushed to assure them nothing was wrong. Sending them into the parlor along with the promise of a story if they would get the book and wait for her, she turned back to the settee.

"Conlan," she whispered, "it will be fine. Your baby is going to be all right. Rachel and I will—" She looked down at the quilt she was wringing in her hands.

The feather pattern! When she had seen how hurt Benjamin was, she had forgotten all about seeing this quilting pattern on the rowdy-boy's coat sleeve in Five Points. She looked from Conlan to the quilt. The little boy no longer needed it. She had promised Benjamin she would send the quilt to him as soon as Conlan no longer depended on it.

"Rachel," she said tautly, "take Conlan with you into the parlor. The other children are waiting for a story."

"He won't—"

"He'll be fine as long as he doesn't see his quilt." She went out into the hall and pulled her bonnet off its peg. Tying it under her chin, she drew on her cape.

"You'll be too hot in that," Rachel gasped, carrying the little boy into the hall.

"I don't want anyone to see this." She tapped the quilt and pulled it back under her cape as Conlan cried out again.

"Why?"

"If what I suspect is true, this quilt may be able to point to more than the person who murdered Conlan's mother." She reached for the doorknob. "And if it is true, I have to make sure Benjamin gets this quilt and stops that person before we all are as dead."

16

SARAH STEPPED OFF THE horsecar not far from 677 Third Avenue, where the conscription lottery was being held. When she had gone to the police precinct station, she had been told Benjamin was here. She should have guessed that, although this was beyond the area he customarily patrolled.

Keeping her cape drawn forward over Conlan's quilt, she ignored the oily drop of sweat rolling down her back. She stared at the crowd gathered in front of the address, which was to one of four doors of a row house. She thought there must be more than a hundred people here. Maybe two hundred, but it was quiet as everyone waited for the drawing to begin.

A few policemen lined the opposite sidewalk. What would a handful of policemen and a pair of men from the Invalid Corps be able to do if trouble started? A wounded veteran leaned drunkenly on a lamppost, a bottle of whiskey balanced on his crutch.

She looked for Benjamin, but doubted she could find him in this mass of people. With a taut smile, she knew he would be at the center of where trouble could begin. That would be inside the house where the drawing was being held.

Pushing her way through the throng in the street, she reached the front steps just as a nearby church's bells began chiming the hour. They rang nine times, and, at the top of the steps, the door opened as promised. She was thrust into the house by the pressure of the crowd.

The large room was bare. A pair of flags had been hung from the ceiling and created strange shadows on the wall as they fluttered over the rush of the crowd. At the front, divided from the rest of the room by a low railing, waited a table where eight clerks sat, ready to write down the names.

Sarah stared at the lottery drum, which was set on a small dais. It was nothing more than a metal barrel with a door cut into one side. A handle had been affixed to it as well as wooden legs.

As more people pressed into the room, it seemed as close as an outhouse. The odors from the people were not much better, and she guessed the stench would only grow worse as the day's heat strengthened. There were only a few other women. Few women could leave their families for the whole day it would take to draw all the names of the men who would be drafted if the war continued on.

A growl halted Sarah as she tried to get closer to the rail, and she gasped. She recognized this man from Five Points . . . and his coat sleeves, which matched the stitching in Conlan's quilt. He had sent her to find Benjamin. When she tried to grab his sleeve, he seized her shoulders and pulled her up tight to him.

"What are you doing here?" he snarled.

"Let me go!" She tried to wiggle away as he pulled her over to the wall where they would not be noticed. Some of the people glanced at her, then away. They did not want anything to prevent them from hearing the first name drawn.

He shoved her against the wall, and the quilt fell out of her fingers as her head hit the boards. He stared at it. "What are you doing with that?"

"What does this stitching pattern mean?" she asked him, trying to hold on to her senses. She did not want to think what he might do if she swooned.

"You'd like to know so you can run and tell your copper friend, wouldn't you?" he demanded in the same low growl. "You're a fine-looking lass, so that explains why he's interested in you."

"He? Benjamin?"

He laughed as his gaze raked along her. "You're as stupid as that copper."

"Just tell me who sewed your coat sleeve. I need to know so I can help two children who have lost their mother."

He spat on the floor. "She betrayed us. So have you." Holding her against the wall with one hand, he reached under his coat with the other. She shrieked as she saw the glitter of a bare blade.

She kicked at him, but her narrow hoops pinned her legs to the wall. His hand slid across her shoulder so his fingers spread across her throat. He jerked her head up and smiled as he withdrew the blade. She took a breath to scream, but his fingers closed on her throat, choking her.

"I should kill you right here," he muttered, "but he says to let you live."

He released her. She sagged, rocking a few steps forward into the crowd. She was steadied by strong hands.

"What in the name of St. Bridget are you doing here?"

Sarah stared into Benjamin's furious scowl. His fierce expression was not eased by the many shades of bruises on his face. She threw her arms around him, knowing no one would pay attention. No one had noticed the man who threatened to kill her.

As his arms enfolded her to the hot, thick wool of his coat, she whispered, "I came looking for you. I went to the precinct station, and you weren't there."

"You could have left a message."

"No, I had to see you." She gathered up the quilt, brushing off the footprints where it had been stepped on. "I wanted to bring you this."

"Conlan's quilt?" he asked, astonished. "He gave it to you?"

She shook her head, trying to keep the tears from her eyes. "No, he no longer wants it. Benjamin, Doreen left and took Birdie with her. Conlan is shattered. I'm not sure if he will ever recover."

"Took Birdie? Why?"

"I have no idea. Maybe her baby was sleeping with Birdie in her basket, and Doreen took the basket not realizing the two babies were in it."

His smile was grim. "You always see the best in people, don't you? I'm surprised you've lasted this long on Second Avenue. I'll put word out to look for Birdie, although finding one tiny baby in this city is going to be almost impossible."

"I know." She bit her bottom lip to keep it from trembling and held out the quilt, taking care that it was shadowed by her cape. As Benjamin reached for it, she whispered, "Look at the quilting pattern in it."

"The feathers?"

"Not so loud!" she gasped, even though his hushed voice would not carry above the shouts in the room as the witnesses to the conscription lottery acted as if this were a party at their favorite public house. "I've been seeing this pattern many places lately, but I never connected them until this morning."

"Where have you seen them?"

"On sleeves. The men who attacked us when you escorted me on the way home from Mr. Winslow's house and again in Five Points and again here." She told him what he had interrupted. "He wanted to kill me."

"But—"

"Someone doesn't want me dead."

"That's what he said?"

"I think so." She put her fingers to her sore neck. "He was choking me."

Benjamin swore as he glanced toward the front of the room. "Captain Potter told me to stay here to make sure the drawing got started without incident. As soon as they start pulling names, I'll take this quilt and the information to him. Then I'll take you home." A smile quirked on his lips. "Thanks for trusting me with this, sweetheart."

"Benjamin, there's more."

"More? You've connected more than we've managed in the past weeks."

She could not return his smile. Taking a deep breath, she wondered if he had any idea how difficult it was for her to say what she must. "I've seen the pattern one other place. On Lorne's sleeve when he called at the Mission."

"That confirms what we'd suspected about Southern agents trying to create unrest here." He stroked her arm gently. "I appreciate you being honest with me, Sarah. If it makes you feel any better, you may have saved a lot of lives, including Lorne's."

"I love you," she whispered. She put her fingers to her lips as she saw his eyes widen. She had not meant to say that now, but her heart wanted to reveal all its secrets.

"Sarah—" He looked over his shoulder as a shout came from the other side of the room. The tension returned to his voice as he shoved the small quilt beneath his coat. "It's about to start."

She followed him as he walked toward the railing that divided the room. The men leaped aside when they noted his copper badge. Hatred burned in their eyes as they grumbled after him. Terror nibbled at her. Never before had she feared so much for Benjamin, but he acted oblivious to their fury. He greeted several men by name, but did not slow until he reached the railing.

A dull sound overhead made Sarah smile in spite of the anticipation that was nearly palpable in the room. She wondered if the child rolling a ball in the apartment upstairs understood that history was being made below. Today, for the first time in United States history, men were being forced into involuntary service in the army.

The wooden rail striking her hip halted her, and she put her hands on its well-worn top. She loosened her cape and put it over the rail as she wiped sweat from her forehead.

As sultry as the street had been, in the overfilled room, the air was even thicker.

Benjamin picked up her cape and handed it to her. "Don't give troublemakers anything to hide behind."

Fear threatened to strangle her again as she saw the intensity in his eyes. This was the Benjamin she had watched keep peace on the streets and risk his life for strangers. Nodding, she said nothing as a door opened beyond the railing.

Sarah watched as three men emerged. Their formal clothes drooped in the heat. They tried not to look at the crowd. When good-natured jeers were shouted, they glanced at each other uneasily.

She understood their shock. This crowd acted as if it were celebrating.

"Who are they?" she whispered.

Benjamin continued to scan the crowd as he answered as lowly, "The man with the black cravat is the provost marshal. Jenkins is his name. The other two are clerks. Carpenter and a man named Southwick, chosen for this duty because they're the least likely to panic in case of trouble." He nodded to the provost marshal, who had glanced in his direction, then looked over the men and women stuffed into the room. "Maybe they've accepted the inevitable."

"Do you believe that?"

"No, I don't believe anything will stop what could happen if it gets started. The police need to contain it before it can spread."

The drum containing the names had been checked and was now in place, and a fourth man took his seat at the table next to the eight men. In front of him was a bottle of ink and paper. It would be his duty to write down the name of each conscript. She did not envy them what could be a dangerous task. With the long lists of dead, wounded, and missing from the battle at Gettysburg flapping from every lamp pole, no one could doubt that the ones drafted here today would be called to serve and to die.

The steady gong of church bells silenced the room. It

was half past the hour, and the beginning of the lottery could wait no longer. Again, almost as if on cue, the boisterous jesting began. No one listened as Provost Marshal Jenkins read aloud his orders to hold the lottery. The crowd did not care that the orders came from President Lincoln. All they wanted was to hear someone else's name called.

As Mr. Carpenter drew off his coat, Sarah slipped her hand into Benjamin's. She needed his touch as time halted along with the breath clogged over her heart. They had dreaded this moment, and now, at last, it was here.

Without ceremony, Mr. Carpenter was blindfolded. When Sarah saw the gestures some of the men made, she flushed. Mr. Southwick stepped forward and began to turn the drum containing the potential draftees' names.

An uneasy silence strangled the last whiff of air as the wheel turned several times, then stopped. Mr. Carpenter's hand was aimed at it. As he stuck his hand into it, a collective breath was inhaled.

Benjamin's fingers almost crushed hers as they waited for the name to be called. *Please don't let it be Benjamin's*, she thought over and over. She wanted to shout that someone should tell General Lee to surrender, that the South had lost its last chance for victory at Gettysburg, but common sense had vanished. All that remained was this lottery of death.

Provost Marshal Jenkins took the paper and opened it. In a clear, steady voice, he announced, "Willie Jones, Forty-sixth Street, corner of Tenth Avenue." He looked up, waiting.

Instead of roaring with rage, the crowd was gleeful to discover Jones was among them. A young man, with ears too big for him, grinned as friends and strangers volunteered to buy him a drink before he marched off to war.

Sarah stared at the crowd, then at the men behind the railing. Provost Marshal Jenkins hid his astonishment at the good-natured jesting, but she guessed he was as uneasy as she was.

"Is it going to be this simple?" she whispered to Benjamin.

"No."

She followed his gaze to knots of people who were not laughing. She looked around the room and saw the man who had nearly choked her.

"Benjamin, there he is!"

"Where?"

"Under the first flag. He . . ." She frowned. The man had disappeared. "He's gone!"

He squeezed her fingers, but lightly. "All rats know how to find a hole to hide in."

The joking continued, its noise obliterating the calling of the next name. Each name brought hoots of laughter and faked sympathy as the men tried to outlaugh each other.

An occasional protest came when a woman heard a loved one's name called, but each time the woman was silenced by more laughter and catcalls. That frightened Sarah more. These men should have compassion for their women. It could only mean that the men were sure they would not be serving in the army. But how . . . ? She shuddered, not wanting to think of what they might do to keep from being drafted.

"Sarah," Benjamin murmured, "I need to report to Captain Potter. You should leave, too. If we get separated in this crowd, go straight home. Stay on the busy streets. I don't want one of these half-drunk fools to take it into his whiskey-sodden brain to follow you because . . ."

He did not have to finish. She understood. Anyone who was seen as the police force's ally today could be in danger.

Edging away from the railing, Sarah fought the crowd that wanted to move forward. She had not gone two steps before she realized she had lost sight of Benjamin. Hoping she was going in the right direction, she pushed toward the front door. The call of names chased her. Already Provost Marshal Jenkins's voice was growing hoarse. She wondered how he would manage until the end of the day when the last name was drawn.

A man stepped aside and tipped his hat to her as she reached the door. Thanking him for holding it open for her, she faltered when she heard Benjamin's name called from the front of the room.

She whirled to see Provost Marshal Jenkins handing a slip of paper to the men at the table. She had watched the motion over and over, but this time he had called Benjamin's name. Her hands clenched as time collapsed to the moment Giles told her how he must do his duty for his "country," no matter the peril. Benjamin was even more determined to do what was right.

Giles had been a trained soldier. Benjamin was a policeman, who was accustomed to dealing with rowdies and drunks. Giles had died, leaving her heartbroken and alone. Benjamin . . . She blinked back tears.

"Miss, are you going in or out?" asked the man, who still held the door.

She fought disbelief. This could not be happening . . . again!

"Out," she whispered.

Hurrying down the steps, Sarah saw the crowd on the street had grown. She tried to see Benjamin among them, but she could spend hours searching for him. He had told her to go back to the Mission.

She walked toward Second Avenue and the Mission. It had been her sanctuary before. It must be again. She was not sure where else to turn. Her heart soon would be as covered with patches as Conlan's quilt.

Conlan! Birdie! Heavens, she could not forget about the missing baby. Maybe Doreen had returned the baby. That thought sped her steps along the sidewalk, which danced in the heat like a sheet of water.

She was assaulted by dozens of questions as she reached her block. Her neighbors wanted to know what had happened. When she told them that the lottery was progressing smoothly, several women pulled their aprons up to their faces and wept. She longed to join them.

The Mission was cooler than the street and quiet. With a pulse of surprise, Sarah realized it was nap time for the younger children. The day, which seemed to be dragging, had sped past as she walked back to the Mission, lost in her grief.

Putting her bonnet and cape on the pegs, she went to the parlor, where Rachel was working with the children and their lessons. She smiled when she saw Rachel grin at Ruthie and give the girl a hug. She fought back the tears that kept pestering her.

"Sarah's back!" Fiona cried, jumping to her feet. "Do you want some lemonade?"

"I can't think of anything I'd like more." That was a lie. She would have liked to have Benjamin's name still in that barrel in a far corner where it could not be drawn. "Bring it into my office, please."

Rachel came to her feet and handed the book to Ruthie. "Will you read the next story while I talk with Sarah?"

Taking the glass Fiona held out to her, Sarah thanked her before going into her office. She waited for Rachel to enter, then closed the door as she asked, "Is Birdie back?"

"No." A single tear flowed down Rachel's face. "I haven't told the children. I've just let them think that Conlan is tired, so that's why he's not playing with them." She hesitated, then asked, "How was the conscription lottery? Was it horrible? What happened?"

Sarah sat on the settee and stared up at her assistant. "Benjamin's name was called just as I was leaving."

"Oh, my!" Rachel knelt beside her. Taking Sarah's hands in hers, she whispered, "Maybe he will not be drafted into the army. I heard that firemen were exempt. Surely policemen must be, too."

"No one is exempt. Any able-bodied man can be called to serve if his name is selected in the lottery."

"I'm so sorry, Sarah."

She brushed Rachel's red hair back from her face. "Thank you."

"I really am sorry." She bounded to her feet, looking no older than one of the children. "You know I didn't want him coming here, but I know you have a great deal of admiration for him."

"I love him." A laugh oozed from her lips. "In fact, I told him that this morning."

"Oh . . ."

Rising, she clasped Rachel's hand. "It's been difficult to hold your tongue about Benjamin being here—"

"I didn't!"

"—and having the Brown children in the Mission." Sarah wandered over to the window and gazed out on the street. No one seemed to notice the day's heat now, because people were clumped together. She knew they were talking about the conscription lottery. Wrapping her arms around herself, she hoped they would not do more than talk.

"I didn't want them here. I thought they should be with their kind at the Colored Orphan Asylum," Rachel said quietly, "but no trouble's come of it. They're good children. Ruthie is so smart, and Mason would do well with his lessons if he did not rush them so he could help Dr. Everett." She held out the bag holding Sarah's quilting. "Sarah, I know this comforts you when I have been very little help. Why don't you work on your quilting?"

She took the bag as if it held a miracle. Sitting again in the chair, she opened it and pulled out the half-finished quilt top. Her fingers were setting the needle to flash in and out of it with easy speed before she even realized what she was doing. Looking up at Rachel, she said, "I'm glad you've changed your mind about the Brown children. I wish others would."

"Sarah," Rachel said, putting her hands on Sarah's shoulders, "I hope the war is over before Benjamin is called to fight. It's not right that you should lose two men you love." She gulped. "Not that Benjamin will be killed. It's just . . ."

She patted her friend on the arm. "I know what you mean. Why don't you bring the children in here? By now, Ruthie should be finished with that story, and I want to see if I can coax Conlan to look at me." She sighed. "I fear it's going to take a long, long time to reach him this time."

BENJAMIN PAUSED AS HE was about to open the door
to the Mission. Red light flowed along the street, but it was
only the sunset. Not blood. Not fire. The day had been
almost anticlimactical, but he was not sure how long it
would stay that way. The taverns, brothels, and public
houses were doing a bang-up business. All that whiskey
and beer was dulling brains and chasing away common
sense. He hoped that the morning would bring nothing
worse than a city filled with heads aching from too much
liquor.

He smiled as the cool hush of the Mission welcomed
him. Voices came from the back of the house, and he
guessed the children were eating their supper. Walking
along the hall, he glanced at the dining room. The police
never had found out the name of the woman who had died
here. Another unidentified soul buried with Father Tynan's
blessing's in the corner of the cemetery reserved for paupers.

A dozen eager voices called his name when he reached
the kitchen door. The one he wanted to hear did not. As
the children jumped up to greet him, Sarah slowly came to
her feet.

He unbuttoned his coat and drew out the small quilt.
Holding it out, he said, "I thought you might like this back
for now."

"That's Conlan's quilt!" Missy exclaimed. "No wonder
he's been hiding in the shadows." She wagged her finger
at him. "You shouldn't have touched Conlan's quilt. Sarah
says that."

"I'll remember that." He almost smiled, but could not
when he saw the desolate expression in Sarah's eyes.

Her smile was brittle as she motioned for the children to
sit and finish their supper. "Fiona, it's your and Ruthie's
turn to do the dishes tonight."

"Ah, Sarah—"

"No back talk!"

Benjamin said nothing as the children stared at Sarah in
disbelief. He had never heard her raise her voice to them,
other than to call for them to go out and play. He cupped

her elbow and murmured, "Sarah, I think we should talk."

"Yes." She put her napkin on the table and released a breath that shuddered through her. "I'm sorry, children. It's been a trying day."

"Go," Rachel said from the far end of the table, where she had been sitting silently. "I'll make sure they do the dishes and get to bed on time."

"Thank you." Sarah was not certain if she should be happy because she had this wonderful family around her or if she should give in to grief. As Benjamin steered her along the hall, she let the numbness consume her again. It was so tempting to feel nothing.

As soon as Benjamin closed the door of her office behind them, he asked, "Is Birdie back?"

"No. No sign of her or Doreen or Doreen's baby." She unfolded Conlan's quilt and put it on the back of the sofa. "Maybe this will help him, but I doubt it. I fear for the poor child's sanity."

"Other policemen are being alerted to look for the quilted design when they are on patrol. Maybe we will be able to pinpoint its source."

"Good."

"Sarah?"

She almost did not look up from the crazy pattern of the quilt. How could she submerge her emotions when Benjamin's were naked in his voice? As she raised her eyes, he put his finger beneath her chin so she could not look away again.

"I want to hold you, Sarah." His voice grew softer. "Sweetheart, I want to hold you while I can."

She closed her eyes to obscure her pain from him and from herself, but it was impossible. "You know?"

"I know. Captain Potter told me on the way to the precinct house. I was outside before my name was drawn."

"How can you be so calm?"

"Because there's no other choice." His eyes met hers squarely as a smile tipped his lips. "I can't stop this war and the conscription any more than I can stop wanting to make love with you tonight and every night for as long as we have together."

He swept her into his arms. Her skirt whirled around their legs as he crushed her mouth beneath his. As she gasped for breath, his surged into her throat. His fingers along her back elicited the luscious longing.

"No," she moaned against his mouth.

Raising his head, he gazed down at her in astonishment. "No?" he whispered. "Are you saying that you want me to stop kissing you?"

"I want to look at you, really look at you, so I can never forget what you look like." She stroked his cheek. "I don't want to lose you or the glorious sensations I've discovered in your arms."

"We'll find a way to work this out." His lopsided grin touched her heart. "Haven't we figured out something with every other problem we've faced?"

"But we've never faced anything like this."

"You have."

She shook her head. "I thought I had. I thought when Giles left, I would die. When I received word of his death, I wished I had. Lorne sent me that newspaper from Vicksburg, and I feared my heart would turn to stone." Her hands uncurled along his face. "Yes, that was horrible, but, Benjamin, this is so much worse. I—"

His mouth covered hers, silencing the sob that slithered up from the depths of her pain. He explored her lips as he drew her into her bedroom. From somewhere beyond the pleasure, she heard him lock the door.

He took her glasses and put them on the night table. When he turned toward her, a roguish grin brightened his eyes. He sent her hair falling along her and loosened the hooks down the back of her gown, bending to press his mouth against her neck. A tremor coursed along her, freeing her from grief as she exulted in this delight.

As eagerly, she slid his clothes off him so she could admire his firm body and savor his rough skin against her. When he untied her hoops and left the rest of her clothes on top of her gown, he leaned her back into the warm lushness of her bed. She drew him with her. The strong muscles of his back rippled beneath her fingers.

His mouth left hers to seek along her neck. Each flick of his tongue created lightning-hot sparks of pleasure. Following the angle of her shoulder, he explored her arm. He chuckled against her inner elbow as she gasped when he nibbled gently on the sensitive skin.

Moaning his name, she tried to bring his mouth back to hers, which hungered for its touch. He smiled as he caressed her cheek, but, with his leg across hers, he pinned her to the bed. She squirmed as her escalating passion took over every thought.

She gasped again when he moved to tease the skin along the inside of her legs. Her fingers twisted through his hair, and she arched to meet each fiery kiss. She drew his mouth back to hers, wanting to share with him this splendor.

He rolled onto his back and brought her to lie over him. Brushing her hair away from her face, he moaned when she tasted the whorls of his ear. His hands on her hips guided her as she brought them together. For a second, she did not move, simply savoring him within her.

His unsated groan fired the sweet madness again, but she fought it to watch his face. Each movement augmented his ecstasy until shimmers of pleasure raced from him to her and through her fingertips back to him.

Suddenly he gripped her arms and pulled her forward until her mouth was only a hair's breadth from his. He whispered her name in the moment before he brought her lips to his. She was captured by their mingled desire. The explosion of ecstasy bathed her in the joy, for she had shared it with him.

∞

REALITY WAS SLOW IN returning. Sarah's cheek rested on a warm surface that moved slowly. Beneath her ear, a steady thump became a heartbeat. When a hand stroked her bare back, she raised her head.

Her hair shadowed Benjamin's face, but not even his

bruises could dim his smile. A single finger steered her mouth to his. Tenderness and love flowed from his lips into her heart.

She opened her mouth to tell him how she loved him, but nothing came forth but sobs. She clung to him, weeping as she had wanted to all day. He held her, his cheek against her hair, without saying anything.

Both of them knew there was nothing to say, except good-bye.

17

"SARAH! SARAH!" A FIST pounded on the bedroom door.

Forcing her eyes open, Sarah groped for her glasses. She settled them on her nose to discover Benjamin was already on his feet and pulling on his trousers. He reached for his nightclub even before he buttoned them closed.

"It's Rachel," she whispered, grabbing her wrapper off the rocker. She pulled it on and unlocked the door, throwing it open. "Rachel, what is it?"

Her assistant stared at Benjamin, but held out something wrapped in dirty rags. "I opened the front door and found her. She's back, Sarah!"

"Birdie!" she cried as she took the baby. Putting Birdie on the bed, she unwrapped the cloth. The baby was naked underneath and almost as filthy as the fabric. "Rachel, she must be starved. Get a bottle ready while I clean her up."

"Yes." Rachel glanced again at Benjamin, then ran toward the kitchen.

Sarah poured water into the bowl and dipped a clean cloth into it. She began to clean the baby. "Benjamin, diapers are upstairs. Second door on the left." As he turned to the door, she added, "Try not to wake the other children."

"I'll be so quiet I could sneak up on a mouse."

She smiled as she cooed to Birdie. Other than the dirt and a few scratches, the baby did not appear to be any the worse for her adventures. "Where have you been, Birdie?" she whispered. "If only you could talk and tell us."

Rachel inched into the room and held out a bottle. "Sarah, I didn't mean to intrude. I didn't expect . . . I—"

"You didn't do anything wrong." She cradled Birdie in her arms and watched as the baby sucked eagerly on the bottle. Drawing it back a bit so Birdie would not drink so quickly that she made herself sick, she sat in the rocking chair. "I'm so glad she's back and safe."

"I think I know someone else who may be," Benjamin said as he came back into the room. He set Conlan on the floor by the chair.

"Look," whispered Sarah, "here is your baby, Conlan."

The little boy stared straight ahead. She had to put the baby nearly under his nose before he reacted. When he tore at the material around the baby, Birdie began to wail. Conlan smiled as he touched her face, then he looked around the room.

"He wants his quilt, Benjamin," she said.

"One moment." He rushed past Rachel into the office and returned to squat in front of the little boy. He held out the quilt.

Sarah quieted Birdie by putting the bottle in her mouth. Biting her lower lip, she looked at Benjamin and Conlan. One was so strong that he ignored the bruises discoloring his face. The other had been hurt even worse, but his wounds were invisible. With his hair tousled across his forehead and sleep weighing heavily on his eyes, Benjamin had a boyishness about him that was as utterly charming as Conlan's young smile. Her gaze was drawn to his bare chest, where his skin was taut across his muscles. During the night, his chest had been her pillow while they slept, while they talked, while they made love.

"Is this what you want?" Benjamin asked.

She almost shouted yes, but knew he was talking to Conlan as he offered the quilt to the little boy. This *was* what she wanted. Being with the man she loved while she worked to help these children who had nowhere else to turn.

Conlan looked at her, and she smiled. "Go ahead. Benjamin is your friend. Don't be scared of the ouch he has on his face."

"Ouch?" Benjamin chuckled as Conlan took the quilt and clutched it to him.

"What we call scratches and bruises here." Looking toward the door, she added, "Rachel, will you take Birdie and get her dressed?"

Rachel smiled as she took the baby. "Of course." Holding out her hand, she asked, "Conlan, do you want to come with us?" She turned toward the door, then paused, "Why do you think she was brought back?"

"That's a good question." Benjamin stood and put his hand on the door.

"Maybe Doreen realized her mistake," Sarah said.

"Do you believe it's that simple?"

She glanced from him to Rachel. "I don't know what to believe right now other than that I'm glad Birdie is back."

Benjamin closed the door as Rachel took the children out into the hall. Picking his shirt up from the floor, he frowned as something fluttered off it. "What's this?" He snatched the slip of paper out of midair before it could fall back to the floor. With a curse, he said, "This must have been packed in with Birdie when she was abandoned outside."

Sarah took the paper. Her eyes widened as she read, *Get rid of the copper, or the next one will be returned to you dead.* She stared at the drawing of a feather at the bottom. Looking from him to the note, she gave a shuddering sigh. Nothing had changed. One way or another, her heart was doomed to be broken.

She folded the page and put it on the dresser. "Benjamin, I think you should leave right away. I'm sure they are watching the Mission."

"Leave? Are you mad? I won't leave you here unprotected."

"I'm going to trade the quilts for whatever I can and get the children out of here."

"No one will give you much for all your work."

"It doesn't matter. We must go." She grasped his arms and tried not to let his bare chest lure her closer. "So must you. You are the danger to us now."

"Us?"

"The children and—"

He buttoned his shirt and stuffed it into his trousers. As he pulled on his boots, he said, "I thought there might be another 'us,' Sarah. You and me."

"I can't let one of the children be hurt or—killed." Her voice cracked. She reached out to him again, but she dared not touch him.

Benjamin strode out of the bedroom before he could say something he would regret. How could he fault Sarah for sacrificing everything—including their happiness—to protect those she had promised to take care of? That was the vow he had made when he joined the Metropolitan Police force. He had never guessed how high its cost could be.

Pounding on the door to the cellar, he stepped back as Sawyer Everett opened it. The doctor was pulling on his suspenders as he peered toward him.

"Benjamin, is there a problem?"

"Yes." He looked back as he heard Sarah's soft footfalls. He did not need the sound. Some part of him was connected to her, so he knew when she was near with a sense that had no definition. "I need you to keep a close eye on Sarah and the children for a few days."

"A few days?" Sarah asked at the same time the doctor asked, "Why? What's wrong?"

"Sawyer," he said, answering the easier question first, "I need to put some distance between me and the Mission to keep my enemies from becoming Sarah's."

The doctor nodded grimly. "That's no surprise. I've seen some unfamiliar characters lurking around here lately."

"All dressed in black?"

"Yes." His brows rose. "So you know who they are?"

Benjamin nodded. "I need to find their leader, and the only way I can do that is to drop out of sight from my usual patrols." He looked back at Sarah.

She had never been lovelier than when he had to deny himself his yearning to pull her back into his arms. Her lips were soft from his kisses, and, in her wrapper, he could admire the curves his fingers and mouth longed to explore anew. Luminous tears glowed in her eyes, but he knew she would not let them fall. Her strength awed him, and he pitied the man who did not take warning from the tilt of her chin.

"It should take no more than a few days," he continued, not taking his gaze from her. "Whatever is going to happen must happen while the Irish slums are all stirred up about the conscription lottery. Only a fool would allow that moment to pass, and General Feich is no fool." Reluctantly he turned back to the doctor. "Will you watch over the Mission for me?"

"I'll do my best."

Benjamin grasped his arm and smiled. "That's all any of us can do. Thank you." His smile slid away. "Now I'd better be on my way."

Sarah came out into the front hall. "Be careful, Benjamin," she whispered.

"I will. You must be, too. Just stay close to the Mission."

"I have to go to the reading of Mr. Winslow's will on Monday morning."

"Don't be foolish. Let the lawyers handle it."

"If I don't go, any money he's left to the Mission will be rescinded." She sighed. "He was my last benefactor, Benjamin. Without this money, I may not be able to find a way to feed the children by summer's end."

He frowned. "Winslow's house is on Lexington, right?"

"Yes."

"If you are careful, you should be all right. Stay away from where the draft lotteries are taking place, especially up on Third Avenue."

"Third Avenue? That was yesterday."

"They didn't finish. Jenkins stopped at 1,236 names, 264 names short. Those last ones will be drawn Monday morning." He buttoned up his coat and reached for his cap by the door. "I didn't like how the crowd was acting when it dispersed yesterday. With a day for the truth to set in, I don't think they'll be as jovial when the drawing begins again. Giving them all day today to think about it was stupid."

"I wish . . ." She lowered her eyes.

He tipped her chin up and wished he could lose himself in those sapphire depths again. "You won't be alone, Sarah. Sawyer isn't the only one who will be watching over you."

"That wasn't what I meant."

"I know." He tasted her eager mouth for only a second, because he knew how little temptation he could endure when he wanted to hand the city over to General Feich if the madman would leave him and Sarah alone to enjoy ecstasy.

Brushing her cheek with the back of his fingers, he opened the door and walked out of the Mission. He tried not to think how long it would be before he might be able to return.

⌘

SARAH HEARD TROUBLE ALONG the street before she saw it. She should have guessed something was amiss when the Third Avenue horsecar did not seem to be running this morning. Worried about being late for the reading of Mr. Winslow's will, because she wanted to get that horrible task done and retreat back into the safety of the Mission, she had set off on foot. Now she was hot and sweaty and staring at Hell.

Banshees ran across the cobbles of this usually quiet neighborhood on Lexington Avenue. Smoke flowed into the sky so thickly from a fire in the middle of the avenue she could not determine what was burning. Wagons were overturned in the road, their contents trampled into the stones.

She ducked as something flew at her. Glass rained down on her, and she covered her head with her arms. The crowd was roaring so much, she could not hear the splinters hit the street. In horror, she stared at the houses on the far side of the street.

Windows were broken and doors thrown open. People were rushing in. When she saw a woman come out carrying a lamp, she could only stare. The looters were the poor who were relegated to Five Points and other slums. More than a hundred of them had broken past those invisible boundaries to invade this haunt of the wealthy. She backed away. She had to get back to the Mission. If this insanity spread—

Gunshots echoed along the street. Cheers erupted.

The Mission! Compared to what these people had, the Mission would be almost as luxurious as the houses here. She had to get back there to be sure it and the children were safe. Let Averill Winslow keep his father's money. If she were hurt or murdered here, the Mission would be closed. Then the children would be shunted off to some large orphanage. She shivered as she thought of Conlan being forced into a lunatic's asylum. She must get back to the Mission!

As she turned, she moaned. A thick pall of smoke shadowed the lower part of the city, erupting from dozens of places. Fire! The city was on fire!

Racing along the clogged street, she could not get back across Lexington Avenue. The current of the mob was stronger. More than once, she bounced off a form and heard a growled curse. When a hand settled on her arm, she nearly screamed.

"C'mon here, dearie," ordered a scratchy voice.

Sarah stared at a woman. Rags as filthy as those that had been wrapped around Birdie were the woman's only clothing. When she grinned, her wide mouth revealed blackened gums. She put her face close to Sarah's.

"Who be ye, dearie?"

The thick miasma of whiskey washed over her. The whole throng might be drunk. She must be careful. "Bridget," she said without hesitation. "From East Twenty-ninth Street."

"Come fer the fun?"

"Yes! It's time they—"

"Yer right!" The old woman lifted her other hand.

Sarah gasped as she stared at the bludgeon. The woman thought she was an ally. She must not change the woman's mind.

"Let's give those three-hundred-dollar-men what they deserve!" bellowed a man farther along the street.

"We're not going to die for them!" came back another shout. "Let them taste their blood first!"

More cheers rang off the houses. Like an ever-tightening coil, fear threatened to strangle her.

Sarah pulled her arm out of the old woman's grip. The old woman rushed as best she could after the mob. Watching them, Sarah eased across the street. She looked for Benjamin, although she did not want to see him here. Any policeman would offer a target for their fury.

The side street was quieter. She jumped back as a trio of young men raced toward Lexington Avenue. They carried brands. One paused to set fire to the leaves on a tree near the corner. He looked back at Sarah and laughed.

She ran until an ache in her side forced her to slow her pace. It was hard to breathe, for the smoke made the sun only a bright arc in the gray sky. From everywhere came shouts and the smell of the city burning.

As she reached the corner of Third Avenue, her eyes widened. Rioters were running wildly along the avenue. She must go across the street to reach the Mission. Looking in both directions, she saw only more people swirling in and out of the smoke. She tried to go north along the street to cross over to Second Avenue. It was impossible. The mob was moving south.

When she heard one man shout directions to the police headquarters on Mulberry Street, she froze. Were they mad to confront the police? They must be.

"Benjamin," she whispered. She hoped he was safe, but knew he would be in the midst of this riot. She shivered again at the very thought of the word.

Sarah bumped into a huge man, who cursed at her in Gaelic. When she was about to ignore him as she had others, she saw a man on his knees behind him. The man was working desperately with wires ripped from the telegraph poles. When she tried to push by the man standing in front of him, she was shoved aside.

At her cry of dismay, the man looked up. His eyes narrowed. "Aren't you Miss Granger?

"Yes. You can't—"

He gripped her arm and pulled her down beside him. In a taut whisper, he said, "James Crowley. I work on the telegraph lines for the police. I'm trying to keep this one open." Raising his voice, he added to the massive man, "It's all right. She's one of us."

The man nodded and turned, his arms folded across his chest as he glowered at everyone passing by.

"I've convinced our buddy there that I'm destroying the telegraph wires," Crowley murmured as he worked quickly. "He's keeping people away. The rioters ripped them down. If we lose them, we'll have no contact with the precincts throughout the city." Again he added more loudly, "Couldn't manage without my friend. He knows how important it is to get these wires out of the way before someone is stung by them."

Although she knew what he was doing was important and dangerous, only one thing mattered to her. "Do you know where Benjamin McCauley is?"

"I don't know where anyone is. This mob took over the streetcar I was riding in. They're talking of forcing the city to surrender to them." He stood and lashed the wires to a pole. "Get home if you can. You aren't safe here." He scanned the street as his fingers worked quickly. "None of us are."

Nodding, she rose. She smiled at the big man guarding Crowley. He must be drunk, she realized when he swayed as her skirts brushed him. No wonder he could not see what Crowley was really doing.

Sarah fought her way through the crowd and found a cross street to Second Avenue. Noise followed her, but faded as she hurried toward the steeple of St. John's Church. It appeared and disappeared through the smoke.

She slowed when she reached its front steps. Again the pain seared under her ribs. Running in hoops was almost impossible. They rocked back against her on every step.

She stiffened as she saw a man emerge from the cloud of smoke. His face and clothes were blackened with soot and smoke. She wondered if she could run away . . . again.

"Sarah!"

She forgot her pain and fatigue as she ran to be crushed in Benjamin's embrace. "You're alive!" she whispered.

"When trouble started, I wanted to be sure you were safe. Rachel told me that you went to Winslow's house." He cursed as he released her. "I didn't think you'd be so stupid."

"It was peaceful when I set out." She gripped his hands. "Benjamin, it's terrible. It's taken me more than an hour to get back from Lexington."

"I hope it was worth it."

She shook her head. "I never got to Mr. Winslow's house. Lexington Avenue is under siege."

Drawing her along the street toward the Mission, he did not slow as gunfire echoed in the distance. "It's spreading too fast. If Captain Potter had gotten the reinforcements he needed, this would never have happened. Headquarters couldn't believe that firemen had set fire to the Third Avenue draft office."

"Firemen?"

"Black Joke Engine Company Number Thirty-three!" He snorted. "Black Joke? Unfortunately the joke's on us."

"But why?"

"Too many of their members had their names drawn Saturday. With all of Saturday night to drink in the saloons and all of Sunday to drink at the station, they decided no one else would be conscripted." He looked past her to the flames, which no fire squad would help douse. "They dumped the barrel with the names on the floor and sprayed the place with kerosene and lit it."

"Was anyone—?"

"Hurt? Yes." His mouth twisted. "Dead? Yes. When I

was alerted to report to duty, I knew there was trouble brewing. It's at a boil now."

Benjamin led her up the steps to the door. "Get inside. Bar the doors and stay away from the windows in case someone breaks the glass. Let no one in or out. When I can, I'll be back to see how you're doing." He opened the door. "Don't trust anyone."

Before she could reply, he was racing along the street. She flinched when she saw him pull a gun from under his coat. If the mayor had armed the police with guns, the trouble must be even worse than she had guessed. She did not move as he turned toward Third Avenue. She knew she might never see him again.

"Come back to me, Benjamin," she whispered, then slipped through the open door.

Rachel rushed toward her as she closed and locked the door. "Sarah, what's happening?" Her face was so pale each freckle looked like a pit.

"Cover all the windows on the first floor. Use the children's quilts. Thank heavens we didn't send them to Mr. Pettigew. Send Mason down to tell Dr. Everett to lock up his office. There's a riot on Third and Lexington Avenues."

"A riot?" She swayed.

Sarah seized her shoulders and shook her. "Don't faint! I need your help, Rachel."

"Are we going to die?" asked Fiona from the stairs.

"No, of course not!" She quickly gave the older children orders to secure the house and check on supplies. She was not sure how long this would last. "Especially the water. If—"

A fist crashed into the front door. Even through it, she could hear shouts. Was it the mob? *Don't trust anyone*, Benjamin had warned her.

Quietly, she said, "Rachel, take the children upstairs. Keep them away from the windows." She glanced at Ruthie, who was holding tightly to Fiona's hand. "Do you understand?"

"Yes." Herding the children ahead of her, she whispered, "Be careful, Sarah."

Giving the children time to get upstairs and out of view from the front door, Sarah unlatched it. The fist kept pounding. She opened the door before the men could burst through it.

She did not recognize the five men and saw no sign of the feather quilting stitch along their sleeves, although most of them were as sooty as Benjamin had been. Holding the door, so she could close it quickly, she asked, "What can I do for you gentlemen?"

Their faces grew uneasy when she did not act terrified. They must not be from Second Avenue, because they would already have known that she would not appear intimidated when she was the only thing standing between her children and a mob.

A man swaggered past the others to push his nose close to hers. She refused to back away. He must not get into the house. If one did, the rest would come in an unstoppable flood.

"You've got two colored brats here!" he growled.

"Here?" She struggled to keep her voice calm. Thank goodness Rachel knew to keep a close eye on Ruthie and Mason.

"No lying, Miss Granger!" he cried over the angry shouts from the men crowding the steps. "We know they're here. The neighbors told us that—"

With frigid dignity, she asked, "And did they tell you as well that I sent them away Saturday evening?"

"If you expect us to believe that, then—"

"I have almost twenty children here. To risk all of them for two would be stupid. When the draft lottery started, I was afraid there would be trouble. I sent them away."

"Where did they go?"

"I don't know." She wrung her hands in her apron as if she was disturbed rather than furious. "Probably the Colored Orphan Asylum."

She started to close the door, but the man blocked it with one of his sledgehammer-sized fists. "If we find out you're lying, we'll be back. You'll rue the day you were born."

"Good day." She closed the door firmly. Locking it, she

rushed into her office and peeked past the drapes. The men stormed along the street, hungry for another victim.

She leaned against the wall and breathed a sigh mingling a prayer and a curse. For the first time, she wondered if anything could save the Mission and all of those inside it.

18

SARAH WASHED THE LAST of the dishes and stacked them to dry. Listening for the children, she could hear nothing over the steady roar from the street. The rioting was edging nearer.

Tiptoeing up the back stairs, she paused to listen to Rachel reading to the children. Her assistant's voice was brittle with fear, but the children laughed along with the story. Maybe they were fooled, but they would not be for long.

She went up to the roof and stared at the dual sunsets. The one to the west was the sun sinking into the Hudson River, but the other was the glow from the scores of fires that had been started through the day. Breathing in the smoke, she wished fresh air would sweep away the madness. Burned-out buildings still smoked not far away. Only chance had saved this block so far.

Suddenly shouts burst out from down the street. Around the corner by the church came rioters. Their chants of "No Draft" echoed amid the tall buildings. She saw Father Tynan on the steps, but the mob did not slow even when he waved to them. A gun fired into the sky, and he ducked back into the church. The rioters cheered.

Sarah stared at the roiling mass and wondered where

their humanity had gone. Her hands clenched as she crouched on the roof. She did not want to find out what the mob would do if they discovered her spying on them. It streamed in every direction like a headless monster. More gunfire crackled, and she flinched.

A scream pierced the shouts. She saw someone race along an alley behind the Mission. A half dozen men and women followed. Even from above, she recognized the slim form.

"Toby!" she gasped. Why were they chasing the boy who sold newspapers on the corner?

One man raised a rifle. It fired, but the youngster catapulted over a fence and fled into the shadows. The drunken shot had gone wide.

More staccato gunfire sent her back down the stairs. It was too dangerous to stay on the roof. She must make sure no one tried the back door. Her lips tightened. Lorne knew how easy it was to get into the Mission through a broken window.

"Don't be mixed up in this," she whispered as she rushed down to the kitchen. "Please, Lorne, don't be part of this." Even though he had lied to her, she hoped he was safe somewhere far from New York. She wished Benjamin was, too.

She looked at a quilt that was draped over the banister. Her love of quilting had died and been reborn, but Benjamin might die before this night was out. Praying for his safety, she clenched her hands on the quilt.

Noise blared from kitchen. Street noise! She ran out of the kitchen to see Rachel by the door.

"Rachel! Close the door! If—" She stared at Benjamin. Her hand over her mouth could not restrain her cry of dismay.

He was not wearing his uniform, warning her that things must be even worse than she had guessed. More bruises shaded his face. Under his ripped coat, his shirt was splattered with blood, and his copper badge hung at a strange angle from his belt.

As Rachel closed and locked the door, Sarah flung her

arms around his shoulders and pressed her face to his smoky shirt. "Benjamin, when you didn't come all day, I thought—I thought—"

He kissed the top of her head. "I came as soon as I could. Potter has been dispatching us all over to try to keep order. It took me a while to find him and get his permission to come here to help you." With a snort of derision, he snapped, "If he'd said no, I would have come anyhow."

"Benjamin!" She stepped back to look into his tense face. "You would have disobeyed him?"

He stroked her cheek. "Don't ask ridiculous questions when you should be gathering up the children so I can get you out of here."

"Leave the Mission?"

"It's better to do so while you still have a choice." He scowled when something crashed on the street. "Have you had any trouble here?"

"Not in the house. They were chasing Toby."

A smile flickered across his lips. "I just saw him. He's fine. Is Sawyer here?"

"No. He was called away to help take care of those who were hurt in the riot."

"Good. He should be safe. No one wants to hurt a doctor who might be needed to bandage them up." Turning to Rachel, he said, "Get the children. I'm taking you over to the church. Father Tynan said you could stay there."

"It's half a block to the church!" Sarah gasped.

"We can get there!" called Skelly from the back stairs. "We're not afraid."

Sarah gave Rachel a shove toward the stairs. "Get what supplies you can and put them in baskets. Not heavy, because the older children will have to help carry them. Everyone has their quilts we've been sewing together. Bring those. I'll take the babies' basket."

"And Conlan," Rachel added. "He won't go anywhere unless you're with him."

"What can we do, Sergeant McCauley?" asked Skelly, grinning.

"Help Rachel and the younger ones! We're all going to

have to work on this together." He drew Sarah to one side of the kitchen as the children rushed back up the stairs.

She sighed. "He's wanted to go outside and fight them off all day."

He lowered his voice. "Fighting is what we may have ahead of us. Second Avenue is clogged with debris and furniture too heavy for the rioters to carry off. It's not going to be a stroll to get to the church."

"The police—"

"You can't depend on the force right now. We're just trying to keep the rioting from spreading. Where it's already going on, we had only the Invalid Corps to help us. They've been overrun. None of the horsecars are running, and most of the telegraph wires have been ripped apart." He drew her against him. "We're on our own here, sweetheart."

The front hall exploded with a crash. Glass sprayed as something struck the staircase with a thump. A fist-sized rock dropped to the floor. From the street came shouts.

With a growl, Benjamin ran to the door. He went into her office and shoved the dilapidated settee into the hall. She helped him push it up against the door. Grabbing another chair, she set it on top of the battered cushions.

"Sarah, get the children into the kitchen," he ordered while he pulled the other settee out of the parlor. "This won't buy us much time." Picking up the rock, he dropped it on the cushions. "I'm sure by now your friend Doreen has shared every detail of the house and that Ruthie and Mason are still here. They'll be anxious to outdo those who set fire to the Colored Orphan Asylum."

"Oh, no!" she cried. "How could they do something so horrible?"

He gripped her shoulders. "Because someone is stirring them up with rhetoric and whiskey."

"If—"

"I'll answer your questions once the children have sanctuary in the church. For now, let's go."

As they entered the kitchen, Rachel ran down the back stairs. The children followed, their eyes wide with fear.

Each one carried a quilt. The older ones held baskets.

Sarah held out her hand to Conlan, who grasped it tightly. Taking the basket Rachel held out to her, she set it on the table and smiled. "We're going to the church to help Father Tynan keep track of all the pews. It's a big job, so we'll need each of you." She winked at the older children, who were looking at her as if she had lost her mind. "Put your quilts over your heads, inside out, so that no one sees your pattern until you have a chance to finish it."

The younger children giggled, caught up in the game.

"I think it's best," Benjamin said, "if we divide up into three groups. Then no one will take note of all the children together. We'll blend into the mob more easily if we're seen."

She turned to Rachel. "Will you be all right if we do that?"

"I won't let anyone hurt these children." She squared her thin shoulders. "You can trust me, Sarah." She hesitated, then said, "You can, too, Benjamin."

"Good." He smiled tautly. "I'll take the Brown children and the younger ones first."

"We'll divide up the older ones," Sarah said. "I'll bring the babies."

"Give us five minutes. Then the next group comes. Five minutes after that, the final group. We should have that much time."

"Five minutes," she whispered as she put her fingers on his sleeve.

He pulled her into his arms and kissed her deeply. "Don't try to be a hero, Sarah. Just get the children to the church. You can't worry about anyone but you and them while you're out there."

She nodded as he released her. Every word he spoke told her that she could not begin to guess how horrible it was along the avenue.

When he pulled two guns from under his coat, Rachel gasped, "No! I will not take one of those."

"Sarah?"

She wanted to refuse, too, but she would have the babies

and Conlan with her. That would slow her. She almost recoiled as he placed the pistol on her outstretched hand.
Putting it behind a half-finished quilt in the babies' basket,
she watched as he gathered the littlest children as well as
the Browns. The instructions he gave them were simple.
Stay close to the shadows ringing the alley. Ruthie and
Mason must remain in the middle of the group, so they
would not be seen.

"Keep your quilts over your heads," she called as he
opened the door.

He looked back and smiled tightly. Then he and the children disappeared into the smoke and darkness.

Sarah locked the door behind them. "Skelly, stay here
and watch the door in case they come back. Fiona, stand
by the hall door and keep an eye on the front door. The
rest of you, come with me."

In quick order, she sent the children upstairs to turn off
the gaslights, so it would look as if they were going to bed.
Everything must appear normal. If no one suspected they
were sneaking the children out, they might all escape.

She ran to her office. When she peered in, she was
pleased that the drapes were still drawn. Upstairs, they had
found several that the children had opened to peek out.

Her hands shook as she lit the lamp over her desk. Its
glow would illuminate the thick drapes. Glancing around
the room, she whispered her farewells. She was not sure
where the Mission would be reborn, but she feared it would
not be here.

Closing the door behind her, she hoped anyone who
broke in would suspect someone was hiding on the far side
and waste time checking. It was a small chance, but she
must take every opportunity to gain them a few more precious seconds.

Going back into the kitchen, she said, "Rachel, it's been
five minutes."

"Let me take Innis. Two babies will be too heavy for
you."

She nodded. "Can you manage?"

"Yes." She put the sleeping baby in another basket. "I'll

have Skelly to help me." She hesitated, then said, "I can wait, Sarah, if you want to go first with the girls."

She shook her head. "Go before I accept your offer."

Rachel hugged her, picked up the basket, and herded Skelly ahead of her out into the night. As the door closed, Sarah tried to smile at Fiona and Missy. It was useless, because they were old enough to understand the danger ahead of them.

"Five minutes." Although she barely whispered, the words knelled through the kitchen.

"Do you think we have five more minutes?" Fiona asked.

Sarah did not answer as she picked up the basket. Birdie was still asleep, her small mouth puckered. Seeing her sewing kit in the basket, she almost took it out. They might need it before this was over. She sat on the bench. Conlan gripped her skirt. Fiona and Missy came to sit beside her. Only Missy spoke as she counted down the five minutes, second by second. Wanting to ask her to stop, Sarah did not. This was the child's way of dealing with her fear. Sarah wished she had a way to deal with hers.

When Missy reached zero, Sarah stood and said, "Let's go. Stay close to me, but if I tell you to run, run. Go to the back of the church. Father Tynan will let you in."

"We won't leave you and the little ones, Sarah." Fiona wore her most stubborn expression.

"We'll be right on your heels." Taking a quilt top from Missy's basket, she ripped off some of the squares to leave the edges torn and uneven. She set it over her head and hunched her shoulders. "No one's going to bother an old lady."

Both girls giggled. Even Conlan smiled as she took his hand.

The girls slipped out the door ahead of her, but did not edge off the steps. She pulled the gun from the basket and slipped it under her gown. The straps of her hoops hid its shape. Then she followed them out. She saw a motion in the back, then heard a dull thud. Someone was using the outhouse. Drawing the children into the shadows, she strained to hear any other sounds to let her know what was going on.

From the street came the same shouts. No other sounds came from back here.

"C'mon," she whispered. She was not surprised when Fiona grabbed her skirt as well as Missy's hand.

Not even Birdie chirped as they inched down the alley. They could walk behind the next two buildings, but then would have to go out into the street the rest of the distance to the church.

A thump came from behind them. Fiona moaned in terror, and Missy hid her face on Sarah's skirt.

"Sarah?"

At the muffled whisper that came from the shadows, Sarah pulled out the pistol and raised it. Her enemies knew her name and could be trying to trick her. Her finger closed on the trigger.

"Sarah?"

She did not shoot as she recognized the silhouette easing through the shadows. "Benjamin! What are you doing back here?"

He took the basket from her. "I thought you might want some help."

"The other children—?"

"Safe. Rachel, too." He drew his nightstick as she hid the gun again. "Let's go."

She whirled when she heard a crash in the Mission. Cheers filled the alley. The rioters must have broken in. It would not take them long to discover the children had vanished.

"Follow me, sweetheart," Benjamin whispered. "Do what I do, and stay quiet."

Fearfully she nodded. With no one else did she and the children have as great a chance of escape. She slipped the pistol into her skirt pocket. Pulling the shawl down around her shoulders, she picked up Conlan and told Fiona and Missy to hold on to her gown.

Benjamin kept their pace even, not too fast and not too slow. No one must take note of them.

Fiona moaned again when they came out onto the street. Hushing her, Sarah tightened her hold on the little boy. They were jostled and knocked aside in the looters' eager rush to get into the Mission.

Benjamin grasped her arm. "Head for the other side of the avenue."

"The church is on this side of the street."

"They'll notice if we go there instead of being part of the crowd breaking into the houses here."

"C'mon, girls," she whispered.

She took only a single step before the quilt was ripped from her head, but she did not stop to get it. Two women fought over it.

"Come on!" ordered Benjamin.

She tried to obey, but bounced off a third woman, who grabbed a handful of the quilt. Sound shriveled up in her throat as she locked eyes with Doreen O'Brien.

Whirling, Sarah tried to push away past the other women. She cried, "Fiona! Missy! Run!"

They hesitated, then obeyed when Doreen shouted, "It's Sarah Granger! Stop her! Stop her before she gets away!"

Hands tried to catch Sarah. She shoved them away as she ran, trying to follow Benjamin through the crowd. She saw the two girls climbing the steps of the church.

She bumped into Benjamin as he came to a sudden halt. Stepping back, she cried out as more hands grabbed at her. She spun away. In her arms, Conlan cowered against her breast, his face hidden. She pulled his quilt over him, so he would not see the drunken faces that were distorted with rage.

Benjamin caught her and held her close. She stared beyond him to see another mob had cut off their single route of escape. She looked behind them to see the others closing around them.

"Don't panic," he whispered.

She glanced at his tight face. "I won't."

"I didn't think you would."

His smile astonished her. As he handed her the basket, he stepped forward to stand between her and the mob. She backed up as he did until the curb hit her heels. Stepping up on the sidewalk, she continued backward until the brick wall of a row house stopped her. She eased closer to the steps.

Putting Conlan on the ground beside the basket, she held his hand as Benjamin paused by the front of the steps. He kept his hand away from his pistol. She waited for him to say something, to tell her what he intended to do, but he remained silent.

"Move aside, mate!" shouted a decidedly Irish voice. "It ain't ye we be wantin'. 'Tis that one behind ye. If she loves coloreds, let her share their fate!"

Applause met his words.

She put her hand in the one Benjamin held behind his back. His touch calmed her. A renewed flash of terror filled her when she realized he would not let them take her while he lived.

"You want to kill Sarah Granger?" he called back.

"Benjamin, what are you doing?"

"Hush," he shot over his shoulder. "This may be your only chance." Much louder, he shouted, "So who will kill her to repay her for her kindness to everyone along Second Avenue?" He pointed to a man. "You? Can you kill her?"

The man shook his head.

"How about you?" he asked, scowling at a woman. When the woman lowered her eyes, he added, "What about the rest of you? How many of you has she fed? How many have found a place to sleep on a rainy night when you had nowhere else to go?"

Feet shuffled in embarrassment. She watched in amazement as the mob's blood-thirst faded. She should have guessed that Benjamin wielded words as well as he did his nightstick.

Suddenly a woman pushed to the front. Sarah's eyes widened. Doreen! In horror, she recognized the man beside her. It was the man who had assaulted her at the conscription lottery.

"How you doing, McCauley?" he bellowed. "Folks, don't you know who this is? It's Copper McCauley!" He stood in front of the crowd. "Maybe you haven't heard. He's Sarah Granger's lover, and he wants your men to die for the slaves."

Instead of shouts, the people murmured uneasily. Sarah fought not to smile. Doreen's friend should have known that Benjamin, too, had helped many of the folks here.

"Get him!" shouted the man. "Get them both!"

No one moved. She dared not breathe. As little as a single breath might throw the delicate situation off balance. Benjamin remained silent, and she realized he must let the mob make the first move. Anything he said or did might bring the rioters upon them like a pack of wolves.

The man looked to his left and signaled.

A man rushed at her. Before the man could touch her, Benjamin's fist sent him reeling back into the crowd. As one, the rioters swarmed toward them. Pushing Sarah to the ground behind him, Benjamin pulled his gun. He fired it skyward. As the thick gun smoke filled the street, the crowd paused.

"This is a revolver!" he shouted. "The next shot won't be into the sky! Go home! Or go and rip the Mission apart. That's what you want, isn't it?"

"We want her!" Doreen shouted.

The man with her bent and picked up a loose stone. With a curse, he flung it at Sarah. It hit the wall above Benjamin's head and showered them with debris. Conlan shrieked, and the baby howled.

Sarah picked up the basket and Conlan. As she straightened, she screamed, for Benjamin had fallen to the ground, mortar broken around him.

She knelt next to him. The mob yelled, smelling victory and ready for the kill. She put her hand on his chest to find the steady beat of his heart. He was alive. A rock whizzed by her ear and crashed against the house. Splinters struck her. She cried out in pain. Blood coursed along her cheek.

Conlan shrieked again, and she saw blood on his arm. Her anguish became rage. She set him on the ground and reached over Benjamin to pull his gun out of his hand.

Lifting it, she stood. The glitter of distant flames bounced off the barrel. "Throw another rock, and I'll kill you!" She held the gun steady and panned across the crowd to aim at the man beside Doreen. "Tell them to stop."

"Why should I?" he shouted back. "You won't shoot me."

"No?" Her finger drew back the hammer, but a hand grasped her wrist. She screamed as the pistol was wrenched from her fingers.

"Lorne!" she gasped.

He put his arm around her shoulders, but looked out at the mob. "Put those rocks down," he called. When they did, he smiled. "Celebration time on Third Avenue. O'Malley found a cache of whiskey. If you want a share . . ."

He did not need to finish as the crowd raced away. She started to kneel to check Benjamin and Conlan, but Lorne tightened his grip on her.

"Lorne, they're hurt. I need to—"

He pressed his hand over her mouth. "You need to be quiet, Sarah," he growled in her ear. "Be quiet, or I'll let them treat you as you deserve."

She stared at him. This was not the gentle, bumbling Lorne she had known, the young man who had followed his older brother to West Point, even though he had not liked commanding others. She glanced at Benjamin. He had not moved. Beside him, Conlan hid his face against Benjamin's coat and whimpered.

"You fools!" Lorne snapped. In amazement, she realized he was talking to a half dozen men who eased out of the shadows. "I thought I told you to keep them away from her house."

"We tried, General, but—"

"Shut up! If you can't control these half-wit Irish, then . . ."

Sarah stiffened. *General? General Feich? Lorne?* This made no sense. He hated telling others what to do.

"We can control them," one of the men boasted. "They're afraid of the death bird's men."

She closed her eyes. Death bird—raven! *Feich* was

Gaelic for raven. No wonder they had frightened the Irish gangs so swiftly. General Feich brought death to any who stood in his way.

"Sarah?"

Hearing the amusement in Lorne's voice, she opened her eyes.

"I think you're ready to offer us some hospitality, aren't you, honey?"

His hand over her mouth kept her from answering. Fear surged through her with a pain as sharp as the rocks. His orders had almost killed Benjamin more than once. She did not want to think what he had planned for them now.

19

WHEN SARAH SQUIRMED AND tried to get away, Lorne
put his foot on Benjamin's back. "Behave, honey, or I'll
break his spine," he growled in her ear. "Understand?"

She nodded.

"Can you keep quiet?"

She nodded again.

When he lifted his hand from her mouth, she whispered,
"Let me check them. Please."

"If you try to escape, I'll kill all of them. Do you understand?"

"Better than I ever did, apparently," she fired back.

He chuckled as he released her. "Honey, that spirit is
what I always liked second best about you." His gaze raked
over her. "A distant second best."

Sarah dropped to her knees and gathered Conlan into her
arms as Lorne turned to talk to his cronies. Even in the
darkness, she could see the stitching of feathers on their
sleeves.

She quickly rolled Conlan's quilt tighter, so its pattern
was not visible. For once glad that the little boy would not
speak and betray them, she put her hand again on Benjamin's back. The slow rise and fall of his breathing brought

tears of relief. She blinked them away. Nothing had changed. General Feich was still Benjamin's enemy . . . and now hers.

Lorne gripped her elbow, jerking her to her feet. "Come with me. I'll take you where you don't have to worry about those half-witted Irish ruffians."

"Where will it be safe?"

"With me, anywhere," he answered with a laugh.

She let him brag. For all she knew, he could be correct. He certainly had shown his power over the mob. As General Feich, he had gained control of the street gangs through death and fear.

A slow smile spread across his face, and she was sure he had guessed her thoughts. As much as Giles had loved Mississippi, Lorne must, too. In that way, the brothers had been alike as only twins could be. Lorne would do anything to see that the Confederacy was victorious.

When he tried to tug her away from Benjamin, who had not moved, she cried, "I won't leave him here! That mob may be back."

"It's just a bump. He'll come around." The coldness of his voice shocked her. How could she have been so wrong about Lorne? She had thought he was the weaker brother. Now he gave orders like a seasoned soldier.

She took Conlan's hand as the little boy cringed against her skirt. "I won't leave Benjamin or the children. Go and do all your mischief. Just leave us alone."

"You'd like that, wouldn't you?" His hand cupped her chin, tilting her head back at a painful angle. "You and your copper all alone?"

His comrades laughed, but became silent when he glared at them.

"They will be killed if they're left here now. The children—"

"Are the least of your worries. You care only about McCauley."

She shook her head. "These children are my responsibility." She pulled her head out of his grip. "I do love Benjamin, if that's what you are trying to find out."

"Giles—"

"I mourned for Giles for two long years. I never thought I could love anyone again."

He sneered, "So you picked this cowardly copper, who chases down pickpockets and drunks, to replace a man who offered his life for his country?"

"Benjamin may have the same chance." She glanced down at him. "His name was drawn during the lottery on Saturday."

"Was it?" Lorne made a motion, and his men surrounded Benjamin.

Sarah opened her mouth to scream. His hand over her lips forced the sound back down her throat as he tugged her back away from Benjamin.

"Silence," he hissed against her ear. "Silence, or you can watch the rest of his blood drain away into the gutter here." Raising his voice, he ordered, "Take him into the Mission. I have a few questions to ask our copper friend. Then we'll finish this where no one can see."

She refused to move as Lorne tried to pull her across the street. When he cursed, she twisted her head free.

"The basket!" she gasped. "The baby is in the basket!"

He released her enough so she could pick up the basket. "Were you always such a shrew, Sarah?"

Her eyes narrowed as she frowned. "I want to be sure you don't leave Benjamin out here to die. He saved my life."

"*I* saved your life!"

"And I wouldn't leave you out here to die either."

Lorne's grin returned. "That's where we're different, honey." Again his gaze scoured her skin. "One of the ways."

She ignored him as his men lifted Benjamin from the cobbles. His limbs drooped toward the cobbles while they carried him across the street.

When Lorne took her arm and herded her across the empty street, she glanced back to be sure the others were following. She winced when he yanked on her.

"Be careful," she whispered. "You're hurting me."

"If I were you, I'd be anxious to find a place to hide before those fools return." He forced her ahead of him up the steps.

Sarah moaned when she saw the shattered front door. Shards of wood covered the stoop and were scattered in the foyer. The settees were broken, and their cushions had vanished.

"Welcome home," Lorne said with a laugh.

She did not look at him. He knew how much the Mission meant to her. Why had she never seen this cruel streak in him?

When he motioned for the men to carry Benjamin into her office, he kept her from following. "Obey me," he ordered. The rest of his threat went unspoken, but she understood. Benjamin would be slain before he gained consciousness if she did not cooperate.

She winced when she heard a thud. Those beasts had dropped him onto the floor as if he were a sack of potatoes. She tightened her hold on Conlan's hand as Lorne shoved her into her office.

Conlan peeked around her dress and shrieked. Kneeling beside him, she set the basket with Birdie on the floor. She turned him so he could not see Benjamin lying as still as his mother had been. Quickly looking around her office, she saw every drawer had been ripped open in her desk. The lock on the closet door was broken, and her bed had been torn apart, the bedclothes gone. The drapes were half torn from the windows, left to pool on the floor.

"Shut him up!" Lorne snarled.

"He's frightened." She wrapped her arms around the little boy, wishing she could do the same with Benjamin. "If you had seen what poor Conlan has seen, you would—"

"Conlan?"

"No!" she cried as Lorne tore the little boy out of her arms. Jumping to her feet, she reached for him.

She froze as Lorne cursed and turned to one of his men. "I thought you said you killed these children."

"I did." The man gulped. "A little boy and a baby girl. Took care of them, just as you ordered, General."

Conlan screeched again when Lorne set him on the floor and plucked the quilt out of his hands. Waving it at the man, he shouted, "I said the child would have *this*! How many quilts can there be like this one?"

"Lorne, please give the quilt to Conlan," Sarah whispered. "He needs it."

"Does he?" He whirled to face her, the quilt bunched in his fist. "Or do you and your copper need it to point the way to me?"

"We don't need it for that anymore." She put her cheek against Conlan's head as he continued to keen like a lost soul. "Conlan needs it to comfort him. Lorne, give it back to him."

"Or?"

She bit her lip and squared her shoulders. This went beyond cruelty. "If you don't give it back to him, I will make certain you don't get any information from Benjamin." She pulled the gun out of her pocket and raised it.

His comrades gasped, but Lorne laughed. "You can't believe that I think you're going to kill him. You love the man, fool that you are. Do you know how hard it is to kill someone you care about?" He laughed again. "We wouldn't be having this conversation if I hadn't been so reluctant to give the order to have my brother's mistress killed."

"Brother? What brother? Giles was your only brother."

He rubbed the quilt against his cheek and smiled when she gasped. The scar had been nothing but greasepaint. "My brother's name is Lorne, Sarah."

"Giles!" she whispered.

"You never suspected, did you, honey?"

"But you died! Lorne sent me the letter telling me you were dead."

"When a bureaucratic error listed me among the casualties, I became a man without an identity. I could do as I wished." He smiled. "And, in New York, I wished to be General Feich. I guessed you might have been able to hide the truth that Lorne was visiting you, but you'd never keep quiet that I had returned from the dead."

In a choked voice, she whispered, "Then Lorne never came here?"

"He came once to familiarize himself with your quaint little project here, but nearly tripped me up with his foolish honesty. 'Twas me the other times when I came to be with Doreen."

"Doreen? Her family thinks you are Lorne!" She tightened her grip on the gun. She had been a fool to believe this man two years ago. She had wasted those two years mourning for a man who existed only in her fantasies. She nearly had lost her joy in quilting and in life. Later, she would be angry about that. Later. Now . . . "You've lied to everyone, but I'll be honest with you. I want you to give Conlan his quilt and get out of the Mission."

"Or?"

"I know how to use a pistol, Giles." She let her smile grow as contemptuous as his. "And you're making it easier than you guessed for me to pull this trigger. I—"

Benjamin groaned and shifted.

When Giles glanced at him, Conlan darted forward and grabbed his quilt. He ran to crouch between the baby's basket and Benjamin. He must have jostled the basket, because Birdie began to cry.

"Our friend is awake?" Giles taunted. "How inconvenient!"

"It won't be if you leave! Now!"

Benjamin heard shouting. Sarah! Sarah was shouting! He wanted to tell her to be quiet. His head ached as if he had been run over by the horsecar. And the baby! Why did Birdie have to howl like the mob in the street?

The riot! He and Sarah and the children had been caught in that. Something had hit him. He had to help her. When he tried to sit, he heard a groan. Only slowly did he realize it had come from him.

"Get out now!"

That was Sarah. He forced his eyes open and stared in disbelief. A half dozen men were staring at Sarah, who held a gun aimed at them.

"If you won't leave," Sarah continued, "we'll leave as

soon as Benjamin is conscious." When one man took a step toward her, she gestured with the gun. "Stay away from me, General Fontaine!"

General Fontaine?

At Benjamin's gasp, the man chuckled. "About time you really woke up, McCauley."

He pushed himself carefully to his feet. He wanted to rest his hand on Sarah's desk, but knew he must not show any sign of weakness. "I thought you called yourself General Feich."

"I did, but Sarah knows me much better as Giles Fontaine."

He saw pain flicker across Sarah's face. Although he wondered what had happened while he was senseless, one thing was clear. Sarah was shocked that her erstwhile fiancé had returned from the dead to cause chaos in the city.

Something crashed out on the street, but he did not look over his shoulder. "It sounds as if you're missing the fun, Fontaine."

"I've been waiting for this ever since you stuck your nose in my business. When I heard you'd seduced my fiancé, I decided to deal with you personally."

"You deal with me?" He laughed as he pointed to Sarah. "You seem at a disadvantage at the moment, Fontaine."

"Sarah won't shoot me," he said serenely.

"I will if you force me to." Sarah's hand shook but she steadied the pistol.

When Benjamin motioned, she edged toward him. Then someone else moved. "Sarah!" he shouted. "Look out!"

She whirled to aim the gun at a man behind her. Fontaine leaped forward and struck her wrist. The gun twisted across the carpet.

Benjamin started for it, but stopped in midstep when he saw Fontaine's hand on Sarah's throat. When her captor took her gun from one of his gang, he pressed it to her forehead. Her eyes strained to see it before looking back at Benjamin.

"I love you, Benjamin," she whispered as Conlan cried out and ran to hide his face in her skirt.

Fontaine ignored him. "Cooperate, copper." He stroked Sarah's cheek with the steel barrel. "Be good, Benny boy. Pretty Sarah would not look so pretty with a bullet in her head."

"Let her and the children go. They haven't done anything to you."

"Sweet Sarah could send me to hang, but she won't." He smiled. "She's coming back South with me to be my wife."

"You're crazy!" Sarah tried to reach for the gun, but he batted her hands away.

He pressed his mouth over hers and tangled his fingers in her hair. Her gasp of pain was echoed by Benjamin's and the dull sound of flesh impacting. Raising her hand, she slashed her broken nails against Giles's face.

With a curse, he shoved her to the floor. He wiped blood from his face. "If that's the kind of loving your copper taught you, we'll have to change that when we marry."

"I'm not marrying you. I don't love you, General Feich-Fontaine. Not anymore."

"I know you think you love this copper." He whirled her to see where Benjamin was thumbing away the blood from the corner of his mouth as he rose from his knees. "But that's going to be over as soon as he tells me what I need to know about the police department's plans."

"Go to hell!" Benjamin said, standing. "I'm not telling you anything."

Sarah stiffened when Giles laughed and said, "Then I guess there's no reason to keep you around any longer. I've kept you alive this long only so you can die knowing that Sarah will be mine—"

"I will not!"

"—and for her to see," he continued, as if she had not spoken, "what happens to those who don't do as I tell them to." He raised his pistol, and Sarah opened her mouth to scream.

The sound tumbled back down her throat as one of Giles's men called, "General Feich, this is the first copper we've caught alive."

"So?" He pulled back on the trigger.

"You said we could draw for who gets to shoot him."
He chuckled. "Our own little lottery."

Sarah held her breath as the room grew silent except for
Birdie's whimpering. She released it when Giles lowered
his gun.

"Make it quick," he ordered. "There must be paper in
the desk. This caterwauling is giving me a headache."
Grabbing the basket from the floor, he shoved it into
Sarah's hands. He opened the closet door and said, "Get
in."

"What?"

"I don't want you doing something stupid. I don't want
to have to shoot you before you give me some of the pleasure you spent so much time denying me." He shoved her
and the children into the closet and slammed the door.

Sarah drew Conlan into her arms and tried to hear what
was being said on the other side of the door. She did not
have much time to figure out a way to save them all. Once
Giles had Benjamin killed, he would have the children murdered, too. She knew he did not intend to make her his
wife. If he let her live at all, it would be as his unwilling
mistress. He wanted her to suffer for every insult, intentional or inadvertent, that she had heaped on him by falling
in love with Benjamin.

Her foot hit something on the floor. She squatted and
picked it up.

The door reverberated as something struck it. She heard
a groan, then a shout. Inching the door open a finger's
breadth, she saw Giles holding the gun on Benjamin again.
One of his cronies lay on the floor, not moving.

She watched as they lashed Benjamin's hands with some
string and forced him to sit not far from the closet. He could
not slip by them and out the door while they drew lots to
see which one would have the pleasure of shooting him.
They laughed at their perverse lottery.

"Benjamin," she whispered, as Giles and his men began
to argue about how the lottery would be handled.

He glanced at her. Sorrow filled his eyes. "Sweetheart,
I—"

"Listen!" She held up one of the cans of ether. "Look what are all over the floor in here. It's Dr. Everett's ether. It's explosive."

Benjamin sat straighter and smiled. "Sweetheart, remind me to speak to Captain Potter about hiring you. You'd be an asset to the force. Can you help me get untied?"

"Turn your back toward me." She eased back toward the basket. There was not enough room to turn her hoops without striking the door. She did not want any sound to alert Giles. "Conlan, can you get my scissors?"

She bit her lip. If the little boy was too frightened to understand, she would have to risk banging her hoops on the door.

"Conlan?"

She counted slowly to ten. She could not risk waiting any longer.

Something cool brushed her palm. She smiled as she closed her fingers around the scissors. Thank heavens! She kissed his head and whispered, "Thank you, Conlan."

Easing the door open a bit wider, she glanced at the men. They were busy doing whatever they were doing. She slipped the scissors through and snipped at the string. Holding her breath, she hoped the soft sound would not reach the men. She opened the scissors and slashed down when the men roared with laughter.

Benjamin settled his hands on the floor behind him, so no one else could see he was untied. "Sweetheart, hand me those cans."

"How many?"

"All you can get quickly and quietly."

With Conlan's help, she passed him four cans. She paused when Benjamin motioned for her to stop. "There are about a dozen more I can see in here," she said.

"I may need them."

"And these." She pulled some of the children's partially sewn quilt squares out of the basket.

He winked at her. "Just what I needed. While I'm stuffing these in the tops of the cans, create a diversion. I'll take care of the ether."

"How can you use it without killing us, too?"

"Just make a diversion and get you and the children out of here." He glanced at the men as one shouted excitedly. "Cover the baby's face, and put the quilt over yours and Conlan's head."

"What—"

"Now! I'll be right behind you."

Scooping up Conlan and the basket, Sarah smiled at the little boy and whispered, "Yell as loud as you can!"

She did not wait to see if he would obey. With a shriek of her own, she burst out of the closet. She ran forward into the center of the room. The men fell back as she whirled with another scream.

Giles tried to grab her arm, but she danced away. "Sarah, have you gone mad?"

"There's a mouse!" she cried. "In the closet." She spun again. "No, there it goes! Behind the desk!" When the men turned to follow the make-believe mouse's route, she cried, "There it is! By the drapes! Someone kill it! Please."

Conlan's cries rang through her head as she paused to take a breath.

"Shut up!" Giles shouted. "Shut him up, Sarah, or—"

The room rocked with an explosion. Fire burst from the drapes piled on the floor. Another explosion sent flames flying through the papers scattered around her desk.

The men shouted.

"It's McCauley! Stop him before he kills all of us!"

As Giles continued to call out orders no one paid attention to, Sarah put Conlan on the floor, grabbed his hand, and ran. Looking toward the front door, she saw people surging up the steps. She turned back toward the kitchen. Her arm was grabbed. Whirled about, she stared at Doreen's twisted sneer.

"Where do you think you're going?" Doreen demanded.

Sarah's fist hit Doreen's chin before she even realized what she was doing. Doreen fell to the floor as the house rocked with another explosion.

Plaster dropped from the ceiling. A thick chunk careened down the staircase. Remembering Benjamin's warning, she picked up Conlan and told him to put the quilt over his head and hers. The floor was as unsteady as the sea, but she fought her way to the back door.

She heard a gunshot behind her. She started to turn. She did not want to leave Benjamin in there to battle alone. Crockery cascaded onto her when another bottle of ether exploded. He must still be alive.

The house wobbled on its foundation. The room filled with smoke. She prayed Benjamin knew what he was doing. She could not risk the children any longer. She threw open the door.

Hands caught her as she stumbled out. She started to scream, then recognized the man in the thickening smoke. "Father Tynan!"

"This way. Quickly."

"Benjamin! He's still in there!"

He pulled her down the alley toward the church. "He'll come out the kitchen door. Listen." When he saw her tense at the sound of more guns firing, he continued, "The rioters are taking target practice on those running out the front door. I heard one of their leaders sent them over to Third Avenue, where a bunch of them were arrested. Now they want vengeance."

Flames flickered in the windows. The house was on fire. She shoved the basket and Conlan into the priest's arms. "I've got to get him out."

"You can't—"

Father Tynan's words vanished as the windows burst outward in red lightning. Tongues of fire sought to taste the air in the seconds before the house shivered. As if exhausted, the Mission swayed as a single brick, then a second struck the street. The rain of stone and wood became a torrent as the house crashed onto Second Avenue.

"Benjamin!" she screamed. She ran toward the ruins.

Hot smoke closed around her. Stumbling, she tripped over loose bricks and chunks of wood. She cried Benjamin's name until her throat was raw. Choking, she dropped to her knees. Hands under her arms pulled her back.

Her eyes widened when she saw Father Tynan and Dr.

Everett working side by side with other neighbors to dig
through the debris away from the flames at what had been
the front of the house. The explosions must have ripped
open a gas line, for the fire soared high into the smoke-
filled sky. She shrugged off the hands and went to help
them.

"Over here!" shouted Father Tynan. He tossed bricks and
boards aside. The men helped him lift someone out of the
debris. The light from the flames glittered off something at
his waist. A copper badge!

Sarah ran to where they placed Benjamin away from the
ruins. She dropped to her knees. He was gray with dust and
plaster. As his eyes opened, he grimaced.

"Don't move," Dr. Everett ordered. "That leg looks broken. How are you otherwise?"

He spit out plaster. "I'll let you know after I get all this
dirt out of my mouth." His hand curled up around Sarah's
cheek. "We did it, sweetheart. We're quite a team."

"I don't think the Mission is going to be quite the same."

He glanced at the house and grinned. "I'd have to agree
with you on that." He cursed as Dr. Everett set his leg and
wrapped it with broken lath from the shattered walls while
the others continued to look for survivors. Slowly he sat
up with the doctor's help. "I'm not sure I'm ever going to
be quite the same."

Conlan pushed forward and held out his quilt. With quiet
dignity, he said, "For Ben's ouch."

Sarah sucked in her breath as she stared at the little boy.
Tears fell down her cheeks, washing through the dust.

Benjamin's eyes glowed as he took the quilt. "Thank
you, Conlan. It will make my ouch better."

As Sarah hugged the little boy, she knew they might
never understand why he finally set aside his pain to reach
out to them. Conlan wiggled in her arms, and she let him
go to spread the quilt across the shoulders of Benjamin's
ripped shirt before he ran back to look into his sister's
basket.

"Conlan finally trusts me with his quilt," he said quietly
as shouts and work went on behind them.

"Yes."

"Do you?"

She did not hesitate. "Yes."

"With just the quilt, or will you trust me with your heart? You know I love you."

"And I love you, Benjamin."

"Enough to be my wife?"

She touched the quilt. "If you want my heart, which is as patched as this quilt, I want to give it to you. My heart and all of me."

"That's a promise I'll see you keep," he said as he drew her into his arms for a kiss that would be only the first in a lifetime of love.

Author's Note

THE DRAFT RIOTS OF July 1863 are an often overlooked part of Civil War history. Other cities, particularly in the Northeast, also had riots, but none as extensive or damaging to life and property as the ones in New York City.

I enjoy hearing from my readers. You can write to me with comments or for information on upcoming releases at:

Joanna Hampton
VFRW
P.O. Box 350
Wayne, PA 19087-0350

or by email at: jaferg@erols.com

FRIENDS ROMANCE

Can a man come between friends?

☐ **A TASTE OF HONEY**

by DeWanna Pace   0-515-12387-0

☐ **WHERE THE HEART IS**

by Sheridon Smythe   0-515-12412-5

☐ **LONG WAY HOME**

by Wendy Corsi Staub   0-515-12440-0

All books $5.99